The River Bend Chronicles

500
KISSES

The River Bend Chronicles

500 Kisses

Renee Kumor

ABSOLUTELY AMA⚡ING eBOOKS

ABSOLUTELY AMAZING eBOOKS

Published by Whiz Bang LLC, 926 Truman Avenue, Key West, Florida 33040, USA.

For information contact:
Publisher@AbsolutelyAmazingEbooks.com

ISBN-13: 978-1945772719 (Absolutelly Amazing Ebooks)
ISBN-10: 1945772719

To all those who keep their Faith,
who worship and pray every day of their lives
as an inspiration to the rest of us.

The River Bend Chronicles

500
Kisses

PREFACE

This is Book 11 in The River Bend Chronicles series. Truth is, it was actually 10.5. I know that looks like odd numbering – but there was a reason it got wedged into my planned lineup. I was wrapping up Book 10, *Deadly Politics* and had already outlined and began the next book in the series, *There's No Explaining Love*, when I was hit, smacked, bowled over, by *500 Kisses*.

Let me explain – I have attended the same church in my town for forty years. All that time there was a gentleman who was our strength – pastors come and go, organists and choir directors come and go – but he was always there, serving in any capacity needed – visiting the sick and homebound, joining a community-wide non-denominational group to create a hospital chaplaincy program ... But you get the picture. So now forty years later, he is over ninety and can no longer do much more than attend services weekly. Someone takes responsibility to see that he has a ride. And I make a point to greet him and give him a kiss as he sits in the last pew. And I have noticed that I am not the only one. Several others stop and hug or kiss him and engage in light banter. He still remembers our names and he still has a sense of humor. And one day, in church, it hit me – 500 Kisses! It's a book that wrote itself. Thanks for taking the time to read it!

- Renee Kumor

Please refer to my website
www.reneekumor.com
to find a list referencing the cast of characters
most frequently active in
The River Bend Chronicles

i

CHAPTER ONE

Lynn Powers could hear the distant sounds of sirens and bells welcoming in another New Year. Quick kisses were shared with each of the family members gathered at her brother's house party.

"I've never been kissed with only one lip before," drawled her husband, Dusty Reid, chief of the James County/River Bend Joint Investigation Unit.

"What do you mean?" she asked as she wrapped her arms around his waist and settled against his chest.

"You're a little distracted."

"These last two months have been a challenge." She gripped him tighter. The party floated around her. It seemed that this was, by tacit agreement, a quiet celebration. Everyone had been affected by recent events.

It all began just before Thanksgiving and the shock waves from the events hadn't stopped yet. In the week preceding Thanksgiving, Teniquia LaMont, one of Dusty's detectives, had been shot during a drug raid and lost her baby. No one had known she was pregnant. At the same time three children were found in a car wreck. It was determined that they were victims of a child porn ring. Fortunately for everyone involved Teniquia and her husband, Lonzo, found it in their hearts to adopt all three children. Although adoption was not an overnight process, Lynn's father, Jim Hoefler, was making certain the process moved toward that end in a timely manner. One of the blessings of the past holiday season was that the children, one boy and two small girls, were beginning to respond to the love and care from their new parents. No one seemed too concerned about "process."

As the adoption solution began to unfold, Lynn's friend, county commissioner Susan Carmichael, was murdered when her car blew up. The explosion left her teenage daughter, Polly, an orphan. To make matters more complex, Susan's murderer was Polly's biological father. In a bizarre turn of events he was also murdered within days of Susan's death. Lynn and her family and friends had spent much of December working on a plan for Polly's future.

Off in a corner Lynn spied her brother-in-law, Tim Powers, in an embrace with his wife, Janet. Though they had been married only months, they were going to take Polly into their family. Tim was scheduled to go to sea in a few days as part of his routine deployment as a long time naval officer. Janet would stay in River Bend and have their baby, while taking on Polly's guardianship.

Lynn smiled to herself. Janet was a local computer whiz who could be very vague at times. Soon she would be the mother of a teenage girl. In addition, Janet and Polly would be living with Janet's parents while Tim was at sea. That would be an interesting household. Janet's father, Bergy Bergman, the retired sheriff, and Lynn's father, Jim Hoefler, were Polly's legal guardians. All in all Polly's care was staying in the family. Lynn only wished the youngster would find even a small smile for the holidays. Polly only smiled for Teniquia's children. They had met in the hospital pediatric ward and had spent many hours during the holiday together in Lynn's attic enjoying Dusty's train layout, a Christmas tradition.

Dusty nuzzled Lynn's ear and she realized they were still embracing. "One good thing about having the party at Will's house is we don't have to wake up and clean." Usually the party on New Year's Eve was hosted by Dusty and Lynn. This year Piper and Will had stepped up because Lynn was still recovering from witnessing Susan's death. She had arrived at the Carmichael home just as the car exploded. She had been seeing a counselor for several weeks to deal with the trauma.

But this was a new year. Lynn withdrew from Dusty's arms, gave him another New Year kiss and moved on to circulate among the family. Moving toward Tim and Janet, she watched as they pulled Polly into their embrace. She heard Tim say, "I'm trusting you to look after Janet. You know as well as anyone how lost she can get."

Polly gave him a measured look, definitely not a smile. "I think you're just saying that because you have to take me."

Lynn held her breath. Polly was proving to be more of a challenge than anyone had expected. She listened for Tim's reply. He put his hands on Polly's shoulders and held her at arms length. "No one is forcing us to take you. That's the first thing you have to remember. The second thing to remember is that both Janet and I will do everything we can to make certain you have the kind of life your mother wanted for you. Next summer we'll move to Japan and we promise that if you think we don't meet your expectations, you can choose to return to River Bend and we'll help you decide on better arrangements." He said all that in a tone that let Polly know he was speaking to someone he respected, to someone he thought could be trusted to make thoughtful decisions, to someone who was mature and for whom he had a growing affection.

Lynn saw Polly's shoulders rise and fall with a sigh. Tim pulled her into his arms and Janet kissed her cheek and ruffled her hair. Polly would stay in River Bend while she finished her freshman year of high school. If she agreed, she would finish her high school years with Tim and Janet while Tim was deployed to Japan. Lynn knew that Polly was eager to leave River Bend and all of its bad memories. The counselor wanted her to stay in town for more therapy. The promise of a relocation in a few months seemed like a solution that might help Polly redefine her life and her future but still be protected by her guardians and her mother's old friends.

Tim and Janet seemed to have this crisis under control. Lynn moved on. "Piper," she hugged her sister-in-law and best friend, "this is a great party."

Piper hugged her back. "It's a quiet party. We're all still recovering from Thanksgiving."

"I agree," said Lynn, "and we all seem to be ready for a new year.

~ ~ ~

It was a cold New Year's Eve, almost New Year's morning. The wind was blowing, carrying dry snowflakes along in its path. The old snow at the edges of the roadway was dirty and crusty from the overnight freeze. No other patrol of the James County sheriff's department was as dismal as that weaving through Portage. What a miserable place! It wasn't even a real town, no one ever bothered to incorporate it, so there it stood in the wind, all tired and dirty and hopeless. Big utility lamps scattered randomly through the town gave a flat, anemic glow to the aging storefronts.

The late night patrol never found anything. The folks in Portage knew how to stay hidden. Although local law enforcement knew a lot went on, nothing ever made it to the surface. The town was run by a family named Masterson. They had been in charge of the town, and surrounding farms, since the first settlement when Portage was the place where settlers crossed the river on the small rafts operated by the Masterson clan. And what a clan! Early travelers had to be wary. Those

Mastersons were known for helping themselves to a passenger's funds, livestock, even a wife, in the early lawless days of the territory.

Over the decades, the Mastersons evolved into criminal nobility. They robbed, pillaged and blackmailed their way to prosperity. By prohibition, they were THE force to reckon with. They said who could operate a speakeasy and who could make liquor and who could sell it. They demanded their share of all illicit profits from prostitution to gaming. In the early twentieth century life was good for the family.

The family mythic hero was Harley Masterson. He organized and executed a plan to rob the Palmer Bank sometime after World War I, managing to strip all valuables from the safety deposit boxes as well as the bank's own safe. However, Harley was caught and hanged. This should have acted as a warning to the rest of the family – maybe crime wasn't going to keep on paying. But prohibition reenergized the family fortunes and Harley was held up to the next generations as a martyr.

After World War II many of the sons who went off to war never returned, or returned with limited interest in the family business. Coming into the twenty-first century the family started to demonstrate a diminishing intelligence for crime. In the recent past, Mace Masterson, one of the last folk heroes of the family, valued because he had done time in prison, was finally sent off for good, having committed two murders in one day, a family record. No matter how the family valued his efforts, the local judicial system put him away for life.

And that's where the Mastersons found themselves. The last acknowledged criminal brain of the family was in prison, and those remaining in Portage worked small time crime: gambling, a steady but slow business in stolen farm equipment, and prostitution.

The current generation was starting to think it was time to rise again, make Masterson the crime worthy name of the past. There was Darwin with his passable computer skills, Lester with his glib tongue, and Chartreuse, yes, even the Mastersons were offering more opportunities to women. Chartreuse was not a sex vender, but a skilled sex blackmailer. Lester and Darwin were afraid of her, and usually let her win all the arguments.

But when she suggested that they start a church as a front for gambling, the boys paused and had to think about that. "Religion," as Chartreuse Masterson liked to say, "keeps people interested as long as you give them what they want. Sort of like Wal-Mart."

The presentation to her cousins was well-organized – no more traveling games, the church would be the front for their gambling operation; no more losing their shirts to skilled gamblers, because robbery came after the last hand; and there would be one less empty store front in downtown Portage. She played her cards right by suggesting that Lester become a preacher. Darwin was happy to find a website that, for a few dollars, licensed Lester to perform marriages and any other rite that suited his religious preferences. They all snickered as they contemplated gambling and sex as their preferences in their new religion, the Church of the Guiding Hands – a time to pray and a time to play.

There was an empty Masterson warehouse across the alley from the backdoor of the Main Street storefront church. Most regular gamblers parked inside that building so the nightly Sheriff's patrol wouldn't see all the extra cars in Main Street and have cause to be suspicious. Only the newcomers parked on

Main Street, but those few cars drew no interest on any given night.

Chartreuse was the brains of the new church. She credited her development of the gambling church idea to an evening when she was stuck at her grandmother's place and forced to watch "Guys and Dolls," an old Hollywood musical where a storefront church was used to cover a gambling operation. Imagine her surprise – there she was humoring her granny while trying to wheedle some cash when she realized she was watching the solution to a family problem.

The church grew slowly at first, as Chartreuse suspected most churches did. Folks had to hear the word and listen for the call. Rolling dice and shuffling cards was the call for a number of local patrons, or congregants, or parishioners. She was never certain which title applied. She supposed it depended on the denomination or affiliation. She snickered, because she thought of her prayers/players as suckers.

Two months of operation and tonight was the biggest crowd so far. New Year's Eve might prove to be the turning point in Masterson family history.

The late night patrol car rolled past the Church of the Guiding Hands. Nothing looked out of line. The patrol car did one more pass through downtown Portage then headed toward the country club to watch for people who shouldn't be driving. In another two hours the next patrol car would be passing through Portage.

In the Guiding Hands sanctuary, as Char liked to call the back room of their gambling palace, the game was breaking up. They knew the patrol timetable and wanted everyone gone before the next sweep in two hours. They had a lot to do before the next patrol because they would be robbing the evening's two big winners – some new guy from Asheville and that stupid

Nevada Utley who was on probation and not supposed to be there. Robbing him, Char reasoned, was really helping the police. Besides, Nevada would never complain, he was breaking his parole. Win-win, thought Char.

The Mastersons had an informal policy, no big winner walked out unmolested. But the new guy proved to be smarter than the Mastersons had expected. This guy, who said he was called Homer, had won a bundle. In fact, Darwin had watched carefully from his apartment overhead where he maintained his security screens. He suspected Homer cheated. But Darwin knew computers and not cards or craps and wasn't certain.

Char had flirted and flounced, trying to get the guy's attention. She was very forward, inviting him to stop by her place on his way out of Portage. Homer declined, "I got a friend who just texted me." He held up his phone. "He's coming to pick me up. He borrowed my truck tonight." He winked at Char and patted her behind. "Maybe next time, doll."

~ ~ ~

The mystery gambler left the fake church under the curious eyes of Char and Lester.

"They try to get you to stay?" asked the driver as Homer climbed into the truck.

"Yeah," nodded Homer, "she promised a lot with that body. I told her maybe next time." The two men were silent for a while as they drove on the slippery country roads back to Asheville.

Homer and the driver were part of a syndicate that ran illegal gambling operations throughout western North Carolina and the part of South Carolina called the Upstate.

"The boss is pissed," the driver, Gilly, reported. "He wants us to end this operation."

"I'm ready," said Homer. The guys planned on a lazy football day tomorrow and a few days with some girlfriends. The boss wasn't expecting to see them until next week. The reliable pick-up truck gripped the icy road as it left the sorry town of Portage behind covered in dirty snow.

~ ~ ~

Char watched Homer walk to a truck parked across the street and climb in. She couldn't see who was driving and phoned Darwin. "You see those guys?"

Whatever else the church might be, it was high tech. Darwin never met the prayers/players and they never saw him. He had placed cameras in strategic spots in the sanctuary that allowed him to watch the games and often to read the cards. In addition, he had placed cameras along Main Street to keep an eye on the nightly patrols. The final camera phase included placing cameras in the alley and in the warehouse. Lester and Chartreuse had been skeptics until he demonstrated his ability to read the cards in a game of poker. Now they were setting aside money for the final security phase, speculating on what other opportunities the cameras would offer.

"No, but I got the tag number." Darwin had created tech central in the rooms above the sanctuary. He studied his camera screen array, stopped the screen of the Main Street camera, and reran the file footage to retrieve the tag number on the truck as it rolled down Main Street toward the bridge. He entered the tag number in a state site that he had hacked months ago. Squinting at the laptop screen he reported on his cellphone. "Owner is Homer Gibson. He lives in Asheville. My laptop always has the answer," bragged the nerdy Masterson.

"Get down here and help us lock up," Chartreuse commanded and ended the call. "He came pretty far on a cold night to gamble," Char mused as she turned to Lester. "Where's Nevada? He won big, too. You didn't let him get away, did you?" Some nights she wondered how long she could work with these two cousins before she killed them.

"Don't worry. He went to pee before he leaves."

Char nodded. "He parks in the warehouse. Walk him to his car."

Lester nodded.

Nevada was dumb and easy pickings. He lingered in the back room counting his money and laughing at his luck, in his opinion, a sign that life in the New Year was looking up. Char congratulated Nevada, offered him one last drink then showed him to the back door, saying, "Nevada, honey, you go this way, and hurry, just in case that patrol car comes back early." He nodded and sauntered out the door, high on winning, liquor and stupidity. Lester was ready. He hit Nevada with a pipe as he entered the warehouse. The young man crumpled to the ground.

Char and Darwin closed down for the night, planning to clean sometime the next day. She picked up a few empty cups and turned out the lights, while Darwin made certain the doors were locked. He let her out the back door and shuffled up the stairs clutching his ever-present tablet. He loved his space above the church with all of his computer equipment and games surrounding him. He wondered if some people felt about their pets that way.

Char followed Lester out to the warehouse in time to find him standing over Nevada's body. He had just extracted Nevada's money from those greasy jeans of his. Char pulled her truck beside the body and helped Lester lift Nevada's body into the pickup's bed. The truck rolled out of the warehouse. Char watched as Lester closed and locked the doors. The Masterson family preacher then crawled into the truck cab glancing at the unconscious man in the back, before closing the door.

"What'll we do with his car?" Lester asked. He knew Char would have a plan. Letting her run things was easy on his brain.

Char thought a moment. "Depends on we let him live or not."

"Not." His answer made her shrug as she thought of her disposal plan.

"We keep his truck in the warehouse," she explained, "We don't have another game scheduled until the weekend. Tomorrow or the next night, late, we take it to Jimmy," the cousin who dealt in stolen farm equipment, "and let him sell it. You know, in pieces like a chop shop." Lester nodded, happy that Char again saved his brain from too much thinking.

They drove to the end of downtown Portage and made a sharp left onto a rutted frozen road that took them under the bridge that crossed the James River – the bridge that decades ago had put an end to the Masterson family ferry service. They followed the old rutted road along the river to a spot where they dropped Nevada's body, pushed it down the bank, and watched it roll toward the river.

With a great yelp of victory, Char and Lester jumped back into the truck and took off for her place to count their money and celebrate the New Year.

~ ~ ~

As the deputy patrolling in the early hours of the New Year crossed the bridge back into Portage, he saw red taillights moving along the old river road. Nobody used that road this time of year. Old timers just used it to get their boats into the water or to fish from the banks. Why was a truck down there? The deputy sighed. It had been a quiet night and now he had to go after some fool kids who were probably drinking and God knew what else. He got to the Portage side of the bridge and drove onto the frozen, rutted road, moving slowly, trying to see if whoever was in the truck had thrown beer bottles along the track. The snow on the riverside of the old road was unblemished. It would be easy to spot any garbage those kids had thrown.

Driving slowly and scanning the roadside, he noticed that the snow was disturbed up ahead. It looked like people had gotten out of a vehicle and, by the indentations in the snow, it looked as though they had dragged bags of trash or something toward the river.

The experienced patrolman paused, scouting ahead to see if the truck was still moving along the old road. It had disappeared. He pulled up to the disturbed snow and angled one of his searchlights into the dried weeds and old branches along the shadowy expanse of riverbank. Did he see a hand? Or was that a rat? He called to the dispatcher and asked for backup. He just had a funny feeling. That truck had been running away from something. He was assured that assistance would be there in ten minutes. He got out of the car. With his weapon in one hand and a flashlight in the other, he crossed the space between the road and the river, making certain that he preserved the snowy imprints. His flashlight reflected off the slow moving water in the center of the riverbed as he pulled the beam back to scan the ice at the edges of the river. He stopped. That was a hand! He made certain his body cam was recording as he flipped his lapel radio to talk with the dispatcher. "I need an ambulance. Some fool was dumped at the river. I bet someone thought he rolled into the water. The ice stopped him."

"Your back-up isn't there yet, why are you out of your car?"

"You gonna send an ambulance or you gonna argue?"

"I already sent it," the dispatcher snarled.

"My back-up's here," said the deputy ending the conversation. He swung his flashlight to guide the other patrol car to the body.

CHAPTER TWO

"**N**ew Year's Day – is there a better day than this?" Will Zubov, Lynn's brother, asked his houseguests. Dusty, Lynn's son, Jason, Piper's three sons, and Jim Hoefler, Lynn's father, were settled in front of Will's giant HDTV – ready to watch football until their eyes could no longer focus. Will had food placed on every flat surface – chips, cold cuts, dips of all sorts, beer and soft drinks iced and ready, cheese balls, cheese sticks and cheese enchiladas. At four o'clock, Mr. Lee was sending Chinese dishes over from his carry out and Piper was bringing pizza at seven just in case anyone was still hungry. "What a great day!"

Two dogs agreed as they sprawled on the floor in front of the TV, ready to sample everything.

Dusty's phone buzzed. Six pairs of eyes stared at him. Would a phone ring in the Sistine Chapel, in the OR, in outer space? "Yeah," he demanded. "Yeah," he agreed. "Yeah," he concluded. He looked at Jim. "Adele Utley is on her way to the hospital. Someone beat the crap out of her grandson."

"You mean Nevada?" asked Jim, Adele Utley's attorney. Dusty nodded. "He's her great-grandson."

Dusty replied, "Whatever. He's in a coma. I told them we would get over there now."

Jim wrapped his cheese enchilada in a napkin, took a last drag on his beer bottle and followed Dusty to his car.

~ ~ ~

Since the men of the family were tethered to the TV all day, Lynn and her sister-in-law, Piper, organized their man-free day to see friends and enjoy the quiet. Their first stop was a visit with the Bergmans to say good-bye to Tim as he left his new family to begin his deployment on an aircraft carrier.

Lynn hugged her brother-in-law as he whispered, "This is not easy." He stared at his new family and sighed. And Lynn understood – it was difficult to leave Janet and Polly in Thel and Bergy's care for a few months. Polly was standing apart from the group with her usual scowl, daring one and all to approach her. Janet looked her vague and detached self, eating something – a new habit since her pregnancy. Bergy, the retired sheriff, slumped in his wheelchair, frustrated that he wasn't recovering from his stroke as quickly as he would have liked. And, finally, there was Thel, Bergy's wife. She seemed to be the only one of the newly formed family ready to take charge, and she had just gotten out of rehab after taking a fall and having hip surgery just before Christmas.

"We'll help them," Lynn whispered back. "You just get on the road. The sooner you're gone the sooner you'll be back."

"What's that? An old wives tale? Like watching water boil?" Tim didn't want to leave.

Lynn laughed at him. "We've got it all under control." She kissed his cheek. Tim made one more round of good-byes with his family and was out the door. He'd be in Norfolk by evening and after turning in the rental car, be on board the carrier by mid-morning tomorrow.

Everyone watched his car leave the neighborhood. Lynn heard a few sniffs. Janet announced, "I think I've lost my appetite."

Polly left the farewell gathering and climbed the stairs to her room as Thel limped to a chair. "You'll all be fine," stated Piper, addressing the rest of the farewell gathering. More hugs then she and Lynn left the house. Outside Piper said, "Polly is going to be a challenge."

Lynn looked at her, surprised. "Why do you say that? She's been very cooperative." It had only been a few weeks since Polly had accepted what she thought of as the 'Tim and Janet solution' to her orphan status. "She's settled in with the Bergmans and is back in school. She's not smiling but she's doing what we ask."

The seasoned educator tilted her head in thought as she and Lynn walked through the neighborhood. "It's my teacher sense," admitted Piper, "nothing specific, but we aren't finished helping Polly face her new situation."

"I don't expect it to be smooth," replied Lynn, "but what are you thinking?"

"That's a good question," replied the tiny principal. "I just think we better stay alert."

~ ~

Mars, one of the detectives of Dusty's unit, was waiting as Dusty and Jim entered the ER. "I sent a car for Mrs. Utley."

"What's that fool done now?" demanded Jim who had spent far too much time, in his opinion as the Utley family attorney, protecting Adele Utley from the antics of her great-grandson.

"Someone hit him over the head and tried to roll him into the river up in Portage."

"It's those Mastersons," concluded Jim. "Go arrest them."

Dusty put Jim into a chair in the ER examining room. "You stay here and wait for Adele. Don't talk about arresting anyone, that's my job." Jim opened his mouth to argue but Adele Utley tottered into the room. Mars and Dusty grabbed her before she fell. The woman was probably ninety years old and weighed ninety pounds.

Jim got up from the chair and they helped Adele

settle in. Mars began the explanation because he was the one who knew all the facts. "Early this morning a routine patrol found Nevada unconscious down by the river in Portage. According to the doc here, he was hit on the head with a pipe or something shaped like a pipe. He hasn't regained consciousness, hasn't said anything and had no ID. That's why it took us so long to get you here, Ms. Utley." He patted the old woman's shoulder.

"It's those Mastersons," she concluded. "Go arrest them."

"Yes, ma'am," replied Mars, "Dusty and I are going out to get our investigation started." Dusty gave him a grateful look and the two detectives left Jim behind with his client.

Out in the hospital parking lot the two men began their discussion. "What do you know?" asked Dusty.

"Nothing," frowned Mars. He then reported what the night patrolman had relayed about the situation. "I think Nevada was lucky that the patrol car found him so quickly. But the doc isn't optimistic. He went into an explanation of the skull and area of the hit." Mars shook his head. "You know, if I was interested in that stuff I would have become a doctor."

"Just give me his conclusion," said Dusty.

"The conclusion is," replied Mars, "he was hit really hard in a bad place on his head and if he doesn't come out of this coma in a few days, he won't come out at all."

Dusty hung his head. Nevada had been a challenge to his great-grandmother for years. Yet he was the only family she still had. They took care of one another as best they could. "What have we learned from the techs?"

"Not much, so far. Do you want to go out to the site?" asked Mars.

"Maybe we better."

~ ~ ~

Per the big game-day plan, Piper and Lynn stumbled into the house with several pizzas. The crowd had grown. In addition to Will and the boys, the room was filled with the usual college crowd that seemed to follow Jason and food. The women were glad they had doubled the pizza order. Most of the kids would be leaving over the weekend to return to campus. This was the beginning of what Lynn thought of as the long good-bye. She knew they would eat nonstop until Sunday when they would pack their cars and head back to campus, to, she was certain, not eat again until they returned to River Bend at spring break.

"Where's Dusty?" Lynn asked.

"And Jim?" asked Marianna, Lynn's stepmother. "I just got here and no one knows where Jim is."

Will pulled his eyes from the TV to say, "Dusty got a call and took Jim with him."

"Is someone hurt?"

"Is there an emergency?" The women had several questions. No one had answers. The two missing men walked in and the women repeated the questions.

Dusty grabbed a beer and a slice of pizza then flopped into a chair. "Nevada Utley was beaten up last night. He's in the hospital unconscious." He downed half his beer. "We took Adele home. She's very upset."

"Can we do anything?" asked Marianna. She had spent the day prepping for her role as director of the senior play at River Bend High School. Casting try-outs would begin next week. Marianna, a retired actress, had accepted the directorship when she married Jim a year ago. She promised to work with the school until Jim's grandchildren all graduated. Jeff, the youngest was a sophomore this year. She was counting down!

"She's fine," replied Jim. "We can check on her tomorrow after breakfast."

19

"How's Nevada?" asked Piper. "I remember him from elementary school."

"He's in pretty bad shape."

"What happened?"

Dusty finished his beer. "That's what we'll investigate tomorrow."

CHAPTER THREE

"**F**ive hundred thousand dollars????" Yolanda Valeri was confused but not speechless at the announcement as she sat in the attorney's office. "You must be joking," she challenged Robert O'Hara, the attorney for Foster Donovan, as he read the man's will.

Yolanda was a woman – fifty-ish or so – her vitality and healthy good looks made it difficult to pinpoint her age. The mother of one of Dusty's detectives, Yolanda Valeri had been a widow for five or six years. Thick black hair with graying streaks, a few extra pounds, she was well known in the community. She led a very full life in River Bend, working part time as business manager and counter help at the family bakery. In addition, she volunteered at the Genealogical Society, the Arts Council, her church and did babysitting when necessary for her grandchildren.

"He was real clear when he dictated this," Robert assured her as to Mr. Donovan's intentions. "That's why I invited Lynn to be here with you. It comes with conditions."

Lynn Powers, executive director of the River Bend Philanthropies, sat up a little straighter. "So there's a reason you wanted me here? Not just to help hold Yolanda's hand?"

Robert, a short lively man with white hair, said, "I wanted you here to help Yolanda understand the conditions."

"So there's a catch?" Yolanda nodded her head, confirming her suspicion that this was too good to be true.

Robert said, "Er...."

I knew it!" Yolanda slapped her knee. "No one gets

that kind of money from someone she hardly knew."

"Hardly knew?" gasped Robert. "Five hundred kisses is what he said."

Yolanda sucked in her breath, then Robert and Lynn watched as tears streamed down her cheeks. Robert passed her a box of tissues. She took several, anticipating a lot of tears, and waving her hand as though chasing gnats, she pulled herself together after a moment. "Five hundred kisses? He counted them?"

"Evidently," shrugged Robert. Yolanda's tears continued as she tried to process the information. Lynn knelt at her side, placing an arm around her shoulders.

"Take your time," said Lynn, as she took the wet tissues and handed Yolanda some fresh tear wipers. "Robert and I aren't going anywhere. We want to hear about your five hundred kisses with a man you say you hardly knew." Yolanda smiled through her tears.

She finally seemed in control and settled back in the chair. "Mr. Donovan sat in the back pew of church every Sunday. When I walked into mass at St. Bridget's he was always there. He had given me money one day for a Lady's Guild raffle. It was a generous donation and I jokingly said that I owed him a kiss. He turned his cheek to me and I kissed him. The next Sunday I noticed him in his usual seat at the back of the church and told him that his donation helped the guild buy extra supplies for the residents of the domestic violence shelter. He just pointed to his cheek and I gave him another kiss." Yolanda dabbed her eyes and smiled at her friends. "And that's how it started. Every Sunday I greeted him and gave him a kiss. He counted them?"

"That's almost ten years of kisses," Lynn reminded her. "You had a very long relationship with him."

"It wasn't ten years," sighed Yolanda. "It was more like three or four. I also kissed him when we met at daily mass. He attended daily and I attend once or twice a week. And sometimes we ran into each other around town and he made a big deal of demanding his kiss." She wiped her eyes again. "He was so sweet." She sighed again. "I guess I did have a relationship with him. When he went into the hospital a few months ago, I visited him. Then he went into hospice care and I only saw him once and he was dead." She wiped her eyes. "He counted my kisses?"

"Evidently," said Robert, "but let me finish this. He has about six million dollars and one son who is F. Mason Donovan. He gets the remainder. You get the five hundred thousand to give away as you see fit and then, if I," here Robert arched his eyebrows, "if I approve your donations, I am to give you a gift for yourself of twenty-five thousand."

"What?" Yolanda gasped, "This is silly – I don't need his money."

"Would you have taken the five hundred thousand if he'd left it to you?" asked Lynn.

Yolanda thought for several minutes. "I didn't think the five hundred thousand seemed real. I thought you were joking. But twenty-five, that seems more real. Am I making sense?"

Lynn laughed at her. "I think Robert isn't making any sense."

"That's why you're here," explained Robert.

"To help you make sense?" asked Lynn.

"No, to help Yolanda give away the money so I can give her the other money. I want to close out this estate and his son wants to sell the house and clean up the other loose ends of the estate and get back to his job."

"Is he mad about the money?" asked Yolanda.

"He inherited all the stock and a lot of other property. You got some of the cash," Robert said.

"Stock and other property?" Yolanda was really puzzled. "He didn't look like he had a lot of money."

"He had plenty. He was pretty generous to the church and his old college. I don't know if he gave money around town." Robert shuffled through some papers.

"I don't think anyone knew he had resources," said Lynn. She knew where all the money was in town. As the executive director of the River Bend Philanthropies she was a professional fundraiser and could sniff out funds. But right now, she was doubting her money sense. How had she missed Foster Donovan?

Robert laughed. "I can see, Lynn, that you're wondering how you missed Foster as a donor." She gasped, then blushed.

"You're right," she admitted. "I never met him. How did he slip through my net?" She turned to Yolanda. "Now what about spending your five hundred thousand?"

Yolanda laughed. "I'll think about it. I think I want to talk to Father Nick. I didn't know Mr. Donovan very well. I'd like to put money into things he supported."

"Fair enough," said Lynn. "I'll give you the weekend and then we can talk about putting that money to good use."

~ ~ ~

"When's the last time we had someone assaulted in Portage?" Dusty asked as he and his two detectives enjoyed leftover holiday cookies with their morning coffee.

"Not recently," replied Danny Valeri another member of the James County/River Bend Joint Investigation Unit. Dusty looked at him in disbelief. "Oh, the ER sees plenty of people and the EMTs get a lot of calls, but no one ever files charges," explained Danny. "So, not recently."

"Any ideas which of the Mastersons might have done this?" Dusty asked.

"Not really. Those still active that we know about are too old. Ever since we put Mace in jail for murder, there's no one young and mean enough to do this to Nevada. At least no one who has surfaced in our patrol reports."

"There must be." Dusty was also a believer – if it happens in Portage, follow the Mastersons.

"We don't know it was the Mastersons," argued Mars, reading his mind. "It could be anyone. We all know Nevada – he could make a saint mad enough to kill him."

The other two in the office had to agree.

"Stay in touch with the hospital. If he comes to, I want one of you there for the interview. In the meantime, make certain the techs are compiling what evidence they find in case this turns to murder."

"Some new year," grumbled Danny.

~ ~ ~

Yolanda was still reeling from the conditions of Foster's will. Half a million dollars to give away! As she thought about it she began to realize that she had two specific goals – first, she wanted to do a great job. Second, she wanted to give it away in a manner that reflected the giving history of Foster – give to the causes and issues he thought were important.

Yolanda pulled into the parking lot at St. Bridget's, deciding that she needed to talk to the pastor, Father Nick. He had spent a lot of time with Foster before his death. Maybe the priest would have some hint, some guidance for her.

She heard scraping and followed the sounds to the side door of the church office. "I thought we paid someone to do that," she commented to the priest who was shoveling the sidewalk.

"We do," Father Nick grinned, "but I needed the

exercise. My robes were a little snug when I said Mass this morning."

She guffawed heartily. No use being dainty and feminine, he was a priest. "You've got to get really big for those things to get tight."

"I'm getting my abs in shape so women will ogle me?" He might be gaining weight but he wasn't losing his sense of humor.

"Is the regular guy sick or something?" Enough of this banter, she had a half a million dollars on her mind. She got the open bag of salt and scattered grains along the shoveled walkway.

"Or something," replied Father Nick. "He was arrested for drunk and disorderly on New Year's Eve. The judge gave him ten days in jail."

Yolanda laughed again. "I can send over my son or my son-in-law to help."

The priest leaned the shovel against the building and brushed the snow from his shoulders. "Did we have an appointment?"

"No, I came to ask you about Foster Donovan."

"You got his money." He stated a fact.

"You knew?"

He grinned. "We talked about it one of the last days he was alive and lucid. He thought you would have fun with it."

"Fun?" she screeched. "A half a million dollars?"

"That much," said the priest in awe. "He never gave me a figure, just the conditions of his will. You don't have to give any to the church. Foster already gave us a bequest. Robert O'Hara told me about it yesterday."

"I want to know more about the man," said Yolanda. She brushed snow off of the shrubbery near the door. "I want to use his money on programs that he supported."

"I can't answer anything specific," said the priest.

"He was very generous. And so was his wife. She didn't attend church here, but they invited me to dinner regularly while she was alive." He led the way into the offices. Yolanda followed, shaking snow from her boots before walking into the reception area.

"Hey, Yolo," called the parish secretary. "There's coffee in the break room."

Yolanda and Father Nick made their way to the coffee pot. The small table was covered with cakes and cookies. "No wonder you were out working on your abs," she said as she grabbed a cookie.

"Mosely, the pastor at First Methodist says I should freeze this stuff. He says things disappear fast and by February you're desperate for even one oatmeal cookie. So I'm following his suggestion." He got a box of freezer bags and began to divide the cookies and cakes. Yolanda fell in step and did her share of sampling and packing. She told herself she would remember this little stockpile when February got dull and boring. Sweets seemed to taste better in a friendly kitchen instead of sneaking bites while hidden in the bakery storage room.

"Give me a little more information about Foster," she prompted the priest.

Father Nick munched on a cookie swimming in powdered sugar. "He made certain any organization that got his money was well managed, kept to their mission and could demonstrate impact for the good of their clients." He poured them both a cup of coffee. "I think he gave you that money because he thought you viewed your charitable work, whether money or time, the same way."

Sipping her coffee, she thought for a moment. "I think you're right. I do have expectations."

The priest licked powdered sugar off his fingers. "I don't know anything more about where he gave money.

I wouldn't worry. You'll do a good job."

She picked up a small bag of cookies. "Thanks for having confidence in me. I'll see you in church." She ran out the door before he could snatch his cookies back.

~ ~ ~

As had become a recent practice in her life, Lynn stopped to see Teniquia LaMont and her new family. During the Christmas holidays Tee had visited The Heights so that her children could enjoy Dusty's train layout. Every Christmas Dusty and his nieces and nephews designed a special Christmas layout under his tree. Once he married Lynn the traditional layout moved to the attic in Lynn's house, and had ballooned to include several additions supplied by Will, Lynn's brother. Or as Dusty's brother, Carl, called it, "HO gauge on steroids."

With Will's enthusiastic support Dusty now had enough track, trains and accessories to fill the attic. Track ran around the attic floor, through a miniature countryside with all sorts of animals and outbuildings. It ran through east village and west village as well as modern village and Victorian village. There was an industrial park and a university campus as well as a hospital, jail and zoo. Will was unstoppable. He spent a lot of time searching the Internet for more.

Needless to say the three children Tee and her husband had recently adopted had been charmed by all of Will's efforts. It had been several days since Lynn had checked in with the new family, so she thought that a drop-in after lunch would do nicely.

Glory, Tee's mother, answered the door. "How you doing, honey?" gushed the older woman, her dark brown face filled with delight. She had taken on a glow since the children had entered her life. The days after Tee's surgery had been tense – the detective had been shot during a drug raid and needed surgery and several weeks in the hospital to recuperate. Deciding to adopt the children seemed to have energized and pleased the family. Lynn always met various relatives and other members of the black community bustling in and out with food or helping with chores. Glory managed all the support like a commanding general.

"I hear Tee is going back to work soon," said Lynn as she entered the crowded little house.

Glory rolled her eyes. "That girl won't listen. She thinks your husband can't do without her."

Tee had been part of Dusty's investigative unit since it was organized. "I'm sure she's correct," smiled Lynn. "They really miss her."

"Hey, Lynn," called Tee from her recliner. She might be home from the hospital, but she still needed her rest. "I'm going to start going in a few hours a day. Moses starts school on Monday and I thought I could be at my desk while he's away. Mama and the others can handle the two girls."

Tee and her husband Lonzo had adopted three abandoned black children – two little girls, barely toddlers and a boy about five or six. The little boy was starting kindergarten at Piper's elementary school. Young Moses appeared at Lynn's side and smiled. "I'm going to school."

"I know." Lynn caressed his cheek. What a difference from two months ago. The youngster was growing in so many ways and his natural charm would help him to adjust and make friends in school. "Miss Piper has a place ready for you. You'll have a lot of fun." He smiled at her and dashed away to play with his sisters.

Tee laughed from her chair. "I'd get up but I did enough today. We looked at a few houses."

"How's the search going?" asked Lynn as she sat on

the sofa.

"I think we found something. I'm waiting for Lonzo to look it over and then have the realtor lead us through the process. It's near the school." She described the interior and the location.

"I know where you mean," said Lynn, "those are solid older homes."

"It's close to my place, too," added Glory who had come into the room with a tray of cookies and some coffee. "You have to eat some food," she instructed Lynn, "Everyone keeps bringing things by. Even Lonzo can't eat much more." Lonzo was a big man.

Lynn couldn't resist a lemon-blueberry scone. It was a specialty of Glory's cousin. "I just wanted to let you know that the guys are dismantling the trains on Sunday. So you might want the kids to have one last look over the weekend."

Tee nodded. "Dusty sent me a text. I'll call before we come. Will Jason be there?"

Lynn's son Jason had become good friends with the youngsters on their visits. "He will. He leaves for school on Sunday. He says he wants to leave before they start dismantling the layout. It always makes him sad to see it put away."

The doorbell rang and Lynn jumped up to answer, calling to Glory as she did. "I'll get it." Piper was standing on the front porch with another woman. "What are you doing here?" both Piper and Lynn asked together. Lynn stepped back to allow the women to enter.

Greeting Teniquia, Piper said, "I brought Moses' teacher to meet him today. I'm sorry I didn't call. But we were getting ready for the kids to return on Monday and I told Ginger about him." She spoke quickly. "Oh, this is Ginger Reyes." Piper motioned the young Latina to come forward. The teacher and the detective shook hands.

Teniquia smiled at the young teacher. "I think he'll be shy at first."

Ginger smiled in return. "That's what I thought. So I asked Piper if we could meet him before Monday. I'm sorry if this is inconvenient." The kindergarten teacher was comfortably round, indicating that her baby might arrive before the end of the school year.

"Oh, don't worry," said Piper as she settled on the couch. "Teachers are never inconvenient." She picked up a lemon-blueberry scone and helped herself to coffee, taking Lynn's cup.

"Who was at the door?" asked Glory as she came into the room with one of the little girls in her arms. Moses and the other little girl followed. "I know you," Glory addressed the teacher. "I see you at the senior center."

Ginger smiled. "Yes, ma'am. I pick up my grandmother when I finish at school."

"Mama, Ms. Reyes came to meet Moses. She'll be his teacher." With that announcement Moses popped his head up and solemnly studied Ginger. In the last two months he had met so many adults who were kind to him. He was always ready to make another friend. He just had to study each one first.

Ginger sank down to be eye level with the little boy. "I will be your teacher when you come to school on Monday. I am very happy that you will be my student." Moses stared. "I have something just for you." She pulled a t-shirt out of her bag. It said I'm a great student at Rathborne Elementary School. Moses moved closer. He studied the shirt as she read the inscription. To everyone's delight, he pulled off his Sesame Street t-shirt and pulled the new shirt over his head.

Piper cleared her throat, and using her

professional voice, so that everyone understood that this was important, she said, "We thought Ginger could do an assessment here where Moses is comfortable and that would help us be ready for him on Monday."

"What kind of an assessment?" asked Tee.

Ginger stood. "I brought a simple instrument we use on all the children when they first enter school. Piper and I have discussed this and think Moses and I would be more successful here than with the distractions of the school. I understand that he has not been around large numbers of children during his early years."

"What do you need?" asked Glory.

"Just a kitchen table and a little privacy."

CHAPTER FOUR

Piper walked into Lynn's kitchen after dinner. Dusty was walking out the door. He and Will were racing out to a North Consolidated basketball game to cheer on Dusty's nephew. Piper was deep in thought as they passed one another without comment. That was unusual so Lynn knew something was on her mind.

"Sorry I couldn't stay while your teacher tested Moses," she explained, "I had to get back to my office. Did everything go all right?"

Piper helped herself to a beer and found a bag of chips. Once she was comfortable at the kitchen table, she said, "That little boy is off the charts."

"So why do you look so worried?"

"I'm not worried, I'm thinking about his future."

"So why do you look so worried?"

"I told you I'm not worried." Piper sighed. "I'm not worried about him, but I keep thinking of all the kids that were caught up in that racket, whatever it was. All the kids we didn't save."

Lynn poured a glass of wine and sat at the table. "I know. But that counselor I'm seeing keeps telling me that there are things I have to let go. And celebrate the positives. So tell me about the kids we saved. What about Moses?"

Piper smiled. "He's a delight. Ginger is in love with him already. She and I have been planning how we'll help him catch up with the class. She thinks it will take him about a month."

"A month? Is that too long or not long enough?"

"Tee and Lonzo have already taught him letters and numbers. He seems to understand about reading–"

Lynn interrupted, "That's because Ricky Mitchell

read the children books every day when they were in the hospital. And Polly worked with them when she was sharing the hospital room with them."

"It's going to be exciting to watch him grow," Piper, the educator, prophesied. Both women had sons; they looked at one another and laughed. "Of course," Piper, the mom, continued, "Tee and Lonzo are still in for some interesting times. We'll just have to tell them some of the things our boys tried to get away with." They laughed again, happy to think about Moses and his future.

~ ~ ~

Martin Healey, Mars to his friends, felt as though he were walking his last mile. It was a new year for God's sake. He had to pull himself out of this funk. He had to get past his broken heart. Fuck! He sounded like a soap opera diva, even to his own ears. His heart was broken. Nancy Rawlings, the young woman he had worshipped for almost his whole life, had broken it. She had allowed him to cherish her, to enjoy her affection and then she told him she liked him for sex, but wasn't interested in family, children, monogamy. After her announcement she had left town at Thanksgiving to join up with her old boyfriend for a few days of gymnastic sex before he returned to his wife and children. She claimed to enjoy her life as a single, rich woman – a life that didn't include Mars in the role of husband. Mars still found it hard to breathe at times. Once she walked out of his life, he had thrown himself into work. He had taken on all extra duty through the holidays, because, if he sat a home, he could hear his heart breaking – just like a soap opera diva.

So it's a new year. Time to try something new. That's why he was walking his last mile of freedom and a life he sort of tolerated. He rang the doorbell. An elderly man answered.

34

"Martin, thank you for joining me for dinner this evening."

"Thanks for inviting me, Uncle Hutch."

Mars, a skilled detective in the James County/River Bend Joint Investigation Unit, felt his stomach lurch as he walked over the threshold to dine with his uncle. It would just be the two of them this evening. Uncle Hutch called this meeting/dinner once a year. He brought Mars up-to-date on the family businesses, the family financial report, the family real estate holdings, and the family ownership of the River Bend First Bank. Uncle Hutch always concluded by asking if Mars had any questions. Mars never did.

Mars was wealthy. His father, Spencer Healey, a recluse and artist living somewhere in Arizona or New Mexico, had been one of three grandchildren of a wealthy construction and land development family. As long as Spencer received funds to support his reclusive, alcohol imbued, creative life style, he stayed quietly away. His cousin, Sophie Grayson, and her son, H. Lawrence Grayson, managed and expanded the family corporation, recently renamed Grayley, Inc., for the remaining family – Sophie, her sister Marge, Spencer, Mars and H. Lawrence.

Mars' mother was Cornelia Dunn, the young, and only, sister of Hutch Dunn. They were the last of a line of heirs of the prestigious law firm of Hutch and Dunn. This law firm had operated in River Bend for over one hundred years, investing in or otherwise controlling and advising most of the wealthy families in James County and western North Carolina. As with the Healey family, he was in the latest generation of grandchildren who would one day inherit and control the family wealth. In the Dunn family there were three heirs, Mars and Uncle Hutch's two daughters who had no children and were beyond childbearing years. Mars was much younger than his cousins and the last of the Dunn line. Someday it would all be his.

Shit. Mars knew first hand that all the wealth in the world didn't matter when your parents fought like cats and dogs, and your fiancée opted for a free-range sex life. His wealth kept him comfortable. It didn't keep him warm and happy.

He walked into Uncle Hutch's den where they enjoyed a glass of scotch as they sat on old, comfortable chairs in front of the fireplace. The old attorney sipped his drink and sighed. "I know you don't like this annual review, Martin. But I also know you understand that in this family, wealth comes with responsibilities. My daughters do what they can. But frankly, the Judge would rather be fishing when she's not on the bench. And Ilona only worries about Botox and looking years younger than she is. And we both know that your mother has relied on me to manage the accounts for years."

"Yes, sir."

The old man smiled at his nephew, then reached out and patted his knee. "Martin, as I look back over my life, I wonder if you weren't the smart one."

Mars stared at his uncle. "The smart one, sir?"

"You chose to work at a job you enjoy, one that allows you to use all your talents, and be exciting at the same time."

Mars smiled at the man. "Sometimes I get shot at, sir."

Uncle Hutch sighed again. "That's when I worry about you. When your colleague, Ms. LaMont was shot, I was devastated. She is a treasure, and we can't afford to lose her kind in our community."

"I agree, sir." Mars shifted in his chair. "But she's on the mend and has adopted those babies. I think her life will be all that she and her husband deserve."

"And that is what I want for you, son."

What was this? Uncle Hutch was making this a different kind of meeting. In fact it didn't feel like a business meeting, but like a family dinner night. Mars sipped his drink and waited to hear what Uncle Hutch had in mind.

"I think dinner is ready," said the old man. "Let's talk about something interesting. We can talk family business later."

"Interesting?" asked Mars.

"That football pool." Uncle Hutch chortled and slapped his thigh as they walked into the dining room. Once they settled in their chairs a maid served the soup.

"The football pool?" He assumed his uncle was referring to the pool that Jason Powers ran from his college dorm on the Internet for his family and close friends.

"Damn," snapped his uncle, "even Nathan Taft won once. I've followed the Panthers since they awarded the franchise to Charlotte. I rarely miss a game. How did he win? He doesn't even know where the end zone is!"

Mars laughed. "I didn't win this year either." And that was the talk for the rest of the meal – sports, River Bend news and family gossip – the kind of evening a man should spend with his only uncle.

Once dessert had been served, Uncle Hutch became a businessman again. He stood. "Let's have a little port in the den. We still have some things to discuss."

Mars followed him back into the comfortable room, took his seat in front of the fireplace and waited.

Uncle Hutch handed Mars a drink and settled in his chair. "Martin, it's time for you to take on some of the family's responsibilities. I can't keep up the pace. I've made certain you understand the business dynamics of our portfolios, but you have to start earning this money."

"Sir, we have this conversation every year."

"Let me frame this discussion a little better," said Uncle Hutch. "I can't do it all any more. My doctor says I have to slow down. My daughters are trying to help. Ilona is coming to town more frequently to help me sort through family records and family treasures. The Judge," his daughter Judge Dunn, "is coming to my office and helping me with the legal aspects of our family trust. We've been reorganizing to make things easier for all of you when I pass."

Mars held his breath. This was a more serious discussion than he had listened to in years past. Uncle Hutch had always liked being the one in charge. Tonight he was acknowledging his age. "Yes, sir. You know I'll help where I can."

"Martin, I have one job I want you to handle. You have a financial background and you're smart and tough." Uncle Hutch sipped his port. Mars waited. The fire crackled and finally the old attorney spoke again. "I want you to replace me on the River Bend First Bank board." He stared at his nephew over his glass.

Mars was silent.

Uncle Hutch continued, "I want you to be there to protect our depositors. At our core we're a hometown bank. And this family owns a big chunk. I want the bank to always work the way our ancestors wanted it to – a bank that serves the community and helps families buy homes and build small businesses. That may not be the current banking philosophy around the country, but it's this family's philosophy."

"Is something happening with the bank board?"

Uncle Hutch chuckled. "That's why you're a detective. You catch nuance. I'm the last of the dreamers on the board. Today they are all interested in taking a bank retreat to Hilton Head and increasing board member perks. But not one of them is interested in helping a family secure a loan for a modest house." He was silent for a moment. "I'm tired of fighting, Martin. I feel as though I've been holding back greed and avarice all by myself. Over the years I've had some allies, but we're all aging. Nathan, Jim Hoefler, Bergy – we've done well by this community. But it's time for your generation to take up our banner.

Mars understood what his Uncle was saying. He knew local history and the role both sides of his family had played in making River Bend a safe and prosperous place to live. And he knew his uncle was right. "Yes, sir," he responded, "It is time. When do you want me to begin?"

"Why," said Uncle Hutch, looking exactly like a man with something to hide, "we elected you to the board this afternoon."

Mars threw back his head and laughed.

Uncle Hutch tried to look innocent.

CHAPTER FIVE

The burden and responsibility of deciding how to distribute Foster Donovan's money weighed heavily on Yolanda. She had talked at length with Father Nick and decided she needed more information from Robert O'Hara. She reasoned that since he had the final say over her funds distribution he might give her some hints as to his preferences.

"Yolanda," intoned Robert, "just as long as it's a functioning, duly recognized nonprofit, I'll approve the donation. God knows there are enough in this town that you could give fifty dollars to each one and still leave someone out." Small town life is informal, so Yolanda had stopped at Robert's home for this early Saturday morning discussion. He was in baggy pants and an old Notre Dame sweatshirt finishing breakfast and reading the morning paper. It wasn't golf weather yet.

"That's so cynical," Yolanda complained. She visited with the O'Haras frequently, especially Millie O'Hara, so she knew where to find the fresh coffee, cup and cream. "You assume any nonprofit is worthless." Having prepared her coffee, she joined him at the table.

"That's not what I said. I just pointed out that there are plenty. As long as you give money to an agency with a valid IRS letter of recognition, you're good. I am not going to judge the merit of any cause you wish to support." He pushed a plate of muffins toward her.

Millie's muffins – they had a bad reputation. Millie wasn't known for her baking skills. Yolanda smiled and ignored the offered plate. "What do you mean by that remark?" she challenged the attorney.

He hemmed and hawed. "I mean, if you want to

give all the money to some Albanian refugee candy makers, I won't comment as long as they have valid papers."

"You mean if they're citizens?"

"Don't go there," he challenged right back. "This is not a human rights discussion. Or a pet rescue discussion, or–"

"Are you saying I can't give the money to groups outside of River Bend?"

"I didn't say that," he paused, "but you know I believe in charity close to home. We have enough nonprofits in this town that you shouldn't have to go anywhere else to find causes you can support."

"I can't send money to an international group serving refugees or elephants in the wild or whales?"

"I didn't say that," Robert growled. "I just said that I like my charity close to home so I can see results and watch how the money is managed." Robert sat back in his chair and studied her. "It's tough, isn't it?" She nodded. "I learned that my first years working with the Philanthropies. How to determine who gets what and how much and are they worthy? I don't envy you. I've kept an eye on the nonprofits in James County and they all do good work. Some are better organized and managed than others but they all seem to stay focused on their missions. Some missions I think are too narrow. It makes sense to me that some groups should merge, but they won't hear it. So they all have to work to get noticed."

"I think I'll let Lynn send out grant requests from her office. That way I can stay as anonymous as possible." She sipped her coffee, feeling smug.

"A will is filed for public record. Once I took all the legal steps everyone knew that you had money to give away – anyone who looks at wills that is. Someone might notice your name. I'm sorry. I should have thought of some way to protect you." Robert frowned into his coffee.

She moaned as her smugness evaporated.

"Now Yolanda, don't get upset and worried—"

"For heaven's sakes, Robert, I can handle this. I just want to do it right. I've started by talking with you and Father Nick. Lynn and I meet on Monday. Next I'd like to find out a little more about Foster. Maybe there were certain things he believed in."

"He gave St. Bridget's a nice donation and also money to some out-of-town organizations," Robert reported as he moved the muffin plate to the kitchen counter. "He made some donations in his wife's memory. She gave money to some projects while she was alive. They seemed like a caring family."

"Have you met his son, the heir you mentioned?"

"Yes, in fact he's coming into town tomorrow. I'll give him your phone number and ask him to meet with you. When he learned about the will and conditions, he asked about you." Robert scratched a note on a small pad. "I'll try to explain your concerns when I ask him to call."

"Thanks." Yolanda stood. "I appreciate your time, Robert. This is just something new to me." The attorney walked her to the door and kissed her cheek.

~ ~ ~

"I don't know why everyone is here," grumbled Dusty. He poked Piper with his elbow as she tried to reach around him for the snacks Lynn had placed on the counter. "You're the one with the new kitchen." A quiet Saturday night as the usual folks gathered at Lynn's for dinner.

"I would have hosted dinner, but I couldn't convince Lynn to leave you at home," challenged Piper. "She thought you should be included and I thought you would probably break something." She shot him an elbow as she attacked the spinach-artichoke dip. "So we had to come here."

Dusty and Piper were always sniping at one another and the family seemed to ignore them, until tonight. "I've had it," snarled Jim Hoefler, Dusty's and Piper's father-in-law. "How long are you two going to carry on –?"

"It's his fault," snapped Piper.

"No, it's not," countered Dusty.

"– pretending you don't get along?" Jim dared them to deny his claim. When they didn't speak, he said, "I know about that thing you do at Piper's school." He stared at Dusty.

"What thing?" asked Carl, Dusty's brother. "He busted her for hitting little kids?"

"I don't hit my students." The tiny principal was getting angry.

"Then what is Jim talking about?" asked Marianna, Jim's wife. Now everyone was staring at Piper and Dusty. Well, not everyone.

Will cleared his throat. "I sort of mentioned your training program." He hung his head.

Lynn gave him a squinty-eyed look. "And they say women can't keep a secret."

Will turned to his sister, "I couldn't let Jim go on thinking that they" he nodded to Piper and Dusty," didn't get along and always fought, or something."

Dusty smiled. "It would have come out soon," he admitted. "We're getting an award from the governor for our" here he used finger quotes, "enhanced community policing curriculum."

"We are?" squealed Piper as she gave Dusty a strangling hug. He peeled her off him and draped his arm across her shoulders.

"I got the letter yesterday. We're invited to a special presentation in Raleigh sometime at the end of

February." The tall detective and the tiny principal smiled at the family.

"But what do you do?" asked Marianna. "Are you teaching Piper to investigate crime?"

Dusty nodded to Piper, acknowledging that she had the floor. He brought the dip to the table and sat down. She began, "We were talking one night about the risks to my students experiencing possible police confrontations as they got older. I didn't want to read that one of my students was shot by an officer for any reason." Piper was principal at Rathborne Elementary in South End, the poor and minority residential area of River Bend.

Dusty took over, "And I was concerned that our training program might not be strong enough to prepare patrolmen for community policing, which is based on building community relationships and avoiding confrontation."

"I thought there already were police officers in all the schools for security and things," said Carl.

"That means those officers have had more training in dealing with youngsters while protecting the students and teachers in a crisis. The training is job specific," explained Dusty.

"We wanted a training component that reached everyone, students and rookies," said Piper.

"We do some training at the department, then we send the rookies to the school," said Dusty.

"We do an orientation at my school and then assign the trainees special tasks that allow them to work with the kids and meet the parents and others in the community."

"What sorts of tasks?" asked Jim.

Piper grinned. "We had to think hard about making certain they kept their dignity, that the kids stayed respectful and that everyone learned to like one another. So they dress out for PE and are assigned lunch tables. They eat with the kids, but they don't have lunch duty like the teachers do. They ride the buses and help the kids get on and off. That way they can meet the parents waiting at the stop. They walk kids home and can learn which kids go to an empty house. They have reading buddies and math buddies and anything else that we can think of."

Dusty plunged a cracker into the dip and popped it into his mouth. "Hey," complained Piper, "You always eat the most."

"I eat the most?" retorted Dusty, "I've seen you put away half a cow and leave nothing for the rest of us but the bones."

Salley, Carl's wife, walked into the kitchen during this last exchange. She sighed, "Can't you two ever be pleasant to one another?"

And the rest of the family rushed to explain what they had just learned.

"Really?" Salley had a gleam in her eye. "Why can't I have a trainee come to the shelter on weekends?" she asked her brother-in-law. "Do you like Piper better? Is she your favorite sister-in-law?" Salley was the executive director for the local women's shelter.

Dusty was smart enough to know that there was no win-win in this situation. He dragged another cracker through the dip. "What have you got in mind?"

Salley was thoughtful as she sat at the table and dipped her own cracker. "For the same reasons you have trainees at Piper's school, you should send some to the shelter," Salley explained. "On a busy weekend your trainees would learn a lot from my clients and they would have some experience with the victims that would be helpful when they're finally on patrol and are called to a domestic violence situation."

Dusty thought for a moment. Crunched another

cracker. Piper crunched a cracker. They looked at each other. "What do you think?" he asked the pensive principal.

"We could amend some of our training goals, redesign the tasks to include things like helping at intake, helping with security." She took a drink from his beer bottle. "We could create a component where the trainees got to listen to the victims and their children in a safe situation."

Salley took a drink from his bottle as she added, "One trainee on a weekend rotation would learn more than you could ever present in the classroom. He or she would see how frightened the women and children are when they arrive. And see the bruises and tears."

Will got more beer for everyone and joined the discussion. "I think that's important. You know that man, the one I thought was my father, used to hit my mother." Everyone gasped. "He only did it twice. I was big enough to scare him." Will was the product of a brief affair between Jim and Will's mother. "And we all know how Amelia was treated."

Amelia Shipley, owner of Amelia's Maids, had been a battered woman who would accept no community support until someone murdered her husband, freeing her from the abusive relationship. Will had known she needed protection but Amelia had refused both his help and help from Salley at the shelter.

"So how much money will you need?" Lynn had been quiet through the whole discussion.

"What money?"

"This sounds like a grant just waiting to be funded," she replied.

"It doesn't cost us any money to work with Piper," said Dusty.

"Will pays for it," said Piper.

"I pay for it?" asked Will, all of a sudden alert to

this money talk.

"I need certain things that aren't in the official school budget," Piper admitted. "I want to pay for the trainees' lunches. And I bought some books for our library that explain law enforcement careers to our fourth and fifth graders. I had a welcome party and will have a farewell party at the end of the school year where we'll give gifts to the trainees." She shrugged at her husband, "Our checking account has the funds," and sipped her beer.

"Why didn't you say something?" asked Dusty. "I might have found some money in my budget."

"It was too important that we have a good program," replied Piper. "Money was just secondary."

"Because I pay for it," Will reminded everyone.

"I expect a grant proposal. In fact," Lynn's eyes twinkled, "I'm aware of a grant request coming out in a few weeks that is designed for your project."

"What grant?"

"I'll make certain all of you are on the e-mail distribution list." Now she was smug – and hungry. Just like the cavalry, Jason and the college crowd plus a few others came through the door with the carryout order from Uncle Chicken. She counted noses and hoped there was enough chicken, ribs and sides for this mob. If not, there were always the New Year's Eve and New Year's Day leftovers in Piper's refrigerator.

CHAPTER SIX

The last of the college crowd waved good-bye. Jason had his car packed. "Happy New Year, Mom." He hugged Lynn one more time. He was still concerned that she wasn't back to her old self after Susan's murder. Dusty had reassured him that things were progressing. "Any weekend you want me home, you just ask," Jason offered his mother. "I always have laundry I can bring home."

Lynn kissed his cheek. She and Dusty had talked about Jason's solicitude. It warmed her to see him maturing and that she was his focus. "You just study so you can get a good job," she reminded him. "Dusty and I will need someone to take care of us in our old age."

"Don't you have an IRA or something?" His voice cracked.

Her teenage son was back. She hugged him harder. "Get on the road. You should be back on campus before dark."

He hugged her, shook Dusty's hand and dashed to his car.

Dusty came up behind her to circle her in his arms. "He's got a good heart, even if he is a little loopy."

Lynn turned in his arms and rested her head on his chest. "I'm trying, Dusty. I haven't had nightmares for several days."

He pushed some hair behind her ear while he held her. "You're doing fine. I think dealing with Polly is also on your mind."

Dealing with the after effects of trauma was proving more of an emotional challenge than either of them had expected. "Just be patient," she mumbled into his chest.

"That's easy to do when I love you." They walked back into the house, finally alone after the hectic Christmas holidays.

~ ~ ~

Mars sprawled across his bed, angling his head to look out the windows. His bedroom had a view of Jefferson Street – a street that ran parallel to Main, but a block over. As with many small towns, it was the block that provided the transition from downtown to residential living. The street was quiet on a Sunday afternoon. The church across the street was empty after the beehive activity of Sunday morning. The small sandwich shop was closed on Sundays and the upholsterer's shop was always shuttered on weekends.

He was staring out his bedroom window because, if he looked out the windows at the back of the building, he would see the bank on Main Street. He was now a full board member of the River Bend First Bank and wondering what it would mean to his life.

Mars had spent years avoiding his wealth. He admitted to himself that he enjoyed what it allowed – he bought what he wanted, followed any whim. But he had learned early in his life that a whim never satisfied as much as dinner with the Bergmans or a run and early breakfast with Danny and Buck.

But he already served the community. He strapped on a gun every day to serve. What more was he to do? He failed to see how being bored on the bank board would serve anyone. But Uncle Hutch needed to step down.

He knew that his wealth also meant power. What would he do with power? Power to do what? He gave that a lot of thought. From his brief discussion with Uncle Hutch, he understood that his bank role would be to keep the greedy and grasping at bay, to protect the family's interests and to serve the community. Maybe he needed to be armed at the board meeting, too.

Here he was in a new year, nowhere near where he thought he would be. Nancy was out of his life – living her fantasy as Cory's mistress. And he was serving on a bank board – not married and not raising a family. He hadn't seen this as his future. He just hoped that this new facet of his life brought him some fulfillment, some enjoyment, and maybe something more satisfying in his private life.

~ ~ ~

"Those kids are so cute," Lynn proclaimed to the darkness of the bedroom. Dusty knew what kids. She snuggled close to him. "I'm glad they got to see the trains one more time. I think little Moses liked helping dismantle the track."

Dusty kissed the top of her head because she had burrowed between his arm and his chest. "It was good that Lonzo was here, too. Someone had to keep Will in line." They both laughed. Will enjoyed helping with the train layout and argued that it should stay together all year. Lonzo had been clear that the trains had to go away or his children would never leave.

As soon as Jason had driven off to school, Lynn and Dusty thought that they would finally be alone for the first time since Christmas break began. Didn't happen. As they walked into the house, Dusty's phone buzzed. It had been a text from Tee

Tee: Trains still running?
Dusty: Y
Tee: Visit?
Dusty: OK
Tee: In 15
And the new family arrived just as Will jogged over

from his house asking, "Need help with the trains?" It had been fun, but it had not been the private afternoon they had planned. Now it was bedtime. They were finally alone again.

"Piper and I were thinking we should warn Tee about raising sons."

Dusty held her tight. "Don't scare her. Besides, Moses doesn't look like he'll be as loopy as Jason." Lynn didn't jump to her son's defense. That made Dusty suspect there was something on her mind. "You think Moses is going to be trouble?"

"No," said Lynn in a slow thoughtful whisper. "I thought Jason showed a lot of maturity this visit. He's thinking about life."

"I'm impressed with the way he has worried about you," replied Dusty. "He's a good kid."

"That's what I mean," said Lynn, struggling to rise up on her elbow. "Should parents raise good kids or good adults?"

"One grows into the other," replied Dusty.

"Maybe not," answered Lynn. "Good kids obey, rely on parents to make a lot of the rules and a lot of the decisions. Good adults have been taught how to make good decisions for themselves." She flopped back on her pillow, which she forgot was Dusty's chest. He gasped for breath. She scrambled to a sitting position and waited for Dusty to breathe again. But of course this was Lynn, so while she waited she continued to talk. "I was wondering if we've raised Jason to always be a good kid, follow rules, play nice, but we haven't raised him to be a leader, think through to a solution, make life-changing decisions."

Dusty got out of bed and padded to the bathroom to get some water. He returned, chilled, and wrapped his icy body around Lynn. "We raised Jason both ways. Just think about it. When you and his father raised him you worked on the listening and obeying thing. But as he grew up and I came into the picture, we set rules, but we didn't hold his hand, he got to figure out how to get there."

"Get where?" She was losing interest in a philosophical child raising discussion as Dusty caressed her.

"Hey," he kissed her ear. "You started this discussion."

"Do you have a lot more to say?" Squirm, wiggle.

He kissed her again. "A little bit. You just made me think about my rookies at the elementary school. We kept them at the classrooms at the community college for eight months, then we let them do some fieldwork. But we don't just give them a gun and a car. So when we send them to the elementary school, it's like junior high. There are still rules and expectations, but we set up scenarios where they can make mistakes and learn, not make mistakes and someone dies. When we finally send them out on the road with a mentor, that's high school and college. Then one day they're on their own."

"Like Jason." Now she sounded wistful.

"That's right," Dusty said, "we teach them to be good kids, and one day we have good adults." He nibbled her ear. "Good like me." He moved his lips down her neck.

"Yes, good detectives."

"That's not the good part I was talking about." More nibbling.

She moved her hands along his body. "You always bring everything back to sex."

"I try."

~ ~ ~

It had been four days since the patrolman had found Nevada Utley at the river's edge. He was still unconscious with tubes and bandages everywhere. The hospital staff had allowed Adele to visit daily, but had been concerned about her spending the night. She was so frail that they wanted her to sleep in her own bed. They had explained their concerns and she had accepted. But it had been so many days, and no sign of recovery.

So tonight Adele slipped into the hospital, late. All those years as a hospital volunteer paid off. She knew how to get around and avoid nurses and security. She would be with her boy tonight. Something pulled her to him this quiet evening.

Checking her watch, she waited patiently in the dark volunteer break room. No one would check this space until the first volunteers arrived in the morning. Hospital staff avoided it after some very embarrassing events years ago when the hospital administrator and a young nurse were caught in an interesting, but unseemly, position by a volunteer who had forgotten a package.

The screaming, the reprisals, the fury, the absolute entertainment of it all – Adele still laughed at the story. After that incident it was determined by the hospital board of trustees that the volunteer lounge was off limits to any and all staff, under threat of dismissal. There were a former administrator and a nurse out there somewhere who could verify that policy!

Finally, the late evening hospital hush settled in and Adele determined the time was right to move. She checked the hall in both directions as she slipped out the door. Nevada's room was close to the ICU nurses' desk, but his room was dimly lit. The nurses all seemed to be involved with other patients. If she were quiet, no one would notice. She slipped a hospital gown over her clothes and tiptoed into his room. Earlier, during her last visit she had arranged the visitor's chair out of the line of sight of the nurse's station. She pulled the grey gown around her, congratulating herself in her wisdom – the gown covering made her dissolve into the shadows of the room. She sat on the stiff chair, resting her feet on the small stool a kind nurse had brought in several days ago. She watched her great-grandson as he slept.

He looked as though he were smaller. He must be losing weight, she thought. All of his piercings had been removed and he looked like the little boy who had won her heart so many years ago. She thought back to that day. His father had dropped him at her home, saying, "I got a chance for a job and my old man don't want to worry about this kid." And that was how her grandson had deposited his son and never returned. Her son had died shortly before her husband and there had not been a word from her grandson since the day he left Nevada behind.

It had been just the two of them for almost a decade. She had tried her best. She loved him with all her heart, but he had been disturbed by his abandonment. For years he asked about his father, about why he was left behind. Finally, the little lonely boy gave up on his father and got lost in drinking and gambling. She still loved him with all her heart.

The night was long. She found it difficult to stay unnoticed, but she had managed to scurry into the bathroom when she saw a nurse coming toward the room for a nightly check on Nevada. Now Adele was finding it difficult to sit up in the chair. She studied the bed and the young man resting and decided that she could make a small space for herself and just take a quick nap. Using the stool to step onto the chair, she moved from the chair to Nevada's side. She was pleased with herself – pretty spry for an old woman! There was enough space for her to cuddle in close. Carefully working around all those tubes she was able to get her arm above his pillow and allow his head to rest on her chest. She could hear him breathing – it was a shallow sound.

She held his fingers with her free hand, being careful again with all of his bandages and tubes. With her head resting on top of his, she began to speak, "We didn't have it so bad, you and me. You were always my little man. Come back to me. I don't want to be alone." She let a tear fall onto his hair. She continued to whisper, bringing up memories of their years together.

"If you can't come back," she concluded, "take me with you. You'll need me to get to Jesus. He might not see how good a boy you are." She stayed there listening to him breathe. The machines attached to him kept up their hypnotic, rhythmic sounds. She may have slept for a bit, she wasn't certain, because Nevada never changed. He was the same as when she had first cuddled beside him.

"Lord," she began her bargaining, "take me if you need someone, leave him here. He's all I got. He'll come to his senses. He'll do us proud."

She rested, waiting for an answer.

All the machines began blinking and buzzing and nurse came rushing into the room. The surprised woman found two people in the bed, her patient and that sad old woman. A quick check of machines and pulses, the nurse knew, Nevada and Adele had moved on together. Adele would help him meet Jesus.

CHAPTER SEVEN

The phone buzzed before the alarm could go off. Dusty yawned as he pulled the phone to his ear. Clearing his throat he said, "Reid." Then he listened to his caller. "Shit," he sighed. By this time Lynn was awake. He tapped the phone to end the call and reported to Lynn. "Only ten minutes before the alarm. We got a good night's sleep."

"What was your call?" She wanted to hear the news as a reward for getting up ten minutes early. And she knew by his response that it wasn't an emergency.

"Adele Utley and Nevada died last night." Dusty pulled Lynn to him and related the story. "It seems she snuck into the hospital and got into bed with him. They found her holding him like she must have held him when he was a youngster. They were both dead."

"Oh, Dusty," she moaned as she brushed a tear. "She must have been so frightened seeing him in that coma."

Dusty held her tighter. "Yeah, Jim said she looked like she wasn't eating and wasn't sleeping. He's been keeping an eye on her."

"What now?" Lynn asked, too sad to even move.

"I've got to get to work. Nevada's death means I have a murderer to find." He kissed the top of her head.

~ ~ ~

Dusty was in the office before Mars and Danny this morning. They found him holding his coffee mug, staring at the white board. He turned as they entered the room. "Nevada died last night."

"What about Adele?"

"She died too. She snuck into the hospital and was with him. The nurse says they went together." He gulped his coffee. "Now we have a murder to solve. Somebody killed that boy with a bash on the head and intended to have his body sink into the river." He flipped a dry marker to Danny and walked to his desk. "So what have we got?"

Danny started making columns for their information. This was the way Dusty liked to start as they organized their thoughts, their information and their hunches. While Danny slid the markers across the board, entering the information, Mars called the ME to get a schedule for the autopsy and then placed a call to the crime scene techs to urge them to get their report completed.

"Hell of a way to get back to work after the holidays," commented Danny. "My grandmother was friends with Adele." He continued to write.

Mars cleared his throat. "Nevada's autopsy will be done tomorrow. They had to autopsy Adele first. The hospital attorneys wanted to be certain Adele died of natural causes." Mars frowned. "They're worried about a lawsuit. I don't know who would sue. She hasn't any other family." The detectives thought about the lonely woman. Mars cleared his throat. "The techs say we'll have their report tomorrow afternoon. Full staff is finally back from holiday breaks."

The phone rang. Mars took the call, then turned to Dusty, "Do you want to talk to Jasmine Fuller? She wants to do a story about the Utleys."

"Tell her to come over. Adele had a lot of friends. Jasmine would do a good story."

Mars and Danny were surprised at Dusty's response since he usually shied away from the press, but Mars relayed the invitation. "She's already in the building," said Mars, "I told her the door is open."

Danny automatically flipped the white board so that Jasmine wouldn't see the case notes. They sat and waited for the energetic reporter to arrive.

Jasmine was a poised young woman, and her years of military service had added polish and confidence to her carriage. She was Teniquia's friend. And as Lynn liked to remind Dusty, Jasmine was one of the up-and-coming black professionals in town. She was fast becoming another of Lynn's good friends.

There was a soft rap on the door jam as the reporter stopped at the threshold, "Gentlemen," she smiled and walked in. Mars pushed out a chair close to Dusty's desk. She sat down. "Thank you for seeing me. I know you want something."

Mars and Danny grinned at her technique. Dusty nodded and looked sad, a response that surprised all of them. Jasmine was immediately serious. "I'm sorry. Was Mrs. Utley a close friend?"

Dusty said, "She lived in this community all her life. She worked hard to keep her family afloat. Her husband wasn't real healthy and her son was a bum. You should think about letting the community know who she was and how much her friends will miss her."

"Who were her friends? Where will I find information?"

"My grandmother," offered Danny.

"The hospital volunteer coordinator," said Mars.

"Jim Hoefler," added Dusty.

"What about this dead grandson?"

"Great-grandson," Dusty corrected. "We will be investigating his death as a murder."

Jasmine opened her mouth to ask more questions, but Dusty said, "You asked me what I want. I want this community to mourn Adele, because she has no one left. We don't have information on the murder because while Nevada was in the hospital, it was just a beating. If he had regained consciousness, we would have asked him to identify his attackers."

The young reporter thought over Dusty's reply. After the murders last summer when she accused Dusty and his staff of not investigating crime in the black community, she had been treated with reserve. Now Dusty seemed to be offering her an opportunity to change that relationship. She could do that, she thought. This was a small town, and she was learning that many people were willing to go beyond the color of her skin to work with a fair and impartial reporter. "When can I get more information about the murder?"

"You can say we're investigating when you do your story today," replied Dusty, "But you won't get any more information from us until we get reports back from everyone. Nevada's autopsy is this afternoon. The ME says Adele died a natural death." Dusty thought it was important to get that fact out to her friends.

Jasmine closed her notebook. "Thank you for your openness. I'll be back for my story on the murder investigation."

Dusty followed her to the door and closed it. He turned to his detectives. "You heard the lady, she'll be back. You boys better have something to tell her."

~ ~ ~

"Let me give you some suggestions and then we can talk about things you would like to consider and what you think Mr. Donovan would have thought was important." Lynn settled in a chair at the worktable in her office. It was Monday morning. Yolanda had had all weekend to come to terms with her new responsibility – five hundred thousand dollars.

"That sounds good," said Yolanda, sitting with her pen poised ready to jot notes.

"First, the basics," began Lynn, "the applicant must have all the official nonprofit paperwork, license to fund raise, letter from the IRS, incorporation papers, bylaws, active board – you want their names. They should have operated in this county for at least three years. You can use the basic front page of the Philanthropies' application. It captures all that information." Lynn placed the application in front of Yolanda.

"Next, set up any parameters you want." Lynn laughed as Yolanda raised an eyebrow. "For example, do you want to give to capital projects, or to operational improvements like new bookkeeping software? Or do you want to offer seed money for a new program?"

Yolanda hung her head because it was already hurting.

Lynn rolled right along. "If it's capital money, you might allow the request to be for only a percentage of the cost and request an outline to see how they plan to raise the rest of the funding. If it's a new program, that should require a similar plan. You might want to ask for a plan for future long-term funding support. If it's operational, you might want to ask for projected outcomes of the improvements, like better management of supplies, or better tracking of services." Lynn shrugged. "This should give you an idea of what you can ask for. You're looking for a response that tells you they won't waste the money."

"You mean the agencies will answer these questions?" asked Yolanda.

"They will," replied Lynn. "Any good agency is asked very similar questions from all their funders and from their larger, more sophisticated donors. No one should have trouble with the questions unless they are not a reputable agency."

"What do you think I should ask for?" Yolanda wasn't above begging for help.

Lynn thought for a moment. "I can think of local agencies who would benefit from funds awarded in any of those categories. For example, the Council on Aging might need operational money because they recently developed a strategic plan and part of it highlighted streamlining office procedures. That could mean new equipment or new office software. And the Hunger Alliance is planning a capital campaign. They have outgrown their building and have found a nice piece of property to build something new and more functional for their programs. And several agencies are working together on a new program based on the services of that old financial management group that was cheating everyone."

"Why would I want to support a group who's going to cheat people?" Yolanda was clearly disgusted by that option.

"No," frowned Lynn, "that's not what I mean. Remember that group that was making bad loans?"

"You mean when they found that man hanging in Glenda's barn?" Yolanda asked. During the summer a man working for a local nonprofit had been murdered after he discovered that the agency that employed him was cheating people. The killers left his body hanging in Piper's parents' barn. It had been a frightening way to wrap up summer.

"That's right," said Lynn, happy that Yolanda understood. "The service that crooked group offered, if it had been legitimate, would have been helpful to the clients of many local agencies. Recently a working group of local government and nonprofit agencies has organized to bring that sort of service to town. You might like to be the catalyst for this project with some of your money."

Yolanda thought over that suggestion. "Foster's money could really make a difference with a service so many people need. I've heard one of Salley's board members talking about it. It would be exciting to have a hand in something new and useful." Maybe giving away money wouldn't be such a headache, she thought.

"I don't think they would need a lot of your money to begin the program, but they could use some funds to pay for a consultant. They have been negotiating with someone who has experience in setting up and running such a service."

Yolanda smiled at Lynn. "I'm starting to get some ideas. I talked with Father Nick because he knew Foster. I've already spoken with Robert O'Hara for some guidance since I need his approval. My goal would be to send out the request for proposals by Friday."

"I can let you use my list of agencies and we can e-mail your announcement and criteria as soon as you're ready."

"E-mail?"

"That's how it's done these days. We can have the responses come to my office to keep you sort of anonymous."

"Anonymous?"

"Trust me," Lynn nodded knowingly, "agencies are not shy about lobbying. And many of these folks are your friends or at least acquaintances. You might like to have that veil of secrecy so you can review the proposals without too much pressure."

"Seriously?" asked Yolanda. "What can they do?"

"Anything they think will raise themselves above the pack."

Yolanda shivered at the tone of Lynn's voice as she recalled that Robert O'Hara had cautioned that everyone already knew about the money. That headache was back.

~ ~ ~

Every lunchtime was the same. Ricky Mitchell walked slowly through the high school cafeteria looking for Polly Carmichael, hoping to find her sitting alone. She never was, alone or in the cafeteria. She must really walk slow he thought, as he watched her get into the food line long after he had found a seat with other friends. No matter how hard he tried, she never seemed to see him – not as a friend, not as anything. Didn't she talk with him all those times he visited her and those kids in the hospital? Then at Thanksgiving he sat with her and introduced her to all the college kids at Ms. Powers' house. And all those days they played with those little kids when Lonzo brought them to see Dusty's trains. All those times – and she still ignored him. Maybe he was invisible.

But today she was different. She looked weird – dressed all in black and her hair pulled back. She walked right past him and he thought she gave him a defiant glare. Then she sat at the table with those weird kids all dressed in black.

He knew he wasn't welcome at that table. It was claimed by the kids who didn't like anyone. They especially didn't like kids who didn't get into trouble and who spoke up in class and who played sports. Three strikes, thought Ricky.

He was staring at Polly and ignoring his food as he sat at the table with his best friend Jeff. The table hosted all the sophomores, including Ricky, who played on the soccer team. "Who's Polly sitting with?" Ricky asked Jeff.

Several of the boys at the table turned and looked. One of them said, "That tall kid was called John when we were in grade school. Now he calls himself Elwrath the Griffin." Someone snickered. "That's what I think, too," said the first boy. He turned to Ricky. "Is she your girlfriend?"

Ricky almost choked, but managed to reply, "Her mom died in that explosion. Jeff's grandfather is her guardian."

Jeff looked at the others around the table. "She's an orphan and wants to leave River Bend."

"So do those kids," said another boy. "Good old John comes from a pretty bad home and he says he's leaving as soon as he turns sixteen."

"Where's he going?"

"Probably to juvie. He's not real smart, but he thinks he knows everything."

Ricky didn't like hearing any of that. But he knew from experience that Polly had no interest in his opinions. "Maybe they live in her neighborhood or something," he suggested.

"They're all just jerks," summed up the team goalie. "Why is she sitting with them? They're sophomores. Isn't she a freshman?"

"Maybe they think it's exciting that her mom blew up."

"Maybe they don't care about her," said Ricky. "Maybe she just wants to hang with people who don't care." He kept an eye on Polly and her friends through lunch. She didn't seem to talk with anyone at the table and they ignored her. Ricky decided that she finally found someplace in school where she felt invisible – just what she wanted. But he didn't think it was a good sign.

A bell rang.

~ ~ ~

Foster's son, Mason, had called Yolanda the day after her conversation with Robert. She had explained her interest in distributing Foster's money among agencies and causes he supported while alive. He invited her to the Donovan home, suggesting that they look through his father's records and see where he was donating funds. Yolanda could then have some idea of his interests. So after her meeting with Lynn she knocked at the door of a unique and well-kept house perched above Hanging Oak with a great view of the river and the national forest.

"Welcome, Mrs. Valeri," Mason greeted her as he opened the door. "Have you ever been here before?" A man about her age smiled at Yolanda. He was tall and fit with a receding hairline of gray-brown hair. His eyes were the hazel warmth that she had admired in his father.

"No," she replied as she took in the view out the living room windows. "I didn't even know this neighborhood was here."

"Evidently my father bought the land in the eighties with some friends. He and Mom built this house and made certain that they placed their home for the views." He laughed. "Pops always liked the feeling of living in the forest. I think it might be because of those years he worked in deserts. You can see he only cut trees to enhance his view. Otherwise this is a jungle. Come on I'll show you around."

Mason took her arm and walked her into a kitchen that could use a remodel, but was very clean and functional. "Once Mom died I think he didn't do much cooking." After helping her with her winter coat he said, "Let me show you the rest of the house." They walked into a master bedroom suite with a commanding view of the river. Mason then took her through the remaining bedrooms, "This is my room, and the next room is Pop's office. Notice that view." Yolanda smiled at the bird feeders hanging from the eaves. "And because this house is built on a hillside, we have a lower level." He turned on lights to brighten a stairwell then preceded Yolanda to the basement. The rooms in the lower level had river views that were obstructed by the trees and not as commanding. Directing her to the next room, he said, "Mom always used this as her projects room. Pop never touched anything in here once she died." The room was filled with quilting fabrics and an expensive sewing machine and other quilting equipment. He led her back to the stairs. "Maybe you can help me get rid of some of these things. You must know a quilter. And down here you'll also find Mom's art supplies and Pop's picture framing equipment. I don't think he had much use for it once Mom quit painting." He took a deep breath and Yolanda patted his arm.

"I'm sorry I didn't know him better and I don't believe I ever met your mother."

Mason smiled. "She didn't go to church. I admire Pop for keeping his faith no matter where he lived and no matter that he did it alone. Mom and I never joined him."

Yolanda shrugged. "Sometimes I wonder what moves some of those older folks who regularly attend services even on the coldest, rainiest weekday mornings. I wonder if my faith is that strong."

"Five hundred kisses?" Mason asked. "Your faith was strong enough for you to greet Pop five hundred times in church." She looked at him in surprise. "Mr. O'Hara told me about your relationship with Pop. I wondered who you were." He laughed. "At first I thought you were probably someone trying to get his money. You know, by marriage or some scam."

She blushed. "You don't think I asked him for this money?"

"No." This time he took her arm and slid his hand down to hold her hand in a very tender clasp. "I know who you are. I had you researched before I came to town."

"You had me researched?" Yolanda was insulted.

Mason caught on. "I don't mean to insult you. I was protecting my father's estate and his memory. I didn't

67

want his name tied to any tawdry gossip."

She scowled. He said quickly. "I'm making a mess of this. I assure you I've learned that you are a kind, hard-working woman. I'm sorry that you've lost your husband, but I also know that you are blessed with children and grandchildren." He eyed her. "Though I must say, I wouldn't have guessed that you are old enough for grandchildren."

She blushed. "You're forgiven."

Mason threw back his head and laughed. It was a joyous sound. "Come on, I'm sure you don't have all day." He led her back to Foster's office. "I've been through his files and pulled out current records, but you can scan through anything here. Maybe you'll find some answers." His phone rang. He checked the caller ID, tapped it and lifted it to his ear, "What is it, Sweetheart?" He winked at Yolanda, and walked from the room.

Yolanda could hear mumbling as Mason settled at his impromptu office at the kitchen table. She focused on Foster's office and the disarray. Clearly Mason had been sorting and discarding records. She pulled a chair up to the desk and began a methodical review of the information before her and blessed her training as a genealogical society volunteer.

Yolanda became aware of the clickety sound of a computer. She looked at her watch and gasped. How long had she been wrapped up in Foster's records? She listened; Mason was again talking on his phone. More typing, more talking. She went back to work.

When Mason returned to the office Yolanda had files organized and ready for him to review. "Wow," he gasped, "I didn't think I was on the phone that long."

She smiled at him. "Was that your wife?"

"I'm not married."

"Oh, I guess Sweetheart was someone else," she

offered embarrassed.

"He's my assistant." Mason grinned. "I'm not gay, but he is and," he shrugged, "we've been together a long time and he is a sweetheart. He speaks the languages I don't. We say we cover the globe. Not that I don't work with women. But in some parts of the world, it's a cultural challenge."

"You don't owe me an explanation," said Yolanda, now uncomfortable. "You obviously live your life and it's not my business—"

Mason laughed. It was a sound she found very pleasing. He sat on the edge of the desk, very close, commanding her attention. "I'm not gay. I'm not married. I have lady friends, I travel a lot and find that a lady friend who has no expectations, in many of my usual spots, is very—" he weighed his next words, "very entertaining and relaxing."

Now Yolanda laughed. "You must think I'm very small town and closed-minded. I'm not passing judgment on your lifestyle. I'm just trying to place you in some sort of framework." She cocked her head. "So you have a girl in every port?"

"Something like that."

"It sounds very adult." Now she looked wistful, but before his eyes she pulled herself together and changed the subject. "Let me explain how I organized these piles." She pointed to the various piles on the desk. "Just to let you know, I volunteer at the genealogical society, so sorting family records is second nature. I have managed to pull together your family records, things you might like to keep for no other reason than they pertain to your father, mother and their families." She went on to detail all the records she had unearthed and what it meant as far as Mason's ancestry. "You should keep all this information. Even if you're not interested now, you might find it offers some hints that could make your travels more interesting, give you some clues to follow when you're in various countries."

"I didn't know Pop did any genealogy," said Mason in surprise.

"I think your mother did it. Most of the letters responding to inquiries are addressed to her." Yolanda moved to the next stack of folders. "These are very old financial records. You may find them interesting because they outline how your father grew his business. They're a genealogy record in a sense, the history of his work. And this final stack should be thrown out. Old warranties and things. What I didn't find are old medical records."

"I have those."

"And old tax records and current banking records."

"I have those, too."

"I thought I'd find information about his charitable giving in those records." Yolanda frowned at all the paperwork. Although she had done a good job sorting Foster's records, she hadn't met her goal of learning about his donations.

Mason stood and indicated that she should follow him. He walked into the kitchen and pointed at the kitchen table. "Tax and banking records."

"If he itemized, all I need are tax records for the last few years to see where he was giving donations. If he didn't itemize, I'd like to scan his banking records for a few years."

"You sit here," he pulled out a chair, "and look things over. There's nothing secret, anyway, I certainly don't expect you to go around town talking about what you learn."

"I would never–"

"I know," smiled Mason. "You work here while I get some information for Sweetheart. He's waiting for an e-mail." Mason took another chair at the table and was quickly lost in his computer screen.

They worked quietly for sometime and then Mason gasped, "I have to get on a conference call."

"I have to leave anyway," replied Yolanda.

"I won't touch anything and you come back tomorrow and finish. Can you do that? I could use your sorting skills. I want to leave town within the week and I'd love to have this all finished so I can have the house put on the market."

Yolanda stood and gave his comments some thought. "Certainly. I'll be back in the morning and try to finish up. And I'd be happy to help you with anything you need to do to close out the house. I've done these after-death-sort-outs before." She thought about the days before Christmas when she and Susan Carmichael's friends cleaned out the house and sorted items for Polly.

CHAPTER EIGHT

Lynn sat at breakfast stirring her yogurt. She pulled out the spoon, looked at the gunk, dropped the spoon back in the cup and sighed.

Dusty kissed her on her head. "Skirt too tight again?"

"Do you think I'm getting fat?" she asked, giving the yogurt a second chance to look appealing. "Nothing is tight, but the holidays are over and I think I have to get back to the gym." She dumped the yogurt in the sink and ran the water to wash it down the drain.

During her struggle with breakfast, Dusty had toasted a bagel, slathered it in cream cheese and honey, then, adding insult to injury, he threw a few slivered almonds on top. While the bagel sat on a plate taunting her, he poured coffee, stirred in sugar and cream – real cream -and pulled a chair up to enjoy his breakfast, including the two eggs over easy that he had managed to cook while Lynn stirred her yogurt.

The only good thing about the morning, thought Lynn, was that she had married an old bachelor who knew how to fend for himself in the kitchen. Maybe he would share a piece of bagel?

"Get your own," he said without even looking at her. "Eat some fruit." The bagel disappeared. The eggs not far behind. He stood and pulled her into his arms. "You don't look fat to me." He continued to hug her. "When do you see that counselor again?"

After Lynn had witnessed Susan Carmichael's death, she had been persuaded to meet with a counselor to deal with the residual trauma. "I see her this afternoon. She thinks I'm doing very well." Lynn hugged Dusty. "She thinks you make a big difference because you're understanding. She says that sometimes family and friends lose patience with people who are working through a crisis that doesn't leave visible scars."

"Sometimes the people I work with have trouble dealing with the tragedies we see. No one is tough enough to weather every crisis." He rested his chin on the top of her head.

"What about you?" she asked. "You always have it together."

"It's easier now that I have you at my side." He kissed her.

"Dusty, what a sweet thing to say."

"It's true," he said as he thought for a moment. "Dealing with all this shit .... Take Tee for example. If you hadn't been there to deal with her family and hold me up, I would have embarrassed us all by breaking down."

She studied her husband's face. "You're serious." She recalled those days in the hospital as they waited for surgery results and consoled Lonzo and Tee's mother after the young detective had been shot.

He smiled, "Love is powerful." He gave her a loud kiss on the cheek. "No matter how fat you get."

"Dusty!" she wailed. "And I'm still hungry!"

~ ~ ~

Danny and Mars were slumped at their desks as Dusty walked into the office. "What have we got?" he asked.

"Nothing," replied Danny, "but Jasmine got a great story in the morning paper." He handed the paper to Dusty. "She talked to my grandmother yesterday and with my Aunt Eloise who is volunteer coordinator at the hospital." Danny smiled. "Jasmine made a big hit with both of them because of the way she talked about Ms. Utley."

They looked at Mars. "I didn't hear from anybody." He cut the article out of his copy of the paper and placed it in Nevada's investigation book. He looked at Dusty. "We gotta talk about something." An unusual request coming from the professional investigator and very private young man.

"Do you want me to leave?" asked Danny.

"No," replied Mars, "but it is personal." Danny's eyes grew big as he wondered what secret Mars had that he didn't already know. But Mars was helpful and said, "Uncle Hutch got me elected to the bank board. He wants me to be there to protect the family interests."

"I knew that," said Danny feeling better about Mars and his secrets.

"What kind of time will you need?" asked Dusty. He had wondered when Mars' other life would begin to demand attention. The family wealth of the Healeys and the Dunns was finally starting to vie for Mars' time.

The young detective sat back in his chair and stared at his colleagues. "I don't know. I'm going to attend my first meeting on Friday. It's a lunch meeting. So I may be gone the rest of the day. I'll come in Saturday to catch up."

Dusty reflected on the new status of his senior detective. "We'll accommodate your schedule. No need to come in extra, we'll just give you on call for the weekend following board meetings."

Danny grinned. He thought he might like Mars' new role. "What do you do at a board meeting? Go after deadbeats on loans?"

Mars shrugged. "I really don't know. Uncle Hutch said I'm there to look out for the people who rely on a hometown bank, because the current board has lost its vision. I'm not worried about all the numbers that I'll see, but I do worry that I won't understand what Uncle Hutch had in mind." Mars' college degree was in accounting with a specialty in forensic account analysis, as in follow the money to the perpetrator.

Dusty patted his shoulder. "You will. Your uncle wants to be certain someone is looking out for people like Adele who are just trying to survive without losing their homes or small businesses." Dusty thought over his statement. "Jim told me a story once about how the board members had tried to deny a mortgage to a small church. He said he and Nathan and your uncle had to fight to get the loan approved."

"What church?"

"I don't know," replied Dusty, "he was telling me the story because your uncle had talked to him recently about a loan that Mazie Doe's son, Reverend Goodson, was applying for to help his church. They want to buy some extra property next to their church. Jim said it had been a fight years ago to get that other loan approved. Ultimately that other church got the money. Without Jim and Nathan on the board your uncle would really have had to fight hard to get those kinds of loans for people."

Mars felt a note of pride after hearing Dusty's story. "So I guess I do the fighting now. Maybe I'll always go to the meetings armed."

The other men laughed and made some inappropriate remarks, things that you could only say to your very rich friend who knew you liked him in spite of his money.

Dusty finally brought everyone back to order. "We better get our act together. Jasmine will be here soon to do a story on Nevada." Organizing the investigation supplanted bank board as the morning topic.

~ ~ ~

The man Chartreuse Masterson knew as Homer walked into an office in Asheville and flipped the *River Bend Chronicle* onto his boss's desk. Jasmine Fuller's story was page one – a long, praise-filled biography of

Adele Utley and a side bar item to remind the readers that there would be more information to follow in the coming days about the murder of her great-grandson, Nevada. "That dead body is one of the guys I played craps with the other night."

The boss scanned the news story as Homer recapped, "He died in the hospital. They found him the morning after the game. There's not much information here. Says they'll have more of a story later."

The man digested the story. "You think those Mastersons offed him?"

"He was the big winner. They could have pocketed about six grand."

"That much?" The boss did some thoughtful calculations. "They're starting to cut into our profit. They need to understand the score."

Homer paced the office in thought. "Gilly hasn't got back from visiting his mother and Antwan went up to Hot Springs to see his girlfriend. He gets back Friday."

"Go visit those Mastersons. You can go alone," said the boss. "What did you tell me, two or three dumb kids?"

"But they just killed a guy." Homer was a cautious man.

"Someone dumber, I'll bet." The boss was wondering why he ever left Florida as he stared out a frosted window. He didn't like this ice and wind and other shit.

"That's true," agreed Homer. "That Nevada fellow was so lucky the other night he couldn't lose no matter how many mistakes he made."

"I guess his luck ran out." The boss got philosophical sometimes. "But, you can deliver the message. Just tell them we'll come by once a month to take our cut."

"I'll pay a visit tomorrow. I meet those kids after

school in River Bend today."

"This business is changing," lamented the boss. "Since them Indians opened their casino in Cherokee, you can't make a decent living on gambling around here."

~ ~ ~

Yolanda's car climbed the steep and curving road to the Donovan place for her second visit in as many days. She had spent last evening working on her grant form. She had given a lot of thought to Lynn's suggestions, but wanted to know more about Foster Donovan's giving so that she could structure her grant application form to elicit proposals that she hoped he would have approved and supported.

As she drove into the yard she saw Mason on one of the decks filling the bird feeders. He waved and ducked back into the house. He had the door open before she climbed from her car. She grabbed a bakery box from the back seat and plowed through the snow to greet him. "I brought some coffee cake."

"That's great, because I have no food here." He helped her with her coat. He sniffed the box. "I'll make a fresh pot of coffee."

"What have you been eating?" she almost demanded as she followed him into the kitchen.

He turned to her and grinned. "Dad has a freezer filled with frozen dinners." When he said it, he saw Yolanda's eyes tear up. "Now you're going to worry that he was alone and ate by himself." She nodded her head as she swiped at a tear. Mason patted her arm. "Don't give it a thought. He was up in his aerie doing exactly what he wanted. After the places he'd lived and the food he had eaten, a frozen pot pie was a luxury." The morning sun was coming in through the skylight and picked up the strands of silver in Yolanda's hair. It also highlighted the thick lashes that outlined her intriguing eyes. Mason was beginning to see why his father had been taken with this dark-eyed woman with the easy smile.

Burying those thoughts, Mason directed her to look at banking statements as he prepared coffee. Yolanda was a woman who did first things first, so she found her way around in the kitchen, putting the coffee cake on a serving dish, locating utensils and plates. Before Mason had the coffee dripping, she had the table set for a pleasant morning break.

"You're very efficient," he commented as he filled a small pitcher with milk. "You and Sweetheart would get along. He anticipates every need."

Yolanda sat at the table waiting for the coffee. "If he's gay, isn't he at risk in some of the countries where you do business?"

"You're not only efficient, you're up-to-date on international customs and mores." Mason sat across from her. "We work really hard to do business and not have any private encounters in those countries. A country that doesn't approve of homosexuality also frowns on adultery. Sweetheart and I just work all day, and spend our evenings doing more work. It's our goal to spend as little time in those countries as possible." He blew out his breath, "That's not to say we haven't met some fine people in all the places we've been. We just respect that they have different views of life than we do. It makes it easier for everyone. Our clients and hired staff don't worry that we'll compromise them by not understanding some religious or government regulation."

They talked over coffee about all the countries in which Mason had lived and worked. Yolanda was mesmerized by his global view and international sophistication. Mason laughed. "There's nothing sophisticated about no indoor plumbing and flies all over your food. But I do enjoy my life and my work. That was a gift from my parents. Every new location was an adventure, always something to be learned and some experience to treasure. We didn't run with the diplomats, we did the work on the ground, building dams and roads and schools. Mom always insisted we live as close to the worksite as possible."

"Why?" asked Yolanda. "Wouldn't that always be primitive?"

"Yes, but she was a nurse and a teacher and always started a clinic or a kindergarten. And when we moved on she left behind several skilled people to carry on her projects."

"Wow, I'm sorry I never met her."

"I used to think that Dad went to church and lived his life as though he believed every word in the gospels. That's how he treated everyone. Mom never went to church but lived the same way." Mason took a deep breath. "They were quite a pair."

"And an example for you."

Mason hung his head. "I never got the altruistic thing. I work and I'm fair to clients and staff, but I don't start clinics and schools. I often wondered if my parents expected me to do that kind of charity stuff."

Mason was silent and Yolanda was uncomfortable listening to him. She hadn't known him long enough to accept his secrets or to advise him on his future actions. So she did what any coward would do, she changed the subject. "Speaking of charity. Where are Foster's records?"

Mason left the table and returned with a handful of papers. "I think you'll find the information here. I have a conference call with Sweetheart and a client in ten minutes. I'll go back to Pop's office." He took his cup of coffee, warmed it up and left the kitchen.

Yolanda freshened her cup and began her search

for Foster's charities. It was straightforward – both Donovans had supported children's causes. Mrs. Donovan liked to also give money to help poor and battered women. And she gave money to groups that loaned funds to women starting businesses as well as a scholarship fund at her alma mater.

Foster liked children and environmental causes. Once he arrived in River Bend, or more precisely in Hanging Oak, he gave money to St. Bridget's, the hospital and several others. It appeared that he made a contribution to most local agencies that asked. To Yolanda's surprise she found a small diary with notes on his giving and his assessment of the success or failure of the agency receiving his funds. She noticed that after the Literacy Council suffered a scandal, Foster had withheld funds until he perceived they had corrected their operational problems. Yolanda remembered that problem – it involved embezzlement and murder. But the new board had reorganized and cleaned house. Today they earned every penny they received from donors.

Foster was very perceptive. His analyses of local groups were on target. Yolanda decided she would ask Mason if she could keep the giving diary.

She was paging through it when he returned. "You found it," he said, "Are Pop's comments helpful?"

"He knew what was happening," she replied. "I would like to keep this." She waved the small notebook.

"Sure," he agreed, "I thought you'd like it. Have you found your answers?"

She nodded. "This diary gives me a lot of direction and will help me respect Foster's giving goals."

He frowned. "I thought he meant for you to give money where you thought it should go."

"I would still like to respect his interests and maybe help his money grow further by giving to an agency that he has supported for years." She cocked her head at him. "Does that make sense?"

Mason smiled at her. "I think I'm dealing with another person like Mom and Pop – a giver. And that's not a bad thing. No wonder he gave you all those kisses, you were a kindred spirit."

"Maybe." Yolanda felt warmed at the idea.

"I'll feed you a pot pie if you'll help me with some other things." Mason offered.

Yolanda laughed. "I don't need a pot pie to help you."

"Yeah, but I want to get rid of them."

"How can I earn a pot pie?" she asked.

"If you found your donation answers, I could use some help making plans to dispose of the things in this house and getting someone in to make some repairs before I put the house on the market." He poured himself more coffee and sat at the table.

"Like what?"

And Mason told her. They spent the rest of the day making plans for the furniture and drawing up a list of minor repairs. They never did eat the pot pies and Yolanda went home hungry.

~ ~ ~

The snow was melting and the sky at school dismissal was clear and sunny. Polly Carmichael missed going to practice. Soccer season was over and she should have been trying out for the lacrosse team, but she still didn't feel comfortable with her old friends – the ones who knew her mom. That's why she was trailing along with her new friends, the Goth group of River Bend High School. She wasn't certain where they were going. The last few days after school they had meandered through the greenway to the park, did nothing then stumbled into an alley downtown and watched each other as they tried to be cool and smoke.

It was pretty boring. She wondered why her new friends chose to ignore all the after school clubs and activities. Then she mentally shook herself. She was ignoring all those things, too. And yes, it was boring but she had an attitude to uphold. Making everyone edgy and frustrated was her new goal. Too bad Janet and Ms. Powers were so nice. BUT – the attitude mattered more. So here she was slogging along the greenway toward downtown River Bend. Probably the same old adventure today.

"You stay here," ordered the chief Goth, Elwrath the Griffin. "I gotta talk to some guy." The others watched as he trotted across the parking lot toward the small outpost that was the bank drive-thru. He stood beside a shrub and waited. Soon a man parked a truck and walked over to him. They spoke for a few minutes, exchanged some papers and an envelope and parted.

Back with the group Elwrath said, "I got some deliveries to make." He was gone.

"That creep," muttered one of the other Goth boys, "he does this every week. Like he can't tell us what his big secret is." The remaining kids smashed the snow mounds along the parking lot edges and shuffled to their usual spot to grab a cigarette.

Polly tagged along. No one had ever offered her a puff. She felt stupid with these kids. They were dumb loser kids, but she had to support her attitude, do things to make herself feel angry and misused. These kids really made her angry with herself and that made her angry and uncooperative with her guardians and with Janet. She stopped. It was really hard to be angry with Janet. She was ... well, it was hard to describe. She was nice and she always gave a hug and smile when Polly came into the house. Polly wondered if pregnant Janet even noticed this new attitude. Sometimes Janet was on another planet.

She leaned against a dumpster and heard a rip. Oh, great. More fuel for her anger and her attitude. She had torn her new winter coat. It was time to go home. She drifted away from the others and slowly walked home as early winter dusk settled on River Bend.

CHAPTER NINE

Darwin Masterson loved his apartment – the second story above the new church he and his cousins had created. It made him laugh. None of them attended any church and now they had their own. His apartment was his church – where he worshipped technology. Char and Lester gave him money every week that allowed him to buy more things.

He had been putting cameras around the church. Cameras in the ceiling so he could watch the gamblers and send hints to Lester. He just had to learn more about poker before that was helpful. He was proud of himself though. Just yesterday he showed Char and Lester the tapes from New Year's Eve. They watched and watched and finally saw that guy, Homer, cheating at the crap game. He was switching dice and sometimes giving that stupid Nevada Utley the crazy dice. Lester had been furious. Their game had been scammed. Homer had robbed them. At least Lester got back Nevada's money.

Darwin reviewed his wall of TV screens, checking the positioning of the online cameras and getting ready to install the new cameras. He had cameras along the street front, the alley, and in the ceiling of the game room, the room Char liked to call the sanctuary. And, next, he would be placing three cameras, two inside and one out, around the warehouse they used as a parking lot.

As he unwrapped his new cameras, the screens cycled through the scenes of the current cameras. He glanced up – and froze. There was that Homer guy in the sanctuary talking to Char. And he didn't look happy.

Darwin quickly texted Lester: C in trouble.

Lester replied: Where

Darwin: Homer in sanctuary

Lester: On it

While down in the sanctuary of the Church of the Guiding Hands, Homer greeted his quarry, "Hey, doll!"

Chartreuse's ears perked up and so did a few other things. Homer was a handsome man. "You come back to visit me?" she asked as she stood in the doorway to the back room making certain he understood how welcome he was. "I always have time for a visitor."

Homer leered as he toyed with grabbing a little opportunity before he scared her shitless. But however much fun he would have, if he didn't get her to understand his message, the boss would not understand the shift in priorities. So, he followed her into the back room, closed the door and held up the newspaper with the headline of Nevada's death. "You and your boyfriend do this?"

"He's not my boyfriend, he's my kin," Char replied, an edge to her voice. "We don't do kinky things. It's unchristian."

"What about murder and probably robbery?"

"That's business." The woman sniffed at his concerns.

Homer ran the edge of the newspaper along her chin as he moved into her space. "Let me tell you about business. My boss doesn't like that you and your kin started a business on our turf. We own gambling in this part of the state."

"This is a Masterson town and we don't share with anyone." Char jutted out her chin and her bosom. Her phone chirped.

Lester sent a message: brg H to warehouse.

She read the message and said, "My cousin saw you come in and wants us to meet him in the building out

86

back."

Homer opened his coat and moved a gun from an inside holster to the outside pocket of his coat. "Let's go meet him, doll."

At the door to the alley Char grabbed her coat. "It's cold out there." She took her time slipping it on and patting her pockets to find her gloves, buttoning her coat and finally slipping on her gloves.

"Come on," urged Homer, unhappy with her stalling tactics.

She opened the door and said over her shoulder. "We're going across the alley to that building. It's where our regular customers park their cars."

Homer took a moment to assess the situation. "Pretty clever," he nodded, "No cars cluttering the street."

Char grinned at him. "We ain't new to this. Mastersons have owned this town for a long time."

"Yeah," he snarled, "tell me about it after you and your kin understand what the new rules are." She opened the warehouse door and walked in. Because Homer was a cautious man, he forced the door back against the wall to make certain no one was behind it. It clanged against the wall and came away, hitting him in the elbow. "Where's this cousin?" he asked as he walked further into the warehouse space. And that was all he said because Lester dropped a concrete block on his head from the loft area above the door.

Char quickly closed the door to the alley while Lester jumped to the floor and searched the body. "He has a gun," she said, as Lester found the weapon. He examined it and was pleased to see that it had a silencer. Placing it against Homer's temple he fired. The gun made a sound like a muted gasp.

As Homer died Char was dragging an old tarp across the floor. "Let's wrap him in this. We can get rid of him tonight."

"We got to think of some place away from here. We can't leave him where we put Nevada." They had been surprised to read about Nevada's death in the newspaper. He was supposed to have sunk into the river. As Char had said, "That stupid Nevada couldn't be counted on to do anything right."

"What's your idea?" asked Lester as he huffed dragging the body onto the tarp.

"I'll think of something," promised Chartreuse. "How'd you know about him?" She glanced down at the body, kicking his arm to make certain there was no movement.

"Darwin sent me a text." He held up his phone. They both laughed. That nerdy cousin was proving to be an asset. "Let's go tell him."

Something was going on and Darwin, the skinny nerd of the cousins, chose to stay in his apartment and scan his cameras. He had watched Char lead the way and Homer follow her into the warehouse. Darwin stared at the screens – they were out of surveillance range. His throat went dry. Was she in danger? Where was Lester? He wondered what he would tell their grandmother.

Then he heard Lester yell, "Hey, dipshit, you just saved our asses."

Darwin poked his head out of his security room and smiled. Char ran up the stairs to his apartment and kissed his cheek. "Show me your movie." Darwin ran the tapes of the last few minutes. There was no sound, but Char explained to the two men just what Homer was saying. They watched the surveillance tape when she scanned her phone as she received Lester's message. The silent drama continued as Char got her coat and she and Homer left the sanctuary. A new screen showed the two of them cross the alley and open the door of the warehouse.

Darwin said, "I just got the cameras for the warehouse. I'll install them tomorrow."

"You do that, sweetie," Char said as she tousled his shaggy hair. "And maybe you should erase any scenes that show this guy was here." He nodded.

~ ~ ~

Several months ago Teniquia LaMont had been the lead investigator in a case involving several murders in the local black community. As she and the rest of her colleagues unraveled a thirty-five year old mystery, new murders occurred. Because of the perceived danger to the community, Jasmine Fuller, a new reporter with the *River Bend Chronicle* had charged that the Joint Investigation Unit was ignoring threats to the black community. It had been a distressing time for Teniquia and many of her long time friends and relatives. Jasmine's media barrage had not helped.

However, as the case unfolded, Teniquia was able to make sense of the murders, identify the killers and become friends with Jasmine. Through it all they learned a lot about the rich, untold story of the past successes of the River Bend black community. Both young women vowed to bring that information to everyone and began planning a Black Forum series to be unveiled during February, Black History Month. And the time was getting close.

Tee and Jasmine knew that they didn't have time to waste. Their long-planned presentations were set for four consecutive Thursday evening sessions in February. They were still having trouble drumming up excitement in the black community. Tee was beyond frustrated. They had promises and interest from their young black contemporaries, but the older folks, the ministers and other presumptive leaders in the community were skeptics.

"I don't understand them," moaned Tee as she and Jasmine sat in Teniquia's dining room watching two children play with all of their new toys. The two little girls were reluctant to stray too far from Tee, and they were leery of Jasmine as they struggled to find a safe distance.

"I wish they trusted me," Jasmine said in a very soft reassuring voice. "How many times will I have to visit before they relax?"

Tee patted her hand as they sat across the dining table where all their notes and cold cups of coffee rested. "It will take awhile. Be satisfied that they aren't hiding in their bedroom. But we're making progress. They come to life when Moses gets in from school."

"How's he doing?"

Moses was the third child Teniquia and her husband Lonzo adopted only a month ago. He was judged to be about six years old and had been enrolled in kindergarten last week. "He loves school," smiled Tee, enjoying motherhood. "He goes to Piper's school and she keeps an eye on him. He seems determined to learn everything in one week. We have to practice saying and writing the alphabet every evening. I think the girls are learning right along with him."

Jasmine studied the girls for a few minutes as Tee cleared the table. "I envy you and don't envy you. Does that make sense?"

Tee nodded. "I feel the same way about myself. Some days I ask myself, 'What have we done?' and other days I can't imagine them not part of my life."

"I think they should call me Auntie Jasmine." The young reporter smiled at the children.

Tee laughed and hugged her friend. "I think that's a great idea. Now, Auntie Jasmine, what are we going to report to Lynn? My mother will be here in a few minutes to babysit so we can keep that appointment."

Jasmine recapped their report and conclusions. Both young women hoped that Lynn could help.

~ ~ ~

While Mason followed Yolanda's direction and organized their work for the days ahead, Yolanda was spending Wednesday at the bakery. It was her usual day to work on the books, pay bills, organize payroll and do a thousand clerical things that Umberto refused to do. She was happy with the extra income the job provided. And she was happy with the solid business that she owned, in part, with Umberto and her late husband's parents.

When she thought about the bakery she always had to smile. She had been drawn to her late husband because he smelled so sweet. In fact that's what she always said to him. "You put the sweet in sweetheart." He had always laughed and hugged her releasing little clouds of flour as he pulled her into him. The bakery had been started by his grandfather. And even though he had had a job as a music professor at Brevard College, only a thirty-mile drive from James County, he still managed to do his share of work at the bakery.

Today in River Bend the bakery, by virtue of its longevity and location, was the spot to stop for a quick coffee and treat. She had thought Umberto was crazy when he reduced the size of the display units and added a few small tables and that long bar with the high stools across the front window. He had argued, "This Starbuckets is on to something. We're going to be ready."

And he had been correct. Coffee shops popped up all over the place, but the bakery seemed to own the downtown area. With the city parking lot in the back of the building, patrons could always find a place to park and Umberto had recently begun his cell lot delivery system. If you called ahead, he was ready with your order at the loading zone in front of the store. He said it was like the airports that now had special cell lots to wait for passengers. He said his cell lot let people wait for great baked goods.

His other idea, as he said, "Catching the coffee both ways," was to supply his pastries to the coffee shops that had popped up all over town. That was another success.

Yolanda remembered when Umberto came to live with her husband's family. He was a cousin who had gotten himself into a lot of trouble in New Jersey. He brought some of that trouble with him, but through determination and affection her in-laws and other relatives had molded him into a great baker and a passable coffee brewer, but never quite got him to understand the bookkeeping. She thought the music had a big part in helping Umberto mature into who he was today. In River Bend the Valeri family was synonymous with music. The family populated the chorale and the symphony. Umberto found his musical skill when he arrived in town. He had never known he had the talent until he was drawn into rehearsals. Her father-in-law always remarked, "Music made him civilized." Umberto soon became a willing student and then an outstanding performer.

"Yolo," he called breaking into her reverie in the quiet bakery office, "I got a cell delivery." She heard the bell on the door ring as he left.

Almost immediately the bell rang again. That was her signal to handle the inside sales until he returned. She walked into the front of the bakery and was greeted by Rory Prentiss, the executive director of the Arts Council, the umbrella organization for the symphony and the chorale and other programs. "When were you going to tell me you got all this money?" he demanded.

She looked at him, trying to understand what he

was saying as she pulled her thoughts away from flour and sugar deliveries. "I haven't sent out the grant announcement yet."

"What announcement?" He was astounded. "Aren't you just sharing with your friends?"

"No. I'm inviting all local nonprofits to make a request for funds."

Rory wasn't happy. "But you know me."

"And I know Salley, and Bertram and everyone else who needs money for a good cause." She leaned on the glassed-in display case. "I plan to give everyone a chance."

"But, the Arts Council needs—"

"I'm sure it does," she agreed.

The bell over the door rang again. Salley Connelly, executive director of the domestic violence shelter, walked in. "Oh, no, are you here to suck up and get her money?" she challenged Rory.

"What do you mean suck up? And what are you doing here? Planning on a little arm twisting?" Rory was ready to take on any threat to Yolanda's funds.

"Yolanda knows my agency does good work and always needs—" Salley dared Rory to dispute her agency needs.

"Yes, I know," interrupted Yolanda. "That's why I will be sending out invitations to everyone in town."

"Nooooooo," wailed Salley.

"See." Rory looked at Yolanda as though Salley's cry demonstrated his point. "You should just take care of your friends."

Yolanda spoke through gritted teeth. "You're all my friends. I want to be fair."

"Hey, Yolo," shouted Bertram Luft as he walked through the bakery door.

"Yolo?" gasped Salley and Rory together.

Then Rory explained his dismay. "Is he some extra

special friend? He calls you Yolo."

"I play music at her place with Umberto." Bertram grinned his million-kilowatt smile. Rory threw an arm around Bertram because he decided to stay close to the guy who called Yolanda Yolo.

"No fair," cried Salley. "I'll be handicapped because I'm not musical." She glared at Rory and Bertram.

The bell rang again. Audrey Decker, executive director of Exceptional Children, came in and cried. "I wasn't quick enough; the money's all gone, isn't it?" She looked at Yolanda accusingly. "You didn't even give me a chance and the group home needs all new kitchen appliances. I thought we were friends."

"So did I," growled the others in the bakery.

Yolanda was now disgusted with the lot of them. Friends, my ass, she thought. This money responsibility was giving her a bad feeling as well as a headache. She slapped the top of the display case. "Enough. I will be sending out grant invitations to all local nonprofits. And I will evaluate your requests."
The bell rang again and Dusty walked in with Umberto. Everyone knew that Dusty stopped by on Wednesday afternoons to eat fresh biscotti. "What's all this?" he asked.

Salley, his sister-in-law, replied, "We came to talk to Yolanda about her grant money."

"Is that the money Lynn said might be available for me and Piper?"

"You and Piper?" cried Rory. "You don't even like each other."

"No fair," cried Salley, "I thought you were going to give me a rookie."

"My clients need money more than you," said Audrey as she glared at Dusty.

"What do you mean?" challenged Bertram, "My agency feeds people. That's the most basic need."

Yolanda threw up her arms and stomped back to the little bakery office. Umberto surveyed the crowd. "Anybody buying anything?" They all looked at him. He made a sweeping motion. "You pester Yolo on her time, not mine. Go home."

~ ~ ~

Tee was a passenger in Jasmine's car and grumbled the whole way to Lynn's office. "Who taught you to drive? You took that curve on two wheels. Do you need glasses when you drive? Didn't you see that stop sign?"

Jasmine growled back, "I should just open that door and toss you out. You're lucky you said I could be Auntie Jasmine to your little angels," Jasmine cut a dark eyed glance at the detective, "because otherwise you would be dead at the curb."

They arrived at Lynn's office after the short, but caustic drive. Teniquia winced as she eased from the car. Jasmine was beside her immediately. "Are you hurt? Is it my driving?"

"Calm down, Auntie Jasmine," sighed the detective, "I still get twinges. Nothing unusual." Jasmine slipped an arm around her waist and helped her into Lynn's office.

Nelda, the office manager, jumped to her feet. "Are you okay?" she asked Tee as she pulled out a chair for the young woman.

"I'm fine," said Tee with a smile, but gratefully sat on the offered chair.

Lynn appeared and announced, "Come into the conference room. I've made some tea." The three women in the office hovered around Teniquia until she was comfortably seated at the conference table with a cup of tea in front of her. "Will you all stop!" she demanded. "I'm going back to work tomorrow. I'm fine." They all sat at the table and stared at her.

"Back to work?" Lynn asked. "Dusty hasn't said

anything."

"I sent him an e-mail this morning saying that Dr. Rita says a few hours a day would be good for my healing process." She lowered her voice, "and for my sanity. Mama hovers just like all of you. Mars and Danny won't hover." She nodded, secure in that knowledge.

Nelda stood. "Well, you have your meeting and I'll keep things quiet out front." She gave Tee one more pat on the shoulder before she closed the door.

Lynn handed Jasmine some tea and sat at the table with her own cup. "Is this about the forum?"

The young women nodded. Jasmine huffed. "We can't get the people to commit to attend. They think we're drawing too much attention to the black community."

"Everyone?" asked Lynn.

"No," explained Tee, "just the old leadership. Our generation is eager to see our history celebrated." She sipped her tea. "We also aren't getting any interest from the white community. A few of the churches have made sponsorship donations, but it's not what I would like to see."

"Do you have a plan?" asked Lynn.

"There will be a series in the newspaper," offered Jasmine, "leading up to the forum. We'll have interviews with some old folks who have some fond memories. We've got a lot of ideas from those tapes. I've done most of the interviews. But I don't know if it will be enough." Jasmine was referring to the audiotapes found at the genealogical society archives that held recorded memories of elders in the black community. They had been produced over thirty-five years ago.

"Any other ideas?" Lynn always liked this part of her job where she helped people find their own solutions.

Tee fidgeted in her chair. "I can't sit too long in these stiff chairs." Both Jasmine and Lynn jumped up to offer something, they weren't sure what. "Sit down. I was just explaining that I can't sit still. Anyway" she continued, "we have one idea. We thought we could get another grant and then not charge admission. That way there is nothing stopping folks from attending."

"How much do you think you need?"

Jasmine brought out her notebook. "We used all your grant money to pay to preserve some of those tapes and photos and other records. We used some money to pay for some displays for that evening, with some blow-up photos and other memorabilia we collected. And the church hall is free. But we want to take out some ads in the paper and run some PSA's on Mr. Warden's radio station. And we want to have refreshments."

"How much?"

"We think we need another fifteen hundred dollars," said Tee.

"The PSAs should be free," said Lynn.

"They are, but they also have some advertising space on a digital sign and space on their website that Mr. Warden will give us at a discount." Jasmine finished her tea. "I think if we do a reasonable job this first time, next year it will be easier. The old folks will see that we were accepted by the community and no one did anything nasty."

"They expect people to be nasty?" Lynn was surprised at that notion.

"There are some old folks who have a hard time changing," said Tee, "and they argue that there are a lot of white folks who also have a hard time changing. I'm sure there are both kinds, but we have to move forward." With hope and courage, were the words she didn't say aloud.

Lynn took her hand. "I think we can find a little more money. There's going to be a grant application coming out soon. I'll see that you get a copy." She really wasn't worried. Her good friend and community benefactor, Nathan Taft, had told her that he would cover any excess costs for this project. But the two organizers shouldn't rely on him. They should solve their own problems because that would make their program stronger in the future. Lynn stood. "I think you have some great ideas. This will be a success and next year even better." She hugged each young woman and led them to the door.

~ ~ ~

Mars and Dusty drove into the farmyard. "Last time I was here," warned Mars, "that old lady chased me with a broom." He opened the car door and climbed out.

Dusty got out himself and walked toward the old house, trusting that Mars had his back because Granny Masterson walked out onto the sagging back porch with a broom in her hands. "What you want, law man?"

Dusty felt like he had just walked into the OK Corral. "Just some questions, Ms. Masterson." He stopped were he was. No need getting within broom distance. "We're talking with folks in the area to see if anyone saw Nevada Utley before he was murdered."

Something changed on the woman's face. She lowered the broom and rested against the porch post. "That be Adele's boy?"

"Yes, ma'am," replied Dusty. "You may have read about his death in the paper. His body was found by the river. He died in the hospital and was never able to tell us what happened."

"And you think us Mastersons did him in." It was a statement.

Dusty looked her in the eye. "He'd been hit over the head and left by the river. If a patrol officer hadn't found him, he would probably have frozen during the night. The whole episode broke his grandmother's heart. She died too, you know."

"I heard," admitted Granny Masterson. "She was a good woman."

"Yes, ma'am, she was," agreed Dusty. "So we're trying to find information that would help us catch Nevada's killer."

"This family wouldn't hurt Adele." That was a strong statement.

"How can you be certain?" asked Dusty.

"Because my kin owe her too much."

"They do?" This was a curious statement from this tough old lady.

She nodded. "When my man was dying from that cancer she always brought me coffee while I sat by his bed in the hospital. She said she understood watching out for your man." The old woman stared at the ground for a moment. "She died with that boy, I hear."

"Yes, ma'am," said Dusty. "They found her in his hospital bed, holding him in her arms."

"Everyone should die with someone they love holdin' on." She pulled a handkerchief out of her pocket and swiped at her nose. "She's happy." With that the old woman walked back into her home and closed the door.

Dusty turned back to his car. Once back on the road, he said to Mars, "She doesn't know anything. But God help the Masterson who attacked Nevada. That woman will kill him."

CHAPTER TEN

Teniquia was finally allowed to return to work part time. So today, with her mother and cousin keeping the children, she walked into the office to start earning her pay. Mars was already at his desk. He looked up and she walked over to him. Taking his hand, she said, "How did she know?"

"Sonny?" Mars shrugged. "She just spoke from her heart."

When Teniquia had been in the hospital recovering from her injury and her miscarriage, Mars had brought her a DVD from Sonny Bosco, a famous movie producer who had chosen to spend her last days in River Bend as she succumbed to a terminal illness. The DVD from Sonny that Mars gave to Teniquia had predicted the loss of her child and the appearance of three orphans in her life. Teniquia and her husband, Lonzo, had heeded Sonny's advice and adopted the children.

"But she knew about the kids. She knew what would happen to my baby." Teniquia gripped his hand harder. Mars stood and put an arm around her.

"She was special," he said. The two old friends hugged one another.

Teniquia wept softly in his arms. "She was right. I'm so happy."

Dusty walked in. "I guess Mars is really glad to see you back 'cause of all the work piling up," he said. The detectives separated. "Do I get a hug, too?" the chief asked.

In an instant Teniquia was in his arms. Danny walked in. "What's this?" She completed the circuit hugging each of her best friends.

A phone rang.

~ ~ ~

Dusty and Mars tramped out behind Joanie's, a restaurant in Verona, a small community in western James County. "Who called this in?" Dusty asked.

Mars looked around at the people gathered by the dumpster. "I think one of the diner workers found the body and called Doug." They saw Doug, that is Doug Fiori, a highway patrolman who lived close by.

"Morning, Doug," Dusty greeted the officer with a bad case of bedhead who was in sweats covered by an old barn jacket clomping around the scene in old farm boots. "Your day off?" It was obvious that the highway patrolman had been called from a sound sleep.

Doug nodded. "I guess it's easy to call me. I only live a block away." He pointed to his small bungalow on the only other street in Verona.

"What's your report?" Dusty knew Doug would have handled this crime scene professionally.

"I got the call about an hour ago. Gerta, one of the older waitresses, found the body when she brought out the trash from the early morning diners. She's cool. She said she doesn't recognize him, so I don't think he was a regular. A couple of the others around town came by to look. No ID from anyone. No one has touched anything." Doug grinned. "You know they all watch those TV shows and have high expectations about the tech crew they'll see. Anyway, watching TV also taught them to leave things be until we process the scene."

"Go back to bed," said Dusty, "we'll call if we need you." Doug gave the detective a grateful nodded. They watched the trooper cut through the snow piles to get back to his home on the next street.

"Poor guy," said Mars, "dragged out of bed to deal with a body."

"This town trusts him," stated Dusty. "He kept

everyone calm and he was a professional. All these people saw the way we spoke with him. They'll all cooperate with us because we're Doug's friends." Dusty understood the nuances of small town law enforcement. "Now get this scene organized. I'm going inside to get some coffee and talk with Gerta.

When Dusty returned outside with a cup of coffee for Mars, they already had an ID on the victim. "We have a name," announced Mars after taking a gulp of coffee to warm up. "The techs were able to take digital scans of his fingerprints and search available data bases. Homer Gibson. He lives in Asheville. Has a record. I called Danny and asked him to follow up with the Asheville PD."

"Cause of death?"

"The medical examiner said all he could see was a bashed in head and a gunshot entry wound, but he'll have a professional response in a couple of hours when he's warmer." Mars took another warming drink. "The lady have anything else?"

"No, she said she gets here at 5:30 to start the grill and turn the heat up. She said she didn't notice or hear anyone once she was here." Dusty pulled a cinnamon roll out of his pocket and gave it to Mars.

Mars handed his cup to Dusty and unwrapped the bun – it was still warm. After one good bite, he asked, "Do you think it's related to Nevada? They both were hit in the head."

Dusty was enjoying his own roll, but answered, "We'll just see what the evidence tells us." In Dusty's opinion speculation was worthless unless he had all the information.

~ ~ ~

Lynn had gotten an emergency call from Thel Bergman. She left her office and rushed over to the

Bergmans' place. "I got here as soon as I could," she told Janet as she walked into the house.

"I don't know why Mom called you." Janet was about five months pregnant and was starting to walk like a penguin. She was living with her parents while her husband was away at sea with the Navy. "I can handle this. Polly is just not paying attention."

Lynn frowned to herself. The Bergmans didn't need someone else in their home who didn't pay attention. Janet was renowned for her vagueness. "What has your mother concerned?"

Janet shrugged and took another bite of her apple. Since her pregnancy Janet had become a foodaholic – and it showed in the penguin waddle. "She doesn't always tell me things."

Lynn followed Janet into the kitchen where her parents, Thel and Bergy, were having a mid-morning coffee. "I'm here. How can I help?" she asked.

Thel looked grateful. Bergy, still in his wheelchair, looked frustrated. Lynn knew that he would be facing any problem head-on if he were healthy enough. But his life had changed and his physical abilities diminished as a result of his stroke. Before retirement he had been the Sheriff of James County and an influential politician. Now he relied on his friends and former deputies to get things done. "That girl is headed for trouble," growled Bergy. "My old deputies are keeping an eye on her. She's picked up with some bad kids at school."

"What can I do?" Lynn asked.

"I want you to talk to her," said Bergy. "Scare the shit out of her."

"Pops!" scolded Janet.

He waved his hand dismissing his daughter's outrage and continued, "You have a son close to her age." Lynn nodded as she remembered some challenges when Jason was Polly's age – the fights with Dusty, the challenges to her authority. It had been unpleasant but they had survived. "Is she skipping school? Lying to you? Not doing her homework? Misbehaving at school?"

Thel said, "She is just too quiet and doesn't talk about school or friends. I think she doesn't feel as though she has to share anything about her life with us." She looked at Janet and Bergy. "And between the three of us, we don't have the skill or energy to look into it." She hung her head.

Lynn understood. All of their lives Bergy and Thel had been strong people, doing a lot for everyone else. Now, as they aged and dealt with some demanding health issues, they needed help. And Janet, their daughter, in addition to being pregnant, was distracted by her high level computer consulting business. Polly was in a household where she could easily disappear. The Bergmans were determined to make certain that they had her attention. So they were calling in the troops.

"Have you talked with Mars?" Lynn asked. Everyone knew that Mars had had a special relationship with the family since his childhood.

"Polly reminds me of him," said Bergy. "She has that same lost look – real quiet." The old sheriff laughed. "We got Mars to come around. But I think we need some help with this youngster."

Lynn nodded. "Tell your old deputies to keep their eyes open. I'll ask around." It was an ambiguous response, but they all seemed to understand one another. "You'll be hearing from me," Lynn reassured them and she left the house.

~ ~ ~

Yolanda had worked with Mason earlier in the week. Today they had no plans to get together but to her surprise, Mason called and invited her out to lunch. There had been light flurries and he told her that he would meet her in town because her light flurries were two inches of snow at his place because of the elevation changes.

He arrived at her home a few minutes after noon. "Dad's house must be in another weather zone. It was good the sun came out to melt some of the ice." His cheeks were rosy from the crisp weather. She stepped aside and invited him in. He came to a halt. The way he stood transfixed at the very ordinary home and its furnishings made her uncomfortable.

"I know it's not the kind of thing you're used to seeing, expensive decor and butlers or something." She felt uncertain about him in her home and began to wonder why he would even want to take someone so plain to lunch.

He took her hands. "Thank you for inviting me in." She looked at him suspiciously. "I was raised abroad in some very primitive settings. Pop dragged us from job to job. Mom said that I was a citizen of a construction site. She always apologized for not giving me the all-American upbringing with picket fences and apple pie." He walked into the living room and tenderly touched the piano. "We always had maids but sometimes not indoor plumbing. I grew up eating the food of the country we lived in at the time. If there wasn't a school for foreign kids I went to whatever was available. It's a great way to learn a language." He threw back his head and laughed – a sound she really enjoyed. "I never went to an American high school so I missed all the experiences in those movies."

Yolanda laughed, "I don't think real American high school experiences are the same as those defined by movies." Then she eyed him with a sly look. "But I can certainly take you to a high school basketball game.

They usually play on Friday night."

He smiled at her. "That would be great. Can I flirt with a cheerleader?"

"Only if you want her father to have you arrested for scaring his daughter because of your age."

Mason looked glum. "I guess I'll have to just soak up the atmosphere."

"You seem to be very familiar with American slang and other cultural references." She tried to collect her random thoughts into a coherent observation. "You don't act like you're from another country."

"I came back to the states every summer once I was about nine or ten and went to summer camp. That's why my parents retired here. I always attended a camp in Henderson County and they would take that time to relax themselves, visit relatives and friends. I'd be here about six weeks, they about two. I usually flew back to our posting alone." He continued to study the room's decor. "Can I see the rest of your house?"

Yolanda took him on a tour of the house she and her husband had purchased twenty years ago. Here they had raised three children, held family celebrations and planted a vegetable garden every year. "I'm sorry you're not here for the summer. My garden is lovely, both flowers and vegetables." She walked toward the back of the house, pointing, "Kids rooms, kitchen." Then she opened a door and took him to the lower level. Although the house didn't appear so, Mason found that the back yard fell away much the same as his father's house, and the lower rooms opened into a lovely yard and patio area.

"The kids entertained their friends here and my husband had his music room." They walked into a room that still held several instruments and an upright piano. "He gave private lessons, and now my son is playing the cello again. He practices here so he doesn't wake up his baby," she smiled, "my grandson."

"It looks like he uses it a lot."

"I use it, too. I play the viola in the local symphony. I've played since middle school."

"Wow! No one ever mentions classical music in those high school teen movies about true American life." Yolanda laughed and gave him a quick hug, surprising both of them.

It was such a quick, spontaneous hug that Mason was certain she had no intention of pursuing anything sexual, but all of a sudden he did. Just something friendly, not too intense, then he studied her as she led him back to the living room. No, it wouldn't be right. He sensed that Yolanda was not like any of his lady friends. She had too much strength and personal reserve. Besides she would know any relationship would be brief and ultimately meaningless, and not, he sensed, her cup of tea. But he was still interested.

He cleared his throat, pulling himself back to Mason-the-grateful-son from Mason-the – lecher. "Where am I taking you to lunch?"

~ ~ ~

Lynn's first stop, once she had the free time to focus on Polly, was the high school where she stopped in to chat with her old friend, Gabe McElvoy, who was the assistant principal. She plopped in a chair in his office and smiled at the man who had been the football coach when she was in high school. He was thirty years older, and as he told everyone, ready to retire, but he loved his job. He stayed fit and wore his gray hair cut short.

"I bet you were never in the principal's office when you were a student here," he greeted her.

She smiled. "Only if I was getting another award."

He laughed. "So why are you here today? We forgot to give you some award?"

"I came to ask about Polly Carmichael. Bergy is concerned that she's hanging out with the wrong kids." They both became very serious.

Gabe nodded. "I'm concerned about her, too. She didn't try out for the lacrosse team. She's one of the better girl athletes in this school. She sits in her classes, does her assignments, but seems to have checked out. No participation – just does what she has to. Her other teachers have noticed, too." He shrugged. "She's not doing anything that raises any flags, so we've been wondering what to do."

"What about her old friends?"

Gabe shrugged. "She's become a loner. I don't see her eating lunch with her old team mates, or others she used to pal around with." He stared out his office window to the school lobby, deep in thought. "I have seen her sort of tagging along with some other loner kids. None of them causes trouble, they all just drift through the day. I don't know who she sees after school."

Lynn blew out her breath and thought for a moment. "Does she need more counseling? I know she hated meeting with the therapist after Susan's death. She's refused to continue."

"I don't know what to tell you," said Gabe. "I've got a thousand kids here and on any given day emotional problems cause more upheaval than academic problems." He was thoughtful for a moment. "I have heard, well, I didn't hear, I got an official letter, that hospice is starting a teen grief counseling project. They wanted me to tell the teachers and counselors. That might be an option." He stared at his former student. "Talk to some of Susan's friends and tell everyone to keep their eyes on her. Maybe you could take her shopping or something – you know, something her mother would do." Coaching was a lot easier, he thought to himself, than trying to stay ahead of kids' personal problems.

Lynn frowned. "I'll check in with hospice and I'll ask Thel about doing some shopping."

They talked for a few more minutes, but Lynn got nothing more from her old friend.

~ ~ ~

It turned out to be a great afternoon, a little cool, but fun. Yolanda and Mason ate lunch at the Main Street Cafe, stopped at the bakery for dessert, and a quick introduction to Umberto, and then they walked along the greenway and sat on a bench in the river park bundled against a stiff wind.

"I think we've done all the Americana that I missed in my life." He dragged Yolanda to Pedro's Casa at the edge of the park so they could warm up. "We need a margarita before we end this lunch."

Yolanda laughed. "It's three-thirty."

"We could just drink for another hour and then have dinner." Mason was hopeful.

"Sorry, I have family obligations this evening," she replied, hoping he didn't ask for an explanation because she was lying. "But we should see a basketball game before you leave town." She pulled a small card out of her coat pocket. It was a game schedule.

"You carry a game schedule with you?" he asked, amazed.

"No, I picked it up at the bakery." She squinted at the card. "They used the really small type this year."

Mason took out his reading glasses then reached for the card. After some study, he concluded, "There's a home game tomorrow evening. JV at five; Vars. at seven?"

"They have two gyms," explained Yolanda, "There will be JV games, boys and girls in the old gym and varsity in the new gym, girls first at seven followed by the boys' game."

"Should we make a night of it?" he asked. "I'll treat. They must sell hot dogs or something at the school and we can grab another margarita after the game."

"Will you have time?"

"Sweetheart made reservations for Saturday. I fly out of Charlotte in the late evening." They sat quietly and finished their drinks.

Yolanda finally nodded. "I really have to get home."

CHAPTER ELEVEN

Yolanda was in Lynn's office early. "I'm ready," she announced. She had felt guilty about lying to Mason, intimating that she had to get home for a particular reason. At home with a free, guilt-ridden evening, she decided to organize her grant application and be ready for her Friday morning launch.

Lynn blinked at her guest, bringing her mind back from the spreadsheet where she had been lost in Philanthropies' finances. "What do you need from me?"

Yolanda took a seat across from Lynn's desk. "I have a packet that I want you to review and then I'd like you to e-mail it to all the agencies on your list."

"All of them?"

"Yes," she nodded, "and I sent a press release to Jasmine so that an announcement should be in the paper tomorrow morning in case we miss anyone."

"A press release?"

"Come on, Lynn," Yolanda encouraged her friend. "I want to get this project started and finished before too long. My daughter is going to have her baby in April and I have to be ready to help." Yolanda was ready to hit the ground running.

Lynn, on the other hand, was ready for the weekend. TGIF! "Let me see what you have." Yolanda handed her a packet of paper. Lynn studied it thoroughly. No sense in letting mistakes get out, that would only mean they would have to recall the grant forms and start again. A bad option for someone ready to run. "You've kept it short, asked for the right information and set good criteria." Lynn shook her head. "But, it's still a very general request for participants. You've set it up so the responses can cover anything from printing a brochure to building an office."

"I know," Yolanda hung her head. "I just didn't want to miss anyone. I reviewed Foster's history of donations. He was a very eclectic donor."

"Do you want to set a limit on the size of the grant?

"Should I?"

"Setting a limit will at least put some constraints on the proposal. No one will ask for more money than you have to give and the skilled grant applicants will try to find the sweet spot of what you're willing to fund to an individual agency." Lynn restacked the papers.

"The sweet spot?" One more consideration to cause a headache, thought Yolanda.

"Whether you know it now," explained Lynn, "there is an amount of money that you have set as a limit for any one agency request. You'll know it when you see the proposals. Some will just seem to be asking for more than you want to give."

"I have a headache already," moaned Yolanda, "I can't even think of a limit." She handed Lynn a flash drive.

Lynn put the drive into her computer, scanned the electronic packet to make certain it was intact, then attached it to an e-mail blast to all local nonprofits. While the computer responded to Lynn's prompts, she asked Yolanda, "Have you seen Polly recently?"

"No, I haven't had time. Is something wrong?"

"I don't know. The Bergmans are worried that she's withdrawn. Gabe says her teachers are noticing the same thing, but Polly has refused to continue to see the therapist."

"I'll ask around the family," replied Yolanda, "someone's kids may have said something." The beauty of being part of a big family in a small town – dozens of eyes and ears. Yolanda had family everywhere. "How long until ...?" She nodded at the computer.

Lynn looked very guilty. "Word has gotten out about the money, folks have been calling me."

Yolanda was not happy. She told Lynn about Wednesday at the bakery.

"I'm not surprised," said Lynn. "It's all over town. Local agencies are just waiting for the request to come out." Lynn smiled at her. "Because of the conditions you've set, some of them may be forced to rework their proposals, but you'll start to see something in a few days."

"I think I'll go home and rest," sighed Yolanda.

~ ~ ~

Teniquia had worked hard yesterday. Her first workday had included a murder victim. That kept her hopping. It also tired her out. But she was back at her desk today, thinking that she would leave by noon. Her body wasn't quite up to her mind with regard to energy and stamina. Stamina, she thought, I've got to start thinking about the gym. She felt her body rebel at the idea. She ran a small training session for some of her friends at one of Bev's Spas. Lynn and Piper showed up regularly and Jasmine had joined just before the shooting. Building up and training with her friends wouldn't be too bad. She was certain not one of them had worked out alone while she healed. The gym – maybe next week.

The idea almost energized her – getting back to her drill sergeant persona might be just the way to snap back, or maybe limp back, into shape. Her phone rang.

At her greeting, a familiar voice said, "You back in the saddle, honey?"

"I am, Dundee." She grinned into the phone as she spoke with an old friend from the Asheville PD. "You get the message about our murder victim?"

"Yeah," he drawled into the phone, "I'll exchange information if you tell me how your life is with all those kids and that midget you married."

Tee had to laugh. Dundee was maybe five foot seven and liked to challenge her husband, Lonzo, to all sorts of strength tests – which Dundee always lost. "Life is good. And my babies love those books you sent for Christmas."

As Dusty always reminded his staff, when Bergy was sheriff he worked hard to build up links and friendships with other regional departments. The joint investigation unit had made friends with everyone. And, today, as usual, it was paying off. "Do you want to give me your report or talk to one of the other guys?" she asked. "I don't know who called you."

"Danny called and he said to talk to Mars. But I'd rather talk to you," he said. She could hear him shuffle papers over the phone. "Here's what we got. Your vic worked for a guy who came up here from Florida a few years ago and opened a used tire recycling place. We think he does some other business, like gambling and maybe drugs, but he keeps that action out of sight."

"So what did our vic do?"

"I think he was muscle," replied Dundee. "There are three guys who work for this outfit and they all seem to stay clean and work at unspecified jobs. Mr. Big–"

"The boss is named Mr. Big?"

"No, sorry his name is Angelo Pontelli. He's clean but raised a lot of interest in Florida and that's why we think he came here. He employs three big guys. One was your vic. He also keeps a few scruffy guys to do the tire side of the business." Dundee paused and she heard him sip a beverage. He continued, "I'd be happy to go with Mars to visit the guy. It gives me an excuse to get inside the operation without a warrant."

"I'll tell him."

They ended their conversation and Tee consulted the sign-out sheet. Mars was gone for the rest of the day. That was odd. He never took free time unless his girlfriend, Nancy, was in town.

"Danny," she called across the room, "where's Mars today?"

Danny looked up from his computer, consulted his calendar and said, "He's doing something for his Uncle Hutch." Danny wasn't certain if Mars wanted his new bank board role talked about. Mars could tell her if he wanted to. "He said he would take on call for the weekend."

She sent a quick e-mail to Dundee telling him that Mars was out today and would contact him early next week. Then she wondered if she could get away early. As if reading her mind, Danny said, "I'm leaving about three. I signed up for basketball duty tonight."

That answered her question. Danny was doing some overtime as security at the high school basketball game. Mars was doing something for Uncle Hutch. Dusty was not in the office. She would stay until Dusty returned and hoped she -

"What are you doing still here?" asked Dusty as he strode into the office.

"Who me?" she asked.

"Go home. You look a little pale."

She laughed. "My skin is brown. How can you see pale?" As Lynn liked to say, Tee was a lovely mocha latte.

Dusty smiled at her. "I can see how tired you are. It's in your eyes. Go home. We'll see you on Monday."

~ ~ ~

The River Bend First Bank board assembled just before noon in a private dining room at the country club. There were fifteen members, plus an assortment of bank personnel deemed worthy of associating with the board. Mars walked into the room in one of his tailored suits, custom shirts, designer shoes and outrageously expensive ties. He also had his weapon in a holster fitted discreetly under his arm. He looked at the group of pompous white men and women and wondered if they thought he was armed. Or if they even considered him a threat. Promising himself he would not embarrass Uncle Hutch, he walked around the room with a smile and greeted all those he personally knew.

Everyone in the room recognized him. He was, based on the wealth he either controlled or would inherit, one of the five richest men in River Bend. He was glad his friends at the office only knew of his wealth in some vague way related to his parents.

"Mr. Healey," simpered one gentleman whom Mars immediately identified as staff. "We are delighted to welcome you to your first board meeting. I'm Renfro Bartlett, vice president of regional commercial loans. Do you know our chair –"

"Of course I know young Healey," boomed an officious blowhard Mars easily identified as John Wilton. "Call me Charger," announced the old college football player. Mars wondered if playing football semi-successfully at a very small college had been the high point of his life. Then he reminded himself, Uncle Hutch expected him to behave.

"Thank you, Charger," replied Mars.

Charger grabbed him by the arm and dragged him around the room making introductions, most of which sounded like, "I want you to meet Martin Healey, old Dunn's nephew. Lot of family history in this bank." Mars shook a hand and they moved on.

Behind him Mars heard some members mutter something along the lines of, "That Dunn is finally gone. Maybe we can quit acting like social workers." and "Heard this kid is a cop. That should make him a realist and not concerned about every single mother in town."

The remarks gave Mars a lot to think about. His respect for Uncle Hutch tripled. How long had the old attorney put up with these people? He smiled to himself. None of them knew he had checked everyone out. He knew the drunk drivers, the men who assaulted their wives, and, of the three women on the board, the one who became the trophy wife after an interesting career in Vegas, and the one who might have a painkiller addiction. Someone was tracking her prescriptions.

As lunch was served the table talk was limited to sports or recent vacations. Mars' lunch neighbor turned and said, "I understand that you work with the police. What do you do? Is it just part time to stay busy?"

By the tone of the question Mars suspected that Charger and his inner circle had dug into his personal finances. "I am a full time investigator in James County," he replied. The talk stopped as everyone tried to listen. For their benefit he explained, "I usually get involved with homicides, kidnappings, robberies, all the things you see on a TV crime show."

"Not in our town," stated one of the women.

"Now, Healey," cautioned Charger, "Let's not scare everyone."

"Yes, sir," replied Mars. He decided to let them think that he would heed direction from the chair.

The formal meeting began. Mars listened to the discussion, asked some mild questions, and demonstrated his ability to understand a balance sheet and profit and loss statement. Before the meeting ended, true to Uncle Hutch's suspicion, someone tried to bring up the idea of a board retreat in Hilton Head. To which Mars stated, "I'm a stockholder of this corporation and wonder what other stockholders would think of that sort of expense."

Charger jumped in to squelch the discussion. "Heh, heh, it's winter and we're all thinking about going some place warmer. Heh, heh." He gave the evil eye to the man who had suggested the jaunt. "I'll entertain a motion to adjourn."

"So moved."

"Second."

The gavel came down. "We are adjourned until next month."

~ ~ ~

Mason was right on time Friday evening. They saw parts of both JV games, ate terrible hot dogs and wonderful popcorn then staked out a seat for the varsity games. It was a great evening. All home teams won. Yolanda seemed to know everyone on and off the court. She maintained a running commentary, "Number five dates my nephew." This was during the girls' game. "Number eleven used to take violin from my husband. The shortest cheerleader is a cousin."

After the game they walked arm and arm through the parking lot. "I can see I missed a lot going to school abroad. We didn't have cheerleaders."

"Did you have sports?"

"No, but we could have used cheerleaders. Although I don't know if the girls looked like that back then."

"You mean a century ago?" asked Yolanda.

Mason stopped and pulled her into his arms. "Were you a cheerleader?"

"No, I played in the school band and orchestra." She didn't pull away, but rested her hands on his chest.

"I've enjoyed my time with you," he said and gently kissed her.

Yolanda was surprised and delighted, then she was confused because a gentle kiss grew into something more. Her confusion turned to active participation until – "Mo-o-om!"

They stopped. Mason held her and with his lips still resting on hers said softly, "We're not finished here."

Yolanda pushed back and asked as only a mother can, "Do you need something, Danny?"

Mason slowly turned around and found himself facing a very concerned and armed police officer. "Hello," he said reaching out his hand, "I'm Mason Donovan."

Danny took the hand with a sidelong glance at his mother. She knew what that meant. He expected an explanation, soon.

"Yes, sir," replied Danny, "I'm sorry about the death of your father. I'm Danny Valeri." Then he stood and waited.

Mason became the international professional businessman. "Yolanda, I have an appointment with O'Hara in the morning then I leave for my flight out of Charlotte. I'll leave the keys for you and some instructions." He addressed Danny, "Can I ask you to see your mother home?"

Danny was caught off guard. "Sir, I'm providing security this evening. But I can call my uncle."

"That's all right, son," Mason said in his business voice, "I'll see her home. It was a pleasure meeting you." He took Yolanda's elbow and guided her to his car.

She was snickering as he climbed behind the wheel. "My son will be in my kitchen at eleven-thirty. That's when his overtime ends."

"Are you saying we'll have to be quick?" He grinned

at her.

"No, I'm saying that I'll see you the next time you're in town."

"I told you," he said in a husky voice, "we're not finished. You can be certain I'll come back."

He walked her to her door and gave her one more body-numbing kiss before he left.

~ ~ ~

Yolanda sat in her kitchen enjoying a cup of tea, thinking about that kiss. She heard the garage door open and waited for her son to walk through the kitchen door. He walked in and glared at her as though she were a child who had misbehaved. "What was that all about?" he demanded.

"What was what all about?" she asked, just to get him riled.

"You know what I'm talking about." The skilled interrogator forgot all he knew. "I suppose you've been having some sort of love fest when you said you were helping him pack up that house."

Yolanda looked at him trying to decide whether to be offended or laugh. She decided instead to be a mother. "Is there a reason you're acting like a little boy?" It was a question she always asked during his teen years when he acted out. She sipped her tea.

Steam seemed to come from Danny's ears. He wasn't disarmed or distracted by her ploy. "Talk about people not acting their ages," he harrumphed, "my mother was out necking–

"Do they still call it that?" She was starting to enjoy this.

"– necking with a man she's only known a few days. Heaven only knows what else you've been doing if you're publicly kissing–"

"You're not my confessor," she replied, "but heaven already knows that I have done nothing for which I should visit Father Nick." So there.

Danny paced in the kitchen, stopping at the refrigerator to help himself to a soft drink. He paced some more, rummaging through the cupboards and pantry until he found something to eat. Throwing a bag of chips and some salsa on the table he sat down and frowned at his mother before opening the bag and helping himself to a midnight snack. "Want some?" He pushed the bag toward her.

"I'm watching my figure now that someone is interested in it." She finally decided to be offended by his attitude.

He understood. "I'm sorry." He closed the bag and put away the food then sat back down at the table. "I was just surprised that–"

"Someone might find me attractive?"

He groaned. "No, that you ... ah ... er." He stopped because there was no way to say why he was surprised without insulting her. He tried another approach. "I was sort of jealous."

"Jealous?"

"You're my girl," he smiled his disarming little boy smile, "I was worried I had lost you to some big, sexy guy."

Yolanda gave him a squinty-eyed look. "I had a date this evening. Mason was charming. He's leaving town in the morning and we may never meet again. But I enjoyed my date. I enjoyed the kiss." She wasn't going to tell him about the other, more thorough kiss, at her door. "It made me feel womanly and maybe not as old as I," here she got even, "or my family believe I am."

"We never said–"

She smiled now. "I know. But I admit all of us sort of decided I was over the hill, or not interested in, you know." Danny blushed. "I have to say, I could be persuaded to, you know. Maybe not with Mason because he's so temporary. But I might like to be in a relationship again. There are nights when it gets lonely around this house." Now she was serious. This was a talk she should have had with herself before she had it with her children, but she was here and so was her son.

"A guy never thinks of his mom like—"

"I'm not going to run off somewhere and go crazy," said Yolanda, "but now that I know there is potential for a new way of life out there, don't be surprised, and don't be hurt if I decide to explore."

Danny took her hand. "I love you, Mom. And I'll always have your back. Just don't do anything that requires me to use my gun."

She laughed and pulled him closer for a kiss on the cheek.

CHAPTER TWELVE

Lynn decided to take Gabe's suggestion about shopping. She was at the Bergmans early Saturday morning. "Hey, Polly," she greeted the youngster as she came into the kitchen. "I told Janet I'd take you on your errands today, since she's feeling a little slow and tired."

Polly nodded to Lynn. "Thanks."

After Polly had a bowl of cereal, they took off for the mall. "What things do we need?" asked Lynn. "I haven't shopped with a teenage girl before. I have no idea about current fashion." Polly stared at her silently. Lynn tried to stop babbling, she could already tell that this was going to be a strained encounter.

They walked through several stores as Polly selected dark clothing. Lynn didn't know what to tell her. Everything the youngster selected suggested sorrow and depression. Lynn recalled the days before Susan's death when she had occasion to see Polly. The young girl had always been dressed in bright clothing – even her school shoes were bright pink. Her current color palette was somber.

Lynn took every opportunity to suggest something brighter. But by the third time she had held up a colorful shirt, asking "How about this?" and had Polly decline to try it on, Lynn quit. She decided she would take her to lunch and try to talk with her.

Lunch didn't work either. Polly didn't want lunch. She finished her shopping and wanted to go home, or as she put it, "I'm done here."

Lynn dropped her at the Bergmans and stopped at the bakery for a snack. "You only eat two cannoli when you got a problem," Umberto, the baker, said to her as she sat at his snack bar.

"It's Polly." Lynn confessed. "She seems to be withdrawing and we can't figure out what to do. Any ideas?" She knew that Umberto had a secret life in this community as a champion of children. Over the years she had known him to quietly step in with snacks and moral support for all sorts of youngsters. He always seemed to know when someone needed quiet support, encouragement or a giant cookie. She thought he had a way with kids because he always allowed them to hang out at the bakery, and they always behaved for him.

"She's a sad one," he agreed. "I'll keep an eye out."

Lynn was reassured there were going to be a lot of eyes on Polly. She only hoped it would pay off with some changes in the youngster's attitude.

~ ~ ~

Mason studied his travel app. There was a big snowstorm blanketing the east coast. Nothing was leaving any of the iced in airports and that had backed traffic up, and was causing cancellations and delays, in Charlotte and Atlanta. Hmm. If he stayed in River Bend a few more days, the traffic tie-ups would clear and he could start his journey back to Saudi.

And ... he would have a little more time to pursue the captivating Yolanda. That's why, after his meeting with Robert O'Hara, he drove to Yolanda's house. His excuse was the snowstorm and his offer was another long lunch. He almost laughed at the look on her face when she answered the door – shocked, and he hoped, pleased.

She smiled and stepped aside to invite him in. "I guess you didn't leave."

"Snowstorm," he replied. "I'm waiting it out here until the planes are back on schedule."

"It's snowing in Saudi Arabia?"

"Smart ass." He gave her a quick kiss on the cheek.

"How about lunch?" He loved her outfit – baggy jeans and a long-sleeved t-shirt that said, "Grandmas are Easy." He hoped that was true.

She walked into the kitchen and he followed – and got hit in the head with something. He looked down at his feet. A Cheerio? "I'm babysitting. So does your invitation include my little angel, Dirty Face?"

"That's what his parents named him?" Mason had never met a baby before. "I'm not certain but I suspect they had something more formal put on his birth certificate." Then he blurted the truth. "I've never met a baby before."

Yolanda stared at him, flabbergasted. "None of your women in all those ports have children?"

"They may, but they keep them away from me. I'm only there for X-rated activities." Which wasn't going to happen here, he told himself.

She laughed. The baby laughed. She wiped the baby's hands and face. "I need to clean up this mess." There were Cheerios and raisins everywhere. "You two go play in the living room."

"Play?" Panic!

"Just let David – see, he has a name – just let him crawl around and don't let him pull any furniture on his head. When I'm done in the kitchen I'll put him down for a nap."

"I don't have to hold him?" Mason wasn't certain about baby protocol. "I don't think I know how."

Yolanda lifted the baby out of the high chair, brushing stray Cheerios and raisins off his clothing, and carried him into the living room, placing him on the floor. "He's a great crawler and he's just learning to pull himself up, getting ready to walk. Just watch him." She left them alone.

Mason spent the most fascinating thirty minutes watching the child crawl, sit, crawl, explore, grin. He was fearless, attacking each piece of furniture. Then he found Mason's leg as the man sat on the sofa. Little David grabbed Mason's shoe lace, tried to eat it, pulled at his socks then began a long struggle to pull himself up Mason's leg. Finally with two chubby baby fists he clung to Mason's knee and grinned in triumph. Mason grinned back.

The baby, acknowledging their new bond, began to gurgle and chatter in some mysterious language, stopping at times to allow Mason to comment. Mason, a man of many languages, talked back in Urdu, threw in some Russian and Korean then ended with a small, timid tickle under the baby's chin.

The conversation was a success. David threw back his head and laughed, promptly finding himself sitting on the floor. His face crumbled and he was ready to cry. Mason, in an unplanned and never before attempted move, lifted the baby up and held him on his lap, talking non-stop in any language that came to his mind. David recovered, grinned and reached for Mason's wristwatch.

When Yolanda walked into the living room she was speechless. Mason was entertaining David, talking and tickling and sharing his watch and car keys. "You look like a pro," she said, as she sat beside him. David reached for his grandmother and, digging his little foot in Mason's crotch, dove at her.

"I'm exhausted," he said as he subtly tried to rearrange himself. "I have never spent time alone with a baby. I'm learning so many things hanging out with you."

"Anything you can use in your world?"

"Probably not, but now I'm prepared in case someone leaves a baby on one of my bulldozers at a construction site." As they talked David snuggled into Yolanda's arms and slowly fell asleep listening to the conversation.

Yolanda held her little treasure and continued talking. "Being in this country must be more foreign to you than any of the other places you work."

"You're right. Except for my time at camp and college, I've never lived in my own country. College certainly wasn't real. Dorm life, parties every night and studies never got me into a private home."

"Never?"

"The other day, when I walked in here, it was the first time since I was a youngster and we visited relatives that I had been in a private American home."

"And I've never been in a foreign home." She stood. "Let me put him in his crib and I'll make us some coffee." She disappeared down the hall and returned shortly, beckoning Mason to follow. In the kitchen she started a pot of coffee. "Have you had lunch?"

"No."

"Neither have I." She opened the refrigerator and pulled out some containers. Walking to the pantry, she brought a few more things to the counter and began to, very efficiently, prepare soup and a sandwich while the brewing coffee pot punctuated their discussion.

Mason watched every move. "None of my women in any port ever fixed me a meal. They all have maids or insist on dining out before things get X-rated."

"I guess that's another reason why I'm not qualified to be your lady in the port city of River Bend." She grinned at him as she placed a bowl of soup on the table.

"I've told you, Yolanda," he held her wrist and pulled her to his side, "we're not finished."

"And I don't understand what you mean." She squirmed out of his reach, placed a plate of sandwiches in the center of the table and sat with her bowl of soup.

He sampled his soup, took a sandwich from the

tray and replied, "I don't either. It's like we have unfinished business."

"Such as?"

"Sex."

Yolanda dropped her spoon on the floor. "I'm to be a conquest? You keep a tally, visit a new town, boink a woman?'"

"I'm not that crude."

She gave him a look only a mother could give as she wiped her spoon before placing it back in the bowl. He looked sheepish.

"I like the time we've spent together." He chewed his sandwich. "With me that usually means an intimate exchange should occur before too long."

"Not gonna happen," she said as she poured coffee.

"Are you sure?"

"Of course, I'm sure," she said calmly. "There's no reason for me to have sex with someone who is only notching his bedpost and whom I'll never see again after his father's estate is closed." She stirred cream in her coffee. "What do I gain?"

"Fun?"

"I look for longer term gains – steadfast relationship, frequent encounters of the non-sexual kind like dinners, hiking, basketball games, you know, life."

"We can do all those things while I'm here."

"You mean until the snow melts in Saudi?" Yolanda didn't know whether to be thrilled or insulted by his approach. And she said as much.

"Insulted?" growled Mason. "I can't believe that other men in this town aren't approaching you with ... er ... invitations?"

"My son wears a gun." A hard fact in her life.

"Yeah, I noticed." Mason stood and carried his dishes to the sink. "I'm serious. No dates?"

"No." Then she smiled. "This was sort of the discussion I had with my son last night."

"He wanted answers, didn't he?" Mason grinned.

"I told him I wasn't dead and I might like to find a companion."

Mason held out his arms as if offering himself. "I have a few days."

"As I told my son," Yolanda said, "I might be persuaded. And as I told you, not by someone just passing through."

"You could reconsider."

The baby cried out and Yolanda smiled. "Not today."

~ ~ ~

A quiet Saturday afternoon and Polly Carmichael sat in her room at the Bergman house. It didn't have much from her old room. The bomb that killed her mother had shattered windows and spread odors and debris throughout the house. Most of her stuffed animals smelled of smoke and had been thrown away. All of her clothes had been replaced. There were a few photos and some drawings that she had been able to save. They had been in her secret drawer. She smiled. Her mother had called it her secret drawer, saying draw-er because both words were spelled the same. And Polly had to admit, she was a secret draw-er. She sat on her bed with the sketchpad balanced on her knees. This was how she talked with her mother. Asking questions and quickly sketching Susan's facial responses.

Polly knew her mother so well that she could almost guess what Susan would say. She began talking softly. "Mom, I'm scared. Those kids met a man in town and now he's dead." Her pencil danced across the paper. Susan's eyes seem to look back in a startled frown. Her mouth turned down at the edges. Polly studied the face. Yes, that would have been her response. Worry, concern. "Don't panic. I didn't talk to the man. I'll be careful." She sketched another of Susan's looks. It was the look that told Polly she knew how to behave so why was she acting out. It was a face that always seemed to intrude on her sketches. "I don't want to talk to my old friends. I don't want to talk to anybody. I want to leave this town."

Her pencil seemed to have a life of its own. Susan's face turned disappointed. "You aren't here," Polly said in a harsh whisper. "I can do what I want. I don't want to be my old self. I don't remember my old self. I think it died with you."

Another face emerged – Susan with the loving eyes and soft smile. "I love you, too. I'll think about it." Polly put down her charcoal and wiped tears from her eyes. Outside the world was winter crisp and bright. In her room things were sad and heavy. She stretched out on her bed and cried softly, while Susan's many faces stared at her from the other pillow.

CHAPTER THIRTEEN

January was already into double-digit days. Everyone knew what that meant – Super Bowl play-offs. Since Piper and Will had hosted News Year's Eve, Lynn and Dusty won the bid for the playoffs. Lynn thought it was like countries bidding to host the Olympics. Only the ones with the resources would win a nod from the committee. In her case, both Will and Dusty had managed to buy big TV screens as their personal Christmas gifts to themselves, so the decision as to host was made when Piper said she hadn't recovered from New Year's Eve. As in, "There's a stain on my carpet I can't get out."

And Will's solution, "Put a chair over it."

Lynn had stepped in to offer her house because she had hardwood floors. "Besides," she had concluded, "When Dusty falls asleep, I won't have to wake him to get him home. I can just leave him in front of the TV with the dog."

So that's why the crowd collected at Lynn's place.

Mason had mentioned that he had never experienced any Super Bowl hysteria. Yolanda checked around. Danny and his family were going to his in-laws. Her daughters groaned at the thought of game mania, both saying they only had enough patience to endure the Super Bowl not all this play-off hype. But she learned that Lynn was having a party.

And that's how Yolanda and Mason ended up in the lunacy that was American football at its most challenging. Just walking into the house made Mason think he was walking through a carnival – the noise, the food aromas, the crowds. If this is play-off activity, he wondered, what is the main event like?

As Mason entered the living room to find a place in front of Dusty's giant screen, he was handed a slip of paper and asked for two dollars. "What?"

"It's the pool," explained Will. "Pick the two winners today and the final Super Bowl winner. Two bucks."

"What?"

"Where are you from?" Carl, Dusty's brother, challenged the stranger. "Give him your money."

"Hold on," cautioned Dusty, "he's new in town." Then he yelled, "Yolanda, your boyfriend needs some help."

"He's not my boyfriend," she shouted back.

"He still needs help."

She found Mason standing in the middle of the living room holding his betting sheet. "Did you give Will your money?" He looked at her sort of dazed. This was an American house party – foreign soil to him. "It's a football pool. We're all betting on the winners. Whoever guesses right wins the pot. You know how to bet don't you? You do gamble? It's not some religious thing?"

Mason finally understood. "Yes, I bet. I gamble." He wiggled his eyebrows at her. "It's one of my more mild vices."

She ignored his response and pushed him into a chair so he could fill out his sheet.

~ ~ ~

"I really enjoyed your friends," Mason said as he made his way to Yolanda's front door. He held on to her tightly because he was a little drunk. "That guy Carl says he can do the repairs on the house for me. And those other people were great, real friendly. They didn't care that I was from out of town."

"Why should they?" Yolanda was holding him up. "I think you should spend the night."

Mason grinned at her. "I was wondering if I would ever wear you down."

"You're too drunk to drive up that mountain to your place." She pushed him into the house and locked the door. Before she could turn out the lights, he had disappeared into the guest room. She ran to check on him. He was sprawled across the bed, still dressed. She slipped off his shoes and threw a comforter over him. It had been fun. And now Mason had another American adventure to check off his list. She wondered of he would be around for Super Bowl Sunday.

CHAPTER FOURTEEN

"**W**e haven't seen Homey for a few days," reported Antwan. A smile lighted his black face as he enjoyed the nickname he had given that white bastard. "I checked his girl and—"

"Look at this," announced Gilly, who had just returned from getting a haircut. He slapped a newspaper on the boss's desk. "They say Homey's dead. Found him behind some diner at a crossroads in the next county."

"I thought he went to see those church people?" asked Antwan.

"He did. They musta killed him." The three men looked at one another. "Close them down," ordered the boss. Antwan and Gilly knew he meant the Mastersons. And in the next breath he said, "Cops. Get out the back and disappear." Gilly and Antwan followed orders.

The boss, whose mother knew him as Angelo, watched two cops talk with the guys out in the yard. He took his disposable cell and hid it in the secret wall compartment and placed his legitimate iPhone on his desk.

"Boss?" called one of the yard guys, "some cops want to talk to you." The man's eyes were wide and curious. But he knew not to ask or answer any questions.

"Send them in."

Mars and Dundee walked into Angelo's office. He almost laughed at the picture they made – one hot, handsome fellow and a dwarf. It was almost like some digital team in a video game. "Gentlemen, may I help you?" He placed the news article regarding Homer's death for them to see. "Yes, he worked for me."

Mars introduced them making certain that the man understood that he was from another jurisdiction and that Dundee had accompanied him in some sort of turf support. "Lt. Dundee and I are aware that Mr. Gibson was your employee and that he has no record of activity that has drawn police attention while he has worked for you."

"Yeah, he's worked for me since I opened this business about three years ago," offered the boss.

"As the newspaper reports, he was murdered." Mars wanted that clear. "That's why we're investigating his background and his contacts."

"He worked for me," the boss repeated, "But we didn't hang out. I mean I got a wife and kids. Homer was a single guy." Angelo wondered what more he could say to be cooperative but obstructive. "He had been gone for the holidays. He was supposed to be back today."

"Did he have friends among his coworkers?"

Angelo threw his arm toward the window looking out into the recycling yard. "Homer was a handsome guy, like you, officer. He didn't hang out with that crew." Mars and Dundee looked at the three disheveled men hauling tires to a trailer.

"What kind of work did he do?"

"Buying old tires. Nothing that got him dirty."

"Do you have other employees?"

"No, sir," smiled the boss. "I'm a real small business. I'm all of the front office and Homer and those guys are, or were, all of the work force."

Dundee asked, "Can I have you cell number in case we have more questions? Then my colleague here won't have to drive all the way over from River Bend."

The boss smiled to himself. He knew they would check his cell calls. And he knew they would find calls related to tires and calls to his wife. "Sure," and he rattled off a number. "Is there any thing else I can do?"

"Do you know if he had family?"

"No, sir."

The investigators left the office and Angelo watched them chat with the yard workers. He could tell by the body language that his men were acting dumb and dumber and the two officers were frustrated, but polite. Once they left the yard he retrieved his disposable phone and called Gilly. "Stay away. Close that game down, then move into my cabin up in Bristol. When you finish that job, I'll find you something someplace else."

"How about someplace warm?"

~ ~ ~

Yolanda found herself at Mason's doorstep again. He had crawled out of her guest room early this morning with a headache and had told her he wanted to be left alone in his pain and returned to his father's house. A few hours later he called. She had been unable to ignore his plea for help. He had given her access to all of his father's records and she had found the answers she sought regarding Foster's charitable giving. She had learned a lot about the man, and regretted that she had not gotten to know him better, or as she told Mason, "Given him at least a thousand kisses."

Mason had laughed and said, "You can give those kisses to me."

Yolanda had blushed and changed the subject, but she was back at his door again today. Was she thinking about kissing Mason? He was charming, fun to be around and very interesting. But was she interested in being one of his lady friends, nothing long-term and nothing emotionally deep? She didn't think so. Then why was she here? It was because of Foster, his father, the man who deserved her devotion. That was it! She was helping Mason because she owed his father. She knocked at the door.

"Great, you're here," said Mason as he threw open the door.

"I thought you were hung over."

"I am," groaned Mason, "but Sweetheart wants me to wrap things up. We've got projects to manage."

Yolanda looked into Mason's bloodshot eyes. "He must have really inspired you to get moving."

"Yes." He pulled her into the house and closed the door. "I researched all the local thrift shops using your list of Pop's donations. Come, look at my list." He led her into the kitchen where he had boxes scattered long the countertop. He offered her his thrift shop plan.

Yolanda studied it. Mason had managed to divide his father's household possessions among several thrift shops in what seemed to be a very thoughtful manner. "You'll make a lot of friends – everyone gets something."

"But I still have some questions." He poured himself some coffee and offered her a cup. They settled themselves at the kitchen table in what had become their routine. "The quilting stuff and that expensive sewing machine. That's really specialized. Do you want it?"

"Not me," she demurred. "I don't have time for quilting. But some of the thrift shops have online sites where they offer specialty items, sort of like an in-house auction. We can check to see if any of the ones you chose do that and suggest they handle the quilting equipment that way."

Mason nodded. "Good idea. I also don't know what to do with some of the furniture.

Yolanda grinned, "This is your lucky day. I have all kinds of ideas." Mason moved closer, she hurriedly said, "I meant about furniture." She was clearly flustered by his apparent interest. Yolanda promised herself that she would take some time to reconsider what Mason seemed to be offering – was she interested, was she too old, was she afraid? This was all too complicated, especially when Mason was so close. She cleared her throat, "I can see I have to be very precise when speaking to you." She tried to give him her most intimidating mom look, but he was unfazed.

"So precisely what is the topic, furniture or something more personal?" He grinned at her.

She blushed. "Furniture." He was preparing to leave sooner than he had intended. She could hold him off for another day or two.

"For now," he replied.

Yolanda's stomach sunk. Mason sounded as though he would be moving up his timetable for her seduction, too. Yikes!

~ ~ ~

Dusty was finally back at his office after wrestling with the county manager at a budget hearing. It was January and the elected officials were starting to plan a budget for the coming year – that annual dance of providing services without raising taxes. He never understood how the sheriff was expected to provide all that was mandated and all that was wanted with no funding. And each year the mandates and the wants grew.

This drew Dusty into a reverie regarding a personal challenge. Every four years, when the sheriff's post was up for election, Dusty was always approached to run for that office. When Bergy retired, Dusty seemed to be on everyone's radar. He had declined and they got Richard, the dunce. Last year Richard had been re-elected, so Dusty had a few more years to decide.

The budget hearing today almost pushed him over the edge. He was ready to be on any ballot that would get rid of that idiot. The man didn't understand his budget, didn't have a plan for staff growth and development, didn't have a professional leadership team in place. What he did have was a network of political friends and relatives who valued their jobs. They worked very hard to support Richard and keep him out of trouble and keep the rest of the community from finding out how dumb he was. Richard certainly looked the part – he was handsome, charming, entertaining. And once in his law enforcement career he had demonstrated courage in the line of fire.

Dusty swore to himself as he thought about that day. Courage my ass, he thought. Richard had stumbled into a robbery at a Quik Mart. He pulled in for a bathroom stop – all day in his patrol car drinking coffee demanded relief. He pushed through the door, ran to the restroom, finished, and returning to the grocery aisles, stopped for a candy bar. He dropped his candy choice and stooped to pick it up as a robber, whom Dusty determined was even dumber than Richard, burst into the mart and loudly threatened the cashier.

Richard rose from the aisle floor and demanded that the perp freeze. The man chose to run, the cashier dove over the counter and flattened him. She was a big cashier. Richard was standing there ready to shoot the perp with his candy bar grasped in his two fisted ready-to-fire grip.

Dusty knew all this because the store's security video caught it all on tape. But no one ever saw the tape after the press created Richard the Hero. Bergy kept a copy, always reminding Dusty that when that day came, Richard could be persuaded to retire.

After spending the whole day dancing for funding from the county commissioners, providing all the answers that no one on the Sheriff's staff could field, he was giving a political career serious thought. He was the chief of the joint investigation unit and he was the one who was justifying the entire Sheriff's budget. Maybe he should run for the job.

But he was interrupted when Mars broke into his thoughts saying, "What a useless trip!"

"What?" Dusty had been mentally far away. He felt like he was being pulled to the surface like a big fish.

"That guy in Asheville," explained Mars. "Me and Dundee went to talk to him about that dead guy. He admitted the dead guy worked for him. He couldn't explain what the guy did. The guys working on the lot didn't know anything. Dundee says it's a legitimate business, but he suspects it's a front."

Danny walked in behind Mars. "Tee go home? Every place I went today people asked about her."

Dusty tried to focus. "She left about an hour ago. She gets pretty tired." He turned to Mars. "Your visit to Asheville got us nothing?"

Mars shrugged. "There was nothing there. The boss man said the dead guy was on Christmas vacation and he had no idea what he was doing in Verona."

Dusty looked at his watch. "Let's go get a beer." He picked up his phone and sent a quick text to Lynn that he would be late for dinner.

"Tough day?" asked Danny.

"You have no idea," groaned the chief budget dancer.

CHAPTER FIFTEEN

Lynn dashed home for lunch, lost in thought about Yolanda and her money. It had been five days since she sent out the grant request. Nineteen requests had already arrived back at the office. She worried her friend would be overwhelmed at the number of grant responses and the detail of some of the requests. All the nonprofits in town took grant writing very seriously. Her inbox was e-bulging.

Her mind drifted from grant writing to dinner. As in what would she prepare. She had seen ads for a refrigerator with a camera. If she had a refrigerator like that she could have just phoned it and scanned the shelves. But she had to go home and scan with her own eyes. Years from now, she thought, that concept would go the way of the landline. Who was she kidding, she still had a landline! So here she was racing home, probably to peanut butter and jelly for lunch, in a rush to scan the contents of the refrigerator and jot down a shopping list. Yolanda and her money were a distant, almost forgotten, memory.

"What now?" she mumbled to herself as she arrived at the house. Will's car and a tired pick-up were parked down near the old barn. She could tell that the door was open. She climbed out of her car and tramped through the old snow to investigate. "Will?"

Two men came out of the barn in response to her call. "Hershel," she greeted Dusty's oldest brother, "why are you here with Will?" Lynn was suspicious by nature where Will was concerned. He always seemed to have an idea that would eventually involve the whole family and any number of unsuspecting strangers. The vast HO train layout in her attic came immediately to mind.

"We were looking for storage space," said Will.

"And?" She needed more of an explanation than that.

"I just bought five acres behind my house," he pointed to the home across the street that he and Piper had purchased a few months ago. "It slopes down to the river and gets good southern light."

"And?" Pulling teeth came to Lynn's mind.

"Hershel said I needed storage for equipment and supplies."

"And?" This time she gave her brother-in-law a squinty-eyed look.

He blushed. "Now, Lynn, honey," Hershel began to babble. He liked Lynn and because he was about fifteen years older sometimes talked to her as though she were his favorite niece. "I didn't tell him to use your barn. He could get one of those prefab things. They just drop them in place and you're ready."

"Storage for what?"

"My vineyard," boasted Will.

"What?" screeched Lynn, and the dog came running from the trees, probably thinking she was in danger.

"It's a real nice piece of property," Hershel tried to smooth things. "He should get a good crop in five years and be bottling his own label in six."

"You're going to sell wine?"

"No, just bottle it for the family," said Will, throwing an arm around her. "Just think, for every family gathering we'll have our own wine as part of the celebration. Christmas, Thanksgiving, birthdays, anniversaries. It's endless."

"I think you'll need more land for that many occasions," ventured Hershel. "You'll get enough for that big party of yours every year." Will and Piper had an end of summer/wedding anniversary party every year. The invitation list included everyone they knew. That would be a lot of wine!

"So why are you in my barn?" Lynn challenged them.

"I need storage for equipment and supplies," explained Will, again.

Lynn stepped into the barn. Her gardening supplies and yard tools and mower took up one side of the aging structure. Jason's motorcycle, bike and sports equipment took up the other side. "Where?" she asked.

"We could move Jason's things, maybe up to the loft. He's young, he can still climb." Will rearranged the tarp over the motorcycle. "I won't take up much space."

"Why can't you get one of those prefab thingies?"

Will hung his head. "Piper said no."

"Now, Lynn, honey," Hershel the peacemaker said, "Will's gear won't take up much space. Maybe in a few years when he's got his barrels in here and a wine press, we may have to work something out."

"Barrels? Wine press?"

"Maybe Piper will change her mind by then," offered Will hopefully, "when she sees I'm serious."

Lynn's cell rang. It was Nelda telling her that her one-thirty appointment was at the office. She ended the call, scowled at Will and said, "I can't grocery shop now. You're buying dinner tonight." She left them at the barn and raced back to her office.

"Do you think that was a yes?" asked Will.

"You are really dumb," laughed Hershel.

~ ~ ~

Umberto suspected that some kids were up to no good behind the bakery. He kept finding cigarette butts and sometimes a beer can. These had to be young kids because everyone knew that his nephew, Danny, the detective, lived in the apartment over the bakery with his wife and baby. Today he thought he was would do a little policing himself and put a stop to any teen antics. He closed a few minutes early and waited in the dark, just inside the bakery's backdoor, so he could hear when they gathered.

He heard the voices and someone kick a trashcan. There were giggles and guffaws. More talking. He heard a few colorful cuss words. It was time to spring. He threw open the back door and found several youngsters too surprised to move. Four boys and two girls gasped and stared.

Umberto reached out and took hold of Polly Carmichael and said to the others, "Get outta here or I'll tell my nephew he has to start coming home earlier." He pointed to the back stairs and the lighted windows over head.

"He lives there?" came an incredulous question.

"The cop?" Another genius, thought Umberto.

"Yeah, the cop. You wanna stay and meet him?" They all took off except Polly who was held in place by the short, but obviously, very strong baker. "You come inside with me."

She pouted and scowled as he pushed her into the bakery kitchen. "What you doing with those creeps?" He flipped on the lights.

She hung her head.

"Not talking?" Umberto ushered her further into the shop and stopped by his office. "Put your things in there." He pointed to a chair. "We're tipping this in the bucket."

Polly looked at him, puzzled. "You mean nipping this in the bud?"

"Whatever." Once she had taken off her coat, Umberto pulled her into the front of the bakery and flipped on more lights. "You got a job every day after school." He handed her an apron and a cloth. "Wipe those tables, sweep the floor, then we'll see what else has to be done."

"What if I—"

"Then we go upstairs and talk to my nephew." He stared her down and she slipped on the apron.

Polly had just enough time to wipe all the tables and sweep the floor. "Time to go home," announced Umberto as he dried his hands. He had been cleaning the bakery kitchen while she worked on the front of the store. "You get here earlier tomorrow and you'll have plenty to do."

~ ~ ~

Teniquia sat on her comfy recliner while her mother and a cousin got dinner ready for her children. Three of them, three healthy (thanks to Dr. Rita) and smiling (thanks to her family and husband) children beginning to understand and enjoy life. She had spent a busy morning in the office. This afternoon she and her husband had found THE house, the one that would suit their new family. It was within five blocks of Rathborne Elementary School, Piper's school, as Tee liked to call it. It was in a solid neighborhood, not all black and not all white and not all Latino – but all families, young and aging. She was certain the house smiled when she looked at it. She could see her young children growing and enjoying the big yard and riding bicycles and walking to school.

Teniquia and Lonzo were members of the successful black community in River Bend. She was a detective with Dusty Reid's unit and was currently recovering from a gunshot wound received during a drug raid – almost two months now and she had returned to work a few days ago. Lonzo was a supervisor with the James County EMS. He was advancing in his career and was respected for the skill he brought to each rescue.

Lonzo had agreed. It was the house he had envisioned. He could see all the things that she saw, but more specifically he could see his son wearing a football uniform and his daughters dressed for Sunday choir. He sometimes even saw a dog and some kittens. That's when he pulled himself together and reminded himself and his wife that they had to get the loan first. Which was what was on his mind. "Baby, that realtor said we made a fair offer. She said we're in a good position. We have two incomes and a good credit rating."

"What happens now?" Tee asked stretching in the recliner. She still got tired after being on her feet for a few hours.

Lonzo paced the living room of the small house they shared with Teniquia's mother. Once they had adopted the children, they had let their lease go on the bungalow they had been renting on the outskirts of town. Moving in with Glory for the short term made sense. They needed help with the children until Tee was back on her feet. "The house is even close enough to Glory so that she doesn't have to think about moving in with us."

Teniquia smiled at her husband. He was looking forward to her healing and their privacy. "Mama is looking forward to her privacy, too." Lonzo grinned. She knew him so well.

"The realtor says she'll take the offer to the sellers and if they accept, she'll get our information ready for the bank."

"It's that easy to get a mortgage?" she asked.

He shrugged. "I don't know. She said it was reasonable to start with the River Bend First Bank and if that didn't work to go to the other banks in town and then look on the Internet." He stared at her, puzzled. "I don't understand any of this. She seemed to think it was normal. We'll just learn as we go."

There was a giggle from the kitchen. "This is the right thing to do," she told him. "I'm glad you found these kids and made us a family."

He kissed her and then ambled into the kitchen to share some laughter with his children.

~ ~ ~

Mars got a call from Janet to pick up Polly at the bakery. When he arrived he used the backdoor because the bakery was closed for the night. When Umberto let him in, he gave the detective a hurried synopsis of Polly and her friends in the alley. Mars understood. He walked into the store's front and greeted the youngster. "Hey, Polly, Janet told me to pick up you and some dessert. And I can stay for dinner."

Polly looked at him, but hid any thoughts. Mars sighed to himself. He had seen this attitude among the kids that paraded through the courthouse. He remembered telling Polly during Thanksgiving that her mother's friends would take care of her. He saw all the signs. It was time for her mother's friend, the detective, to step in.

Umberto handed Mars a box tied with string and Polly hung up her apron.

"Remember," said Umberto, "You be here right after school. This place gets messy and I need help."

"Great idea," said Mars, speaking to Polly, "You want a little extra money and you found a job."

Polly looked at Umberto. "It found me." She said it in a low, controlled voice.

Mars patted her shoulder. "Umberto knows talent. Let's go home. Janet is probably starving." No one spoke as they drove through town to the Bergman place. When they got out of the car, Mars asked, "Do you have a lot of homework?"

"No."

"Are you playing any sports this semester?" Polly was one of the talented girl athletes at the high school.

"No."

"In any after school activities, besides your job?"

"No."

They climbed the wide stone steps to the front porch. But before Mars knocked, he placed his hands on Polly's shoulders and turned her to face him. "You better find some new friends at school. This isn't a warning. This is an order." Umberto had been specific when he told Mars about the kids in the alley.

Polly stared at the ground.

"I told you before, we look out for our kids. And you are not going to turn into some kid your mother wouldn't recognize." He put a finger under her chin and lifted her face so that he looked into her eyes. "Find new friends. Hang out with your old friends. But those other kids are history. You may think Thel and Janet can't keep up, but the rest of us can. Susan's friends are on the job."

"She left me." Polly stared back at him as tears streamed down her cheeks.

He pulled her in for a fierce hug. "She didn't do it on purpose. And we're all going to succeed at this and make her proud."

"He's dead." She was sobbing now.

"I know she's dead, sweetheart." Mars held her.

"No, he's dead, the man in the parking lot."

"What are you talking about?" Mars could feel her quivering tension.

Polly explained about being with the kids from the lunch table. "We usually all walk into town after school. Last Tuesday the older kid, Elwrath said he had to do something for his job. And he met with that guy. I didn't meet him, I just stood by that machine that gives you the parking tickets. I didn't hear what they said, but I saw him."

"Saw who?" The detective had a feeling that something had shifted.

"The dead man." Polly was starting to feel as though she attracted the dead. "The one you found behind the dumpster."

Mars became still. He processed what she was saying through her tears – which now seemed close to hysteria. "I'll give Janet this food and then we're going some place quiet." Polly nodded.

The porch light came on and Mars said quickly as Janet opened the door, "Here's dessert. Polly and I gotta run. Eat without us. We won't be late." He almost dragged the youngster back to his car.

~ ~ ~

"Wine?" Dusty was standing at the kitchen counter in The Heights, waiting for Lynn to serve dinner. He already had the plates and things out. She was puttering around the kitchen getting the rest of the meal together. "He's growing grapes?"

"Yes, grapes, and wine," she repeated, "Didn't you know?"

"Bootleggers don't usually invite the law in for consultation."

"Making your own wine isn't illegal," Lynn reminded him. "I was surprised that your brother is involved and that they plan to use our barn. I thought you must know if they're using our barn." She pulled another plastic container from the refrigerator.

Leftovers, Dusty thought to himself as he stared into the small pot on the stove. For days they had been eating holiday leftovers. Lynn must have frozen bits of every meal served since Christmas. Finally, tonight a beef stew that smelled great but looked like it was the end of the ends. There was pounding on the kitchen door and Mars barged in towing Polly Carmichael. Dusty just knew dinner would be delayed. He picked up the dinner plates and the placed them on the counter. "Yeah?" he asked as he sat down.

Lynn was quick to catch on and quietly put all the other food away. She sat down, too, certain that things were going to get interesting.

Mars placed Polly at the table and sat beside her. "Polly knows that dead man."

Well, thought Dusty, that got my attention. "What dead man?"

"The dumpster guy." Mars sniffed and looked around for some food. Lynn got up and started ad libbing a meal as she turned the heat up under the stew.

Dusty sat back, looked at Polly and said, "Maybe you should help Mars out here. He's not making any sense."

Polly nodded and began her explanation of the kids, the alley and being frightened. She hadn't told Mars that part. But she was relieved to finally have the opportunity to spill her guts. "We should bring in those kids," said Mars.

"No," Polly almost shouted, "They'll blame me."

"Where did you see this man?" asked Dusty.

"Behind the bakery in that parking lot. The man and Elwrath talked over by the bank drive-thru."

"Cameras," Dusty and Mars said together. Then Mars explained, "There are security cameras over that section of the lot because of the bank. We can look at the tapes and identify anyone in the parking lot. That'll give us a reason to call all you kids in for an interview. Depending on the time of day, we can say someone recognized him from the newspaper story and told us they had seen him in the parking lot."

Polly thought about that. "Okay, but you have to call me in, too."

"Do you want to be handcuffed?" asked Mars with a grin.

The youngster looked at him and for the first time in several weeks, gave everyone a soft smile, just as the kitchen door burst open.

Piper announced, "I don't know why, but Will said he had to provide dinner tonight. Hi, Mars, Polly." The tiny principal carried two bags from the Chinese carry-out and plunked them on the table. Mars began unpacking dinner.

Will followed with two more bags and Jeff came in last with a delighted grin. "They let me drive from Mr. Lee's place." Then he gasped because Mars, the ultimate in River Bend law enforcement, was opening a container of moo shu pork at the table.

"Don't worry, pal," drawled the detective, "I can be bribed with egg rolls."

Lynn nodded to Polly who jumped up to help put out dishes, a task she had been assigned while living in The Heights last month. Jeff joined them to help with drinks and gave a shy grin to Polly.

"So, why is Will buying dinner?" asked Piper.

"Wine," said Dusty and the discussion took off.

As Polly had learned, never be surprised at the number of people who streamed through Lynn's kitchen or what was said – going from murder to wine just about covered everything.

CHAPTER SIXTEEN

The doorbell rang for the third time today. This time the florist had two more plants in his arms. "More?" gasped Yolanda as she let him in.

"I got three more in the van," he replied. "No one died in your family? Or did I miss something?" Small towns! But he was correct, no deaths in the Valeri family recently.

Somewhere between the last three bouquets and plants he brought, Yolanda had cleared a space on the kitchen counter. The kitchen table had two edible arrangements and five boxes of candy. Once she let the florist out of the house she called Lynn, "Tell them to stop," she raged into her phone. "I will not give money to anyone who wastes money by sending me gifts."

Lynn laughed. But Yolanda heard typing. "I just sent a mass e-mail out to all local nonprofits. If anything more arrives it was already ordered and couldn't be stopped." Lynn laughed some more. "Anything good?"

"Flowers and candy, like I'm being courted."

"You are. Why don't I come over and help you eat your candy and we'll develop some guidelines to review the proposals."

"More guidelines?" Yolanda rubbed her forehead. "Come on. I might as well get started. So it will be over."

She cleaned off space at the kitchen table, began to dismantle the edible arrangements thinking David would love all that fruit, leaving a few strawberries for Lynn to eat, because she knew, as well as everyone in town knew, that Lynn preferred chocolate but would fake interest in a little fresh fruit.

There was the doorbell again, more flowers? She

shuddered at the thought. Flinging open the door she said, "No more, send them back." Mason stood there with a quizzical look. "What are you doing here?"

He laughed that joyous sound of his. "Sweetheart's trying to get me out of town, but there's a revolution."

"In Saudi Arabia?"

"No, I was flying into Saudi and driving into Yemen with some body guards."

Yolanda shivered. "Why are you going someplace where you need bodyguards?"

"I always have body guards, or more specifically security staff." Mason gave her a kiss on the cheek and walked into the house. "There is a lot of fighting on the ground and Sweetheart closed up our operation and went back to South Africa." He threw an arm around her waist and pulled her close to nuzzle her ear. Mason was proud of himself. He was working his way into Yolanda's heart. Soon she'd see that they should have some more adult exchanges. He'd always been able to convince women that they needed more intimate knowledge of his character and skills. What was taking her so long? Was it because he was older? After all he wasn't that brash, young engineer who skittered around Asia, Africa and the Middle East anymore. Brash had faded, sort of. But he was certain he still had style and charisma, didn't he? So what was her problem?

"I'll be in town for a few more weeks." He pulled her closer.

"Weeks?"

"I thought I might help with your grant project." Another peck on the cheek.

"Help?"

He walked with her into the kitchen and was overwhelmed by the fragrance – and dazzled by the display of flowers. "What's all this?" He hoped it wasn't all the secret admirers in her life.

"Bribes," came her voice from behind a bouquet of birds of paradise, using the plants as her defense perimeter.

"To get you to do what?" Now he was really curious, because he hadn't thought of flowers. Darn!

Her head popped from behind the flowers and she held something that looked really strange. "They want me to give them money."

"Who? And what is that?" He nodded toward the strange sculpture in her arms.

"It's an edible arrangement. See? Fresh fruit and it came with a cream cheese-strawberry dip." She pulled a spoke off the globe. "Taste. It's honeydew on a stick."

He took the offering and enjoyed some fresh honeydew. "Interesting. What else have you gotten?"

She threw her arm out encompassing all the flat surfaces in the kitchen. "Fresh fruit, cakes, flowers, plants, and lots of chocolate." The doorbell rang.

"I'll get it," Mason offered as he walked off with his honeydew on a stick. "It's not another bribe," he shouted back to the kitchen, "it's Lynn." He stepped aside to invite her in.

"Edible arrangements?" she asked.

He nodded as he walked back to the kitchen to grab another refreshing stick of honeydew.

Lynn greeted Yolanda by handing her a gift-wrapped box. "This was on the mat in front of the door. Where's the chocolate?" She began rifling through the boxes on the table. "Any from the locals?" The region was blessed with three chocolatiers, charming little shops filled with, in Lynn's opinion, heart melting, heart stopping chocolate temptations.

"All of them," replied Yolanda, as she began to unwrap the package Lynn had delivered. "This looks like more candy, but not handmade." Lynn scowled in disappointment, but took heart at the options already available to her. She and Mason were searching through the candies when Yolanda screamed.

"They're dead!" She waved the opened box in front of their faces. "Five dead mice!"

"Who sent that?" demanded Mason.

Lynn picked up the card that had fallen from the box. Opening it she read, "The Church of the Guiding Hands gets half that money or something happens to your family."

"Who delivered that, the bakery, the florist?" Mason asked Lynn.

"No one. It was there when I arrived at the door." Lynn frowned at the dead mice as she smudged the card with chocolaty fingerprints.

"Who would send you something like this?" he challenged thin air.

Yolanda took the card from Lynn as she read the letterhead. "It came from the Church of the Guiding Hands – A real Christian congregation." She dropped the letter.

Mason placed the box of mice bodies on the floor and pulled her into his arms. "We can call your son," he suggested.

"I don't want my son investigating anything with people who want to hurt my family." She looked at Mason to make certain he understood her reasoning, since it wasn't really clear to her.

"Then I'm moving in." Mason understood safety and security.

"You can't, my son–"

"We tell him or I move in." He also knew how to negotiate.

"Move in." She rested her head on his shoulder.

Lynn watched this little bit of drama, and said, "I can do a little investigating. As long as you're safe,

Yolanda, we don't have to tell Dusty or Danny." She was certain there was a reasonable explanation for this note. She just couldn't think of it right now.

"Investigating?" asked Mason.

Yolanda seemed to sigh with relief. "Lynn always helps Dusty investigate things." Lynn blushed at the praise. "She's found bodies and been attacked and shot at. She knows what to do."

Mason looked at the woman he had assumed was a charming, but somewhat delicate and refined person who, well, he didn't know what else he thought, but a murder investigator and seemingly a police combat veteran was not on his list of assumptions. "Shot at?"

Lynn demurred, confirming his opinion of delicate and refined. "They were just trying to scare me."

"What about the guy you attacked at the hospital who was kidnapping those kids?" Yolanda reminded her.

Lynn winced. "I had help. Ricky," she turned to Mason, "he's fifteen. Anyway Ricky helped me hold the kidnapper until the police arrived. But let's not talk about me. We have to worry about Yolanda." She stared at Mason.

He studied Lynn for a few minutes, then nodded. "Can you stay here so I can run home and get a few things to spend the night," he wiggled his eyebrows, "or nights?"

"Of course," agreed Lynn. "Yolanda and I wanted to talk about criteria to review the proposals."

Mason grabbed another honeydew on a stick and dashed for his car. Lynn could barely wait until they heard his car drive away. "Spending the night? What's going on?"

"If you want to eat chocolate," threatened Yolanda, "you will forget you heard any of this. No mice, no overnight Mason." Then she popped a handmade chocolate truffle into her mouth.

Lynn stared at her as she enjoyed the treat, licking her lips after she swallowed the delicious confection. "OK," agreed Lynn. "But you better share details."

"Nothing's going to happen," prophesied Yolanda, "he has girlfriends all over the world. I don't want to be his River Bend bedmate."

"Really?" Lynn's eyes grew big. "All over the world? He told you?"

Yolanda flopped down in a kitchen chair. "Yes, we've had some interesting conversations. He gets around. And I don't want to think about it any more or I'll not let him stay."

"He has to stay or we tell Danny." Lynn was firm. "I'll do a little investigating but by the end of the week, we'll have to tell Dusty and the team."

"I suppose you're right. We can't let someone else be threatened by this group." With that the two women focused on giving Yolanda some guidelines to use when she reviewed the grant requests.

~ ~ ~

Antwan and Gilly watched the Church of the Guiding Hands for two nights. They saw the gamblers come in and out the alley door. They watched Char and Lester lock up and walk into the warehouse where they kept their truck. They never saw Darwin because he lived in the upstairs apartment. By Wednesday evening they figured they had enough information.

From Char's point of view it was a slow week. She was disappointed when Wednesday's game came to a close. No big winners, so they didn't hassle anyone. No big money changed hands. Maybe they should use those crazy dice. It would make things interesting. She and Lester closed up for the evening. Darwin was away on a mission. Granny Masterson had called him because she was having problems with her Netflix account. He was probably out at her place eating and watching Star Wars movies.

"Let's go to Gran's after we close up. Darwin can't have all her food," whined Char.

Lester grinned. "Yeah, she probably bought him pizza." They finished locking up and dashed across the alley to the warehouse and Char's truck.

Walking into the warehouse from the alley, Char said, "Those bums left the street door open." The regulars were supposed to close the door as they left the warehouse, keeping the parking garage a secret from the night patrol.

"It was probably one of the new–" Two guns with silencers fired, ending the conversation.

Antwan and Gilly put away their weapons. They closed and locked the alley door, walked out the big garage door to the street, closed it and walked over to the next street where they climbed into their truck and drove to the boss's cabin in Bristol.

~ ~ ~

It was after dinner and Mason was settled in comfortably at Yolanda's. He was helping her read the grant proposals that had already been submitted. She had set a deadline for Friday to receive proposals because Lynn had told her, "Everyone knows and is already getting their requests together." And it seemed very few agencies needed the entire seven days to send in their requests.

Mason had been surprised at the response, and Yolanda had explained all that she had already learned about nonprofits and grants from Lynn. "Nonprofits can field a creditable grant request in a day." Mason raised his eyebrows. "Lynn says they always have something ready or can easily rewrite something to fit a request." She straightened the stack of papers and handed Mason the one on top. They began to read silently, prepared to make notes and comments for future discussion.

Prepared to give this effort her best shot, Yolanda was stopped by the Hospice proposal – her first review! They wanted to begin a program for children who had lost loved ones. They weren't asking for much, and they had a plan for continued funding. The proposal just stated that this request was for the desk and computer and a few other things the staff person would need. Yolanda thought about Polly. She put the hospice proposal on a corner of the dining room table, the spot she now considered as the holding area for possible grantees. She was elated, her first review, and she found something that she personally knew was needed, needed by someone she personally cared about. Success!

And then Mason rained all over her victory. "This isn't right," he said as he flipped back to the beginning of the proposal he was reading and began to reread it.

She looked at him over her glasses. That's how relaxed she was around him. She wore her glasses and was wearing sweats this evening. "What's not right?" Mason was looking over one of the one million applications she had received requesting her money. Well, maybe not one million and maybe not her money, but she was stressed.

He waved the pages at her. "This construction proposal." He read the front page. "The Church of the Guiding Hands. It says here it's an interdenominational religious retreat and prayer center."

"They sent the mice. We're not considering them." Yolanda had her own criteria.

"It's a good thing." Mason continued to scan the proposal, "They want money to build a prayer center and it sounds like a spa – not a religious retreat. Listen to this, saunas, locker rooms, meditation rooms with hot salt steam and flowing mud."

"I said we're not giving them any money."

"Will the other grant proposals be as frivolous as this one?" Mason didn't want to waste his time.

"No, Lynn says we'll get good proposals. I set out some criteria requiring certain levels of organization like incorporation papers and by-laws."

"Hmm." Mason was intrigued. "I don't deal much with nonprofits. How does Lynn know so much?"

"She's the executive director of the Philanthropies, our community funding group, like a community foundation. She has a nose for bad nonprofits."

"Bad nonprofits?"

She laughed. "Dusty says he can't believe how much trouble some nonprofits can cause." With that explanation she ran through a brief history of local nonprofits and some of the mischief they had caused.

"Embezzlement? Selling children? Getting murdered? Fake loans?" His face paled and he looked as though he didn't believe a word she said.

Yolanda stared back, deep in thought. "Yes, murderers, embezzlers, kidnappings. It keeps the detectives busy. And Lynn, she always seems to get involved."

"She does?" Mason still found that hard to believe. For the next hour they ignored the grant applications as Yolanda gave a very detailed accounting of Lynn's exploits into the steamier side of local nonprofits.

"Wow." It was a slow sound of surprise.

CHAPTER SEVENTEEN

Mason was making coffee wearing an old t-shirt and a pair of sweat pants and in his bare feet. He heard a noise at the kitchen door and realized too late that he was going to be caught in Yolanda's kitchen – in the very early morning.

David squealed as he and Danny came through the door. "How ya doing, pal?" Mason greeted the baby as he poured a cup of coffee and offered it to Danny.

It was all the detective could do to stay calm, place the baby in the highchair and accept the coffee. He stared at Mason.

"Having a little one makes your day start really early," observed Mason in a relaxed conversational tone. "You and your wife must have to be pretty organized to get him ready and yourselves to work on time."

"We manage." Icy stare.

"Do you have time for some eggs?" Mason asked. "I told Yolanda I would cook breakfast"

"Where is my mother?"

"In the shower."

At that moment Yolanda called from the back of the house, "Mason, Danny will be here soon. Maybe you should get out of–" she stopped at the kitchen door, "Good morning, grandma's little angel." David squealed his happy greeting. His grandmother ignored her son and poured a cup of coffee.

"I asked Danny if he had time for breakfast," said Mason.

Yolanda looked at her son as though she just noticed him. "Did you run this morning?" He nodded. "You must be hungry. How about some eggs?"

Danny scowled, but managed to be civil and polite. "I'm in a hurry this morning. We have a meeting on Nevada's murder."

"Poor Adele," sighed Yolanda, "That boy gave her one challenge too many. Her church is planning a double funeral tomorrow."

Mason took some eggs from the refrigerator and a pan from the cupboard. He ably began to prepare breakfast. No one spoke until Danny said, "Thanks, I gotta go."

Once they heard his car leave the yard, Yolanda burst out laughing. "Are you going to tell him about the mice?" asked Mason.

"I'll wait to see what Lynn finds out. She said she would do some investigating." The eggs began to sizzle.

~ ~ ~

"Let's get ourselves organized," announced Dusty, as he walked into the office, coffee in one hand and files in the other. "This is the autopsy report for the second guy. Call those techs and get their report on the site where his body was found. They say this Homer guy and Nevada were killed in the same location. They both have concrete dust and seeds on their clothes and hair."

Dusty looked up and noticed that his three detectives were huddled around Danny's desk. He was scowling while Mars and Tee were trying not to laugh. No one was listening to the chief.

"Is there a problem?" asked Dusty. Usually his early morning orders were met with quick, professional responses. Was he losing control of the unit?

Tee grinned. "We were catching up on River Bend gossip."

Dusty was clever enough to understand that there was something going on that wasn't gossip and wasn't detecting or crime solving. He waited.

"Some people were surprised this morning to learn

about certain private lives," remarked Mars. He leaned against Danny's desk. Dusty waited.

Finally Danny threw a pencil across the office. "She's my mother. Why does she have a guy spending the night? And my son is over there now in that den of … of …"

"Sin?" offered Mars, helpfully.

Dusty looked at Danny. "Whether your mother has a house guest or not doesn't solve our murders. Your son will keep things on the up and up. Let's get to work."

"But, Chief, she's alone—"

"No, your son is there and so is her house guest."

"That's my point. My son is nine months old. She's my mother and —"

"She's healthy and attractive and we should be minding our own business." Dusty understood trying to develop a romantic relationship with an attractive woman who had a son. He had pursued Lynn, but her son had been a challenge to any alone time. And dealing with her father had been worse. So Dusty was sympathetic to Yolanda's circumstances. A good-looking woman should be allowed a little latitude – as long as it wasn't his mother.

"Let's get to work." He outlined the work for the day. "I want us to finish looking at those security tapes and get Gabe in here to prepare to talk to those kids we find on the tapes. I want us to do those interviews tomorrow."

~ ~ ~

Lynn was still thinking about the awful box of dead mice that Yolanda had received. She was trying to remember if she had ever heard about this group claiming to be a church or some church-like charity. She walked into the coffee shop in the business park, lost in thought.

Someone called her name and she focused on a table with three men. All of them local clergy. Father Nick from St. Bridget's said, "Lynn, join us, we have a question."

She smiled at Father Nick, then grinned at the other two men, Rev. David Mosely from First Methodist and Rev. Tilson Butler from the Lutheran church. "Starting a new church?"

"Smart ass," replied Rev. Butler. They had gone to school together.

"Now, Tilly, I'll tell your mother you're swearing." She then turned to the other two men. "Once in second grade, because his mother was our second grade teacher," Lynn relished telling this story, "Tilly made an outrageous comment using several inappropriate words. His mother grabbed him out of his seat and put him over her knee." Lynn started laughing, but got control of herself because she could see that the other two men were entertained with her story and wanted to hear more. "She sat down on a chair, threw him over her knee and proceeded to thwack him on his back side with a ruler."

"And she wasn't even a nun," laughed Father Nick.

"Did his dad come to school and complain?" asked Rev. Mosely.

"No," replied Lynn, "but no one ever used a swear word again in that class." Everyone laughed.

Tilly wiped tears from his eyes. "The rest of the story. Mom told Dad and I got tenderized again at home." More laughter.

"Hey, over there," Kew Lee called to the church group. She was in the coffee shop this morning helping her brother. "You guys are laughing too loud to be praying." There was agreement with her statement from a number of coffee shop patrons.

"Clergy laugh," Father Nick announced and dared

anyone to challenge him.

The patrons all booed. Ah, small towns. No one got a free pass. Everyone was fair game for ridicule.

Lynn took a seat at the clergy table as Kew brought over a cup of coffee. "Sorry we laughed at your prayer meeting," she said with a grin and placed a small dish of macaroons on the table.

They each grabbed a cookie and sipped and chewed for a few minutes. "Is this a secret pastor meeting for your secret club?" asked Lynn after dunking her macaroon in her coffee.

"Why do you always call it a secret club?" asked Rev. Mosely. "You and everyone else in town know we pastors meet frequently."

"Yeah," seconded Tilly. "We need to join forces to keep evil at bay in River Bend."

Lynn finished her cookie, "So what evil has your attention this morning?"

"Officially," began Father Nick, "we're the membership committee for the secret pastors' club. We want all pastors working with us. Coordinating services to people in need is more efficient if we share information and resources."

Tilly nodded. "Everyone knows that the James County Hunger Alliance was the result of pastors in years past coming up with a solution for hunger in our county."

Rev. Mosely nodded. "But you know that, Lynn, because your mother was a big part."

Lynn didn't know. It was something she would talk to her father about, but she asked, "Does that mean you're working on another big solution for something?"

"Not today," sighed Tilly, "we have smaller fish to fry. Remember, we're the membership committee. We were just discussing that Reverend Goodson at the church —"

"He doesn't want to join you?" Lynn gasped.

"No," said Father Nick, "We want to invite him, but we don't know him. Do you?"

"Yes, I'd love to introduce you."

"That solves one problem," said Tilly. "Do you know anyone at that new church in Portage, Church of the Guiding Hands?"

Lynn looked at them aghast. "You want them to join?"

"Not when you use that tone of voice," said Tilly.

She took a deep breath. "I had never heard of them until yesterday." She related the story about the mice. "I'd be suspicious. They may not be a real church."

"That's an understatement," replied Rev. Mosely.

"Did I hear you mention that church in Portage?" asked Bev, owner of Bev's Spa's, as she passed the table on her way to order a latte. She had just taken her seat on the county commission as an appointee to replace Susan Carmichael who had been murdered a few months ago.

The three ministers jumped to their feet to greet and congratulate her on her new role in the community. For years Bev had been managing and growing her business in River Bend and surrounding communities. Public service as a political figure was a new role for her.

When they had drawn another chair to the table and were all seated, Lynn asked, "What do you know?"

Bev said, "This isn't government stuff, this is beauty salon gossip." They all nodded, knowing it was probably more accurate than government stuff. She drew closer and lowered her voice. "Bernice, she owns Bernice's Beauty Boutique in Portage," they all nodded, "she says that something funny is going on at that place. But she can't say anything because the Mastersons are running the place and they're her landlord. But, sometimes people sneak out of their part of the building and slip into her shop and out into the street. She complained and tried to lock the adjoining door but Chartreuse Masterson–"

"Chartreuse?" asked Father Nick.

Bev rolled her eyes. "You want this story or you want to ask what saint she's named after?" She shot the priest a threatening glare. He shut his mouth and Bev continued. "Chartreuse told Bernice that the door had to stay unlocked or else."

"Or else?"

Bev looked at Rev. Mosely and replied. "In Portage everyone knows that a Masterson 'or else' would not be pleasant."

Tilly added, "Those people are crazy. Didn't someone just murder someone?"

Lynn nodded. "A few years ago, one of the Mastersons was arrested and convicted of killing Lily Seymour. He's in prison now."

Bev reclaimed the stage with her narrative. "Bernice keeps her door unlocked and strange men still sneak through, but she's got an electrician coming in next week to rewire so she can move her hair dryers away from the door. She said she'd feel safer if she could sort of isolate the door. The men could use it but her clients wouldn't see them."

"Where is her shop in Portage?" asked Lynn.

"She's on Main Street in that group of buildings – a hardware store, her salon, the fake church and that Asian grocery. Across the street is a laundromat and that empty building that used to be a lawyer's office until he didn't keep that Masterson from going to prison and had to leave town." Her listeners gasped.

"It's a tough town." Bev looked around the table. "So why did you want to know?"

"We wondered," said Rev. Mosely whose wife got

her hair done at Bev's, "if they should be invited into our pastors' club."

"You mean the secret club you all have?" asked Bev.

"It's not secret!" chorused the ministers.

Lynn wrapped up the discussion. "The conclusion is that your not-so-secret club should blackball the fake church for membership."

Tilly finished the last of his coffee. "I guess this meeting of the membership committee is adjourned."

"That's right," said Rev. Mosely, "we must have souls to save someplace."

They all wished one another a Happy New Year and went on their divine ways. Bev and Lynn stayed behind to gossip a little more.

"How's government?" Lynn asked, bursting with curiosity.

"The other commissioners are tiptoeing around me. I don't know how Nathan and your father managed my appointment, but the commissioners seem to think I have a lot of power and influence."

"You do," said Lynn. "You got yourself appointed and the competition didn't."

"I think you and your brother had more to do with it than you have admitted," said Bev. "But the real challenge will be when I run for election. I've got a few months for the voters to get to know me and evaluate my work."

"You'll be fine," prophesied Lynn. "All your Bev's Spa clients have your back." With that they wished each other a Happy New Year, waved to Kew, and left the coffee shop.

~ ~ ~

"Everyone says talk to the Mastersons," said Tee. She had been on the phone all morning checking in with the volunteer fire department in Portage. Those guys knew everything going on in their district. "The fire captain says there's gambling going on at that church the Mastersons formed."

"What church?"

"They opened a storefront called the Church of the Guiding Hands." She looked at her notes. "The fire captain swears none of his guys go there, but they've heard stories. The Masterson family owns several of the buildings on Portage's Main Street. They opened a church in one of the empty stores."

"Why haven't we heard about this gambling?" asked Mars.

"The captain says they just started operating around Thanksgiving." They all looked at one another. "We were pretty busy with other things then."

"Let's have some lunch," said Dusty, "then Tee, you stay here and collect more information and we'll go to church and see if we can match the concrete floor with our bodies."

"Do we need a warrant?" Danny asked.

"Not yet," replied Dusty, "we can always say we came to pray."

Everyone groaned.

CHAPTER EIGHTEEN

It was late afternoon when Darwin returned to his apartment. He hadn't seen or talked with Lester and Chartreuse since yesterday. He hated it when they left him out of their fun. He thought they would come to Gran's last night. There had been a lot of pizza. He ate the leftovers for breakfast and lunch before he left her farm.

So where were they? Doing things without him? Laughing at him? But Char had kissed his cheek last week when he saved her with his cameras. His cameras. That's right. Maybe he could get a clue from last night's tapes. He fast-forwarded through what looked like a boring evening. There they were soundlessly talking it up, encouraging people to spend more money. Every now and then Char looked into a camera and winked. Darwin grinned. Maybe she liked him a little.

He moved to the new warehouse cameras and gasped. He froze the frame and checked the time stamp. At what would have been an hour before the game ended, he watched two shadowy forms sneak into the warehouse. They seemed to scout positions and set up a sort of hunting blind. It was really clever; they didn't rearrange anything, just angled things. When they were finished Darwin was certain no one would notice, especially in the dim light. The only lighting for the area was the outdoor lighting that streamed into the warehouse from the windows high up on the walls. It was enough to help everyone find their cars without having to light the inside and draw attention for the cops to investigate.

He felt as though he were observing a suspense thriller as he watched the strangers hide. He fast-forwarded to when people began to enter the warehouse and leave in their cars. He switched back to the sanctuary cameras and watched Char and Lester lock up for the evening. He flipped to the alley camera and followed them into the warehouse. He wanted to shout and warn them like he did when he watched horror movies. But like a movie, the story was already determined. He couldn't save them.

As a result he watched them be murdered on the screens and watched two strangers close the warehouse and walk away. He placed his head on the console and cried.

~ ~ ~

Lynn walked into the empty room using the connecting door from Bernice's Boutique. It was a dusty, eerie space with papers scattered about the floor and footprints that seemed to be running in all directions. A lonely round game-table sat in a corner, seeming to ignore the nearby chairs. Nothing moved. No sunlight found its way into the room even though there was a small window near the ceiling that brought in light from the adjoining room. The late wintery, dry cold kept the room's temperature at just above freezing. She pulled her coat tighter, stuffed her hands in her pockets. She was not interested in picking over the papers or searching the desk or filing cabinets.

There was a rustling sound. Mice? Snakes? No, too cold for snakes. Besides she heard whispering.

From the window high on the opposite wall she saw interruptions in the light, like something caused a blink. She gasped at the movement. Shadowy threads were reflected off the ceiling that she could see in that other room. Was someone out front? Well, now she was certain it wasn't mice or snakes whispering. Considering all those footprints, was it someone who had come back for the scattered papers? Lynn scanned the room. There was the door she had entered – too far away. And two other doors – both closer. She listened to the shadows in the next room talking in whispers. She would hide – that smaller door must be a closet. She could duck in there and call for help. Dusty could get someone here in five minutes, ten tops. She tiptoed toward her door of choice, slowly turned the handle. It was unlocked. She gently pulled, trying to keep quiet. There was a push from the other side. It wasn't a closet! She clutched her phone in her pocket as the door swung open pushing her against the wall with the doorknob in her ribs. A head inched around the door.

"What are you doing here?" demanded her husband.

"What are you doing here?" she countered. She looked over his shoulder and saw Mars and Danny, both quietly holstering their weapons.

Dusty looked around the empty office. "How did you get in here?" She glanced at the door on the opposite wall. "You had a key?"

"The door just opened."

He raised an eyebrow.

"It wasn't locked." She decided to get huffy.

He walked to the door, opened it and looked into a room with two women sitting under hair dryers, another woman with foil in her hair and a fourth getting a pedicure. He turned back to Lynn. "What is that place?"

"A beauty salon." How could anyone be so dumb, she wondered. "Bernice's Beauty Boutique."

His mouth gaped. Mars and Danny were leaning against the wall, always entertained by the chief's relationship with Lynn, the nexus of crime and nonprofits. He just stared at her.

Lynn swallowed. She was now facing a professional interrogator. "I was at Yolanda's with Mason, helping her wade through all the grant proposals and gifts people were sending her," Danny rolled his eyes at the mention of his mother, "and while we were talking a small package arrived with a crazy application from the Mastersons and their fake religion." She watched as Mars and Danny looked into Bernice's Beauty Boutique. They returned to Dusty's side and grinned at her.

"I know there's more," said Dusty as he planted himself in front of her.

She swallowed again. "I told Yolanda I would look into the church. Then today when I was having coffee with the membership committee of the pastors' club," she hesitated and Dusty made a rolling motion with his wrists to indicate that she should continue with her story. "Bev stopped by to chat with us."

"You're a member of the pastors' membership committee?" asked Mars

"No," replied Lynn. "The committee just asked me for information." She tossed her head in defiance. "Some people in this town think I know things."

Dusty snorted. And Danny asked, "Who's on the committee?"

"Tilly and Father Nick and Reverend Mosely from the Methodist Church."

"Tilly?" scoffed Mars. He poked Danny. "Did you ever think he would get religion?" They both laughed.

"Just finish your story." Dusty gave the evil eye to all three of them. Everyone wiped the smiles off their faces.

Lynn continued. "Anyway, Bev stopped at our table. We were in the coffee shop. She had heard us mention the Mastersons. She said Bernice was complaining about them. The Mastersons used a door in her place to sneak out on people. Her clients were frightened because the Mastersons are mean and scary."

"And you're here because?" asked the professional interrogator.

She blew out her breath. "I thought I would see if there was something here to report?"

"Report to whom?"

"You." Lynn was getting good at withstanding Dusty's interrogations.

"I'll bet I was at the top of your list," scowled Dusty. "What were you looking for?"

"Something to prove this isn't a legitimate nonprofit." Lynn started to pace the room, kicking aside papers and trash as she walked. "I thought I could find something concrete so Yolanda didn't have to worry about their threats."

"Their threats?" Danny almost shouted.

"She didn't want you to worry," explained Lynn, "The Mastersons sort of hinted that to deny them half of the five hundred thousand dollars might be harmful to their cause and her family."

"How come I didn't know this?" demanded Yolanda's son. He snapped his fingers as he had an epiphany. "That's why Mason moved in."

"Sort of," admitted Lynn. "They didn't want to worry the family. And the Mastersons sent a box of dead mice with their letter. You know all the other nonprofits were sending flowers and things. Their gift arrived like all the others."

"Dead mice?" Danny paled.

Dusty rubbed his forehead. "Did you or Yolanda even consider reporting this threat?"

"It only came yesterday. We thought I could snoop around a little first and not cause any bad publicity for Foster's money or other nonprofits. Things were getting a little crazy – you know, flowers, food, candy. Yolanda thought maybe the Mastersons were just trying to make an impression."

"An impression?" Danny was beside himself.

Lynn frowned at his lack of understanding. "We were dealing with nonprofits vying for grant funds. It's a very competitive atmosphere. We thought the mice were just some exaggeration."

Dusty made a strangled sound. Mars stepped in with logic. "Did some of the other nonprofits seeking funds make threats?"

"No, but they did send outrageous gifts." The three men were very interested so she explained. "Yolanda got house plants, bouquets of flowers, edible arrangements, lots of chocolate." Lynn thought over all the gifts she had seen. "Each gift came with a letter explaining the nonprofit mission and proposals for the use of the funds. A few even sent videos. One, the symphony, I think, sent a CD with very clever lyrics to Les Miz." She smiled. "So you see, a threat might just have been an agency trying to get noticed."

"With dead mice?"

"Maybe we were too accepting," she acknowledged the flaw in her thinking. "But why are you here?" She had forgotten that she wasn't the only one interested in this fake agency, or religion or whatever they were claiming to be.

"We're in an active investigation," Dusty stated.

"Don't give me your attitude," Lynn scoffed, "You'll want to know what I know, so I'll expect something in return." She waited.

Dusty swore. Danny said, "So we heard about this place. The volunteer fire department thought they were gambling. We don't know what they do here. Do you?"

"It's confusing. Bernice thinks the same thing. One of her regulars said her husband couldn't cover his bet and they broke his finger as a warning." She thought a bit. "Lois, the day manager at the laundromat across the street, thought they did poker or other gambling in this room with no the windows. She said she always saw men leaving in the early morning when she was opening up. But the Laotian couple at the corner grocery and produce store–"

"Laotian?"

"We're a very diverse community," said Lynn with a smug tilt to her head.

"And how do you know how diverse we are?" pushed Dusty.

Lynn smirked. "Their daughter won a Philanthropies' scholarship last year." Dusty signaled for her to continue. "The Laotians thought all the traffic coming into the church was drugs, but changed their minds when someone from here confided that they would stay out of the drug trade and not interfere with the Chinese gang operation." The detectives looked confused. Lynn said, "The Mastersons thought the Laotians were Chinese." She marveled at such ignorance. "So, why are you here?" She asked again.

"Two dead bodies and a lot of suggestions to look at Mastersons."

"Is Bernice a Masterson?" asked Mars. "She lets them use her shop as an escape."

Lynn shook her head. "They're her landlord. They don't want her door locked during the day. She says that the shops along here are owned by the Masterson family. It's been years but business is picking up. Everything is rented except this church and the empty lawyer's office across the street. There's a sandwich shop. Bernice brags that Portage is slowly coming out from under Masterson control."

"I guess we should go talk to Bernice."

~ ~ ~

Darwin raised his head, thinking he heard voices. He flipped through his camera screens in real-time and saw people in the sanctuary. People armed with guns. He looked closer and recognized that detective, Dusty, the one who had arrested his cousin, Mace.

This time Darwin was happy to see the police. He rushed downstairs crying, "Help! They're dead!"

Although Mars and Danny had put away their weapons, ready to follow Lynn to interview the ladies in the beauty salon, they retrieved them quickly as a strange man ran from a stairway toward Dusty.

"Mr. Dusty," sobbed the man, "they're dead."

Dusty stopped the man by holding him at arms length. "Darwin?"

"Yes, sir."

"Who's dead?" Dusty asked.

"Chartreuse and Lester. I saw them on the camera." Darwin sobbed and Dusty motioned to Danny who ran into the other room to get him some water.

"Sit here and tell us," said Dusty as Darwin settled on a chair, too distracted to take the water.

"They're dead in the warehouse. I saw them."

Dusty gave another nod. Danny and Mars went out the alley door. They were back in minutes. "Two bodies," reported Mars. Darwin wailed.

CHAPTER NINETEEN

It had been a late night securing the crime scene and moving the bodies and finally getting Darwin to make sense. So Dusty was rushed to get into the office on time, but managed his usual, "What have we got?" before anyone noticed he didn't have his coffee mug with him.

Danny checked his notes and said, "The techs got Darwin's video. You can see a truck from one of the outside cameras. Doesn't tell us much, but we're checking for any surveillance at banks or all night gas places to see if we can spot it leaving the area."

Mars said, "Gabe called from the high school. He'll have those kids ready at their lunch break."

"We'll all meet for lunch at the high school," said Dusty.

Teniquia cleared her throat. It was her first action since her return. "I'm going with Mars this morning to canvas the businesses along the street in Portage."

"Danny, you get everything ready to talk with those kids," said Dusty. A phone rang. Mars answered.

"That was the tech," he reported. "They think they can do something to the warehouse video and ID the shooters. Give them a day or two."

Dusty stopped at his desk, jotted some notes. "I'm going to Adele's funeral. Tee, find some time to get Lynn's story over the next day or two. She's got something about mice and Danny's mom and some preachers that we probably want in the file. And talk to Yolanda Valeri."

"My mom?"

"I thought we cleared that up last night," said Dusty. "That guy only moved in because of the dead mice." Dusty turned back to Tee. "Just get the story straight."

Then he added slyly, "And keep the sex out of it."

"Hey!" shouted Danny while Mars and Tee laughed.

~ ~ ~

Polly's information about the victim meeting kids in the bank lot was a boon to the investigation. When the detectives reviewed the tape they saw three kids talk with the victim at separate times. In addition, they identified another seven who were walking through the parking lot during that time.

Dusty suggested that Teniquia help interview the kids over at the high school. That was one of her talents – talking to witnesses. She was warned, though, not to smile at Polly, and heaven forbid, not to even think about hugging her. The youngster was to be treated as a witness – period.

At River Bend High School, Gabe McElvoy, assistant principal, was just thinking how different school administration was to teaching in a classroom. Today he had lined up interviews with a group of youngsters about their contacts with a murder victim. What were these kids up to? Were they in danger? Was the school in danger? Today was a day he would rather be teaching about some obscure American history event. Then he caught himself, The History Channel was un-obscuring every American history event and there was no event that was as scary as the murder discussion facing his students today.

According to Dusty's instructions, Danny and Teniquia would be talking to the kids. The detective had requested that none of the students be aware of the others being questioned. They had discussed notifying parents, but Dusty had argued that his detectives would just be asking if the kids had noticed the victim, because they were on the security tape near the time the victim was. Gabe suspected most of the kids would be happy to answer the questions as long as no one brought parents into the equation. Dusty had agreed to allow Gabe to sit in as the kids' advocate in the questioning. He would be allowed to intervene if he thought the situation needed a parent.

The interviews would take place in a small workroom beside his office. Sometimes they used the room for tutoring or sometimes for when he had to give a teacher a place to have a melt down before the next class. Maybe he should be grateful that none of the teachers was seen on the tape talking with the murder victim!

Gabe had asked the guidance counselor to pull the individual students from class. She was a perky young woman whom the kids adored, so this would not raise any questions among the other students. Every student counted it as a lucky day when this popular teacher invited him out of class.

Danny and Teniquia were settled in the workroom with the security tape cued on their laptop. When the first student entered, Gabe was pleased with the way Teniquia set the tone, asking for help, and not once hinting that the youngster was more than a casual bystander. All of the interviews went something like this:

Gabe: "Thanks for coming in. The detectives are here to ask for your help in a murder investigation. They will explain what they need, and I'll stay with you. If you feel that it is necessary, we will ask your parents to come in before I allow the detectives to question you."

The student would nod.

Teniquia would explain the security tape and make it clear that she didn't care why the student was in the area. She and Danny only wanted to know if they had noticed the man and anything they could report. After that statement, Danny would run the portion of the video that involved the student present.

Most students then said, "Wow, that was the guy you found at the dumpster?"

A couple of the students admitted that they had seen the man speaking to another student. Each interview was brief, including the one with Polly. Then the detectives brought in each of the three students who had been on tape talking with the victim. These interviews were more intense, and one student asked for his parents.

By the end of the day Teniquia and Danny had collected some interesting and helpful information.

Back at the office, Dusty asked as they entered, "What did you get?"

Danny went to the white board and boxed in a space he titled Kids' Interviews. "Those kids who talked with him were runners." He wrote their names and began to list information under each one. "They are all boys and they bring him receipts or cash from gambling operations."

"Cash?" asked Dusty.

"I guess he had them scared enough that they are honest and he seems to be fair when he pays them." Teniquia shrugged. "He doesn't hurt them and gives them some money. I think those kids need the cash to survive, not just for extra spending money."

"So what are you telling me, this guy is a social worker?"

"He hired the kids, seemed to treat them fair and paid on time." Danny then went on to give a mini bio of each youngster. He started with Elwrath. "This is Polly's friend. He lives with a drunken father. Gabe suspects abuse, but the kid is real quiet. I think he's saving his money to bolt as soon as he turns sixteen." He stared at the board for a moment. "I don't think I blame him. We've hauled his father in enough to know he's a bad actor."

Danny went on to talk about the other two kids. "This kid lives with a single mom. He's only fourteen and tells us he needs the money to help with family expenses. He's from Piper's school. He has siblings there."

"The third kid, Jackson, asked for his parents. His father just lost his job." None of the kids knew more than their own part. Each one had a route where they collected stuff and delivered it to the victim every Tuesday. After school they would make their rounds, meet up at the parking lot, get paid and go home."

Mars had not been a part of the interviews but he could see that they had taken a toll on his colleagues. Kids always brought out the social worker in Danny; and Tee, as a new mom, saw things in a new way. "I'm surprised there're so many gambling opportunities in River Bend. I thought we knew everyone. But did we get any information about who's in control?"

Dusty stared at the information and weighed what he had heard. "Right now we could break up some illegal activity, but possibly bring reprisals down on these kids. And we also are starting to see a network that may take us up the food chain to the head of this gaming operation." Dusty tapped the white board. "Let's give this information to the regional vice team. We don't need to be distracted from our murders."

"But those kids?" Teniquia asked. "We have to do something for them."

Dusty looked at the wall clock. "Not tonight. Go home and think about our options and we'll build a plan come Monday morning."

"Yipes!" gasped Danny, "I have to pick up the baby."

~ ~ ~

Lynn knew something was wrong. Janet came into her office dragging Polly and with no food. Janet with no food was a real clear indicator that there was a problem – something so big, so distracting and so important – that Janet in her foodaholic pregnancy wasn't hungry. A foodless Janet was only a small sign because one look at Polly and Lynn knew – rebellion was close at hand. And why not? Didn't every crisis happen on Friday just as she was closing the office?

"Did you know she was interviewed by the police?" Lynn had never seen Janet so furious. "Danny and Teniquia talked to her at school."

Polly sulked. Lynn mumbled. Yolanda came through the door.

She turned to Lynn, "Janet wanted me here. What police?" she asked Janet.

"Your son."

"Why?" asked the detective's mother.

"I don't know," stated Janet, ready to fight. "No one told me anything." Lynn sort of shuffled her feet. Janet and Yolanda stared at her.

"Let's go sit in the conference room. Polly and I will explain things." She shot a burning glance at the youngster. Once Lynn had everyone settled, she began, "Mars brought Polly over to the house Tuesday night–"

"The night Umberto said he hired you," accused Janet.

"He said he hired me?" Polly thought about that information and its relationship to reality.

"Don't you have a job there?" asked Janet.

"Yes." The youngster hung her head.

Lynn swallowed and jumped in with a tiny fabrication. "As I was saying, Mars brought Polly over because she had confided in Mars that she had seen that murder victim in the parking lot behind the bakery when she was going in to apply for a job last week." Polly sunk into her chair.

Janet gasped. "Is she in danger?"

"No."

"Then why was she questioned at school?" demanded Janet.

Lynn took a deep breath, grateful that she was back in a truthier area. "Once Polly told Mars about seeing the man, Dusty and his staff pulled all the security tapes from the bank and other shops around the parking lot. They interviewed several kids who walked through the lot after school to see if they had noticed anything."

"Did you?' Janet asked Polly.

"Only that he was there and then I saw his picture in the paper."

"Danny was nice to you, wasn't he?" asked Yolanda. She had a suspicion that she wasn't getting the whole story. She would grill Umberto and Danny later for the real picture.

"Yes, ma'am. He and Miss Tee talked to us and Mr. McElvoy stayed in the room with us." Polly gave a semi-grateful look at Lynn.

And then Lynn pounced. If she was going to hide the truth from Janet, she wanted something in return. "You know, Polly, Yolanda and I understand that you don't want to see that counselor any more. But we have heard about a teen grief group meeting at Hospice. It's for kids your age who have had a recent loss." Lynn gave the youngster a squinty-eyed look. Game on.

Polly swallowed. "I might not have time because of my job."

"Nonsense," chimed in Yolanda. "Umberto would want you to have this opportunity."

"Yes, ma'am."

Janet let out a big sigh. "Do you have any food here?"

Crisis over, appetite back.

~ ~ ~

Mason had been staying with Yolanda for a few days. When Danny burst into the kitchen, he stared in amazement. Mason was sitting at the kitchen table feeding David while the baby giggled and smiled in his highchair and Mason spoke to him in Italian.

"Italian?" asked Danny, as he closed the door. The baby waved at him and took another mouthful of buttery orzo.

"Connecting him to his roots," said Mason as he kicked out a chair inviting Danny to take a seat. "Do you speak it?"

"A little. It helps when I have to try to understand some of our clients who speak Spanish." Danny thought a moment. "I think my Spanish is pretty good, my Italian not so good." He watched the new man in his mother's life feed the baby. "How long are you in town?"

"Do you mean what are my intentions?"

Danny turned red and looked at the floor. "I guess," he mumbled.

"Since you carry a gun," said Mason, "I'll be honest. Your mother and I are friends." He looked at Danny and smiled. "She turned me down for anything else. But the truth is I like spending time here anyway. My pal here is one of the reasons." David squealed and reached for the feeding spoon. Both men laughed and the tension in the room evaporated.

"Your mother tells me that you solved a murder and the church people are dead."

Danny sighed. "We found them dead but still haven't solved the murder." As he related the story about meeting Lynn at the fake church, Mason laughed. And then Danny continued with Darwin interrupting their search to report the murders and the discovery of the bodies.

"Wow. I thought I was in a small safe town." Mason

wiped David's hands and face and lifted him from the high chair.

"You are. We think this murder had something to do with a dispute over who runs illegal gaming in our county." Danny took his son from Mason while the other man cleaned up the bits of orzo and other food scraps. "Where's Mom?"

"She's running errands or at some meeting or something." Mason shrugged as he dried his hands on a kitchen towel.

"You're baby sitting?"

"Sort of." He smiled.

CHAPTER TWENTY

Jim walked into Lynn's kitchen at lunchtime on Saturday. "I'm here looking for food."

He opened the refrigerator and brought out some lunchmeats and mayonnaise.

Lynn was in the middle of cleaning out her pantry. Jason had been home and she knew from experience that several of the cereal boxes would be empty, that some food that should have been refrigerated had not been, and that she would find several strange things that had dropped into the open bag of bird seed stored on the pantry floor. She had been so busy that this was the first chance she had found to attack the big closet. And now she had a guest.

"Marianna throw you out?" asked Piper as she strolled in behind Jim. She reached into the pantry and pulled out a bag of chips. "Get those rolls by the microwave." She and Jim moved to the table ready to prepare a meal. And now Lynn had two guests, and birdseed on her socks.

"Will throw you out?" Jim asked.

"I'm thinking of throwing both of you out," remarked Lynn as she put plates on the table. Jim and Piper were just like the kids – no plates, no forks. She brought out some remnants of dips and salsas, some grapes and a few other edible things from the refrigerator. Joining them at the table she asked, "No spouses?"

"Marianna's casting the play today."

"Will went to the farm with Dusty, remember?"

Jim worked on a sandwich as he spoke. "He's becoming quite the farmer."

"Who, Will?" asked Piper as she piled roast beef on

her bread. "He's designing some attachment for a tractor. He and Dusty's brothers have been working on it for months."

"A new invention?" asked Lynn.

"Something broke and no one can figure out how to fix it."

"Pithy family conversation over boring sandwiches," cried Jim, "Does life get any better than this?"

Lynn laughed. "Do you want me to heat up some soup, too?"

"Wouldn't hurt," said Piper, and Jim nodded.

As Lynn puttered around the kitchen, reheating the leftover soup no one ate earlier in the week, she said, "Dad, I was talking with David Mosely from the Methodist Church and he said Mother had helped organize the Hunger Alliance. When did she do that?"

Jim thought for a moment, stirring the soup Lynn placed before him. "I'd forgotten all about that. Maybe when you just started high school, before she got sick. She came home from a bridge game and talked about, hmm," he reached for a memory. "Some preacher's wife was in the group and talked about hungry people and all the ladies were shocked that River Bend had people in need of food." He sipped his soup. "Your mother did some research and found out that each church seemed to be helping several people eat. She went to that pastors' club and volunteered to host a meeting where they could discuss the need and find solutions."

"They all listened to her?" asked Lynn. She knew first hand that sometimes getting all the players to a meeting took a lot of finesse, cajoling and political blackmail. "How did she do it?"

"Finesse, sweet talk, blackmail," replied Jim. "Your mother was a master at sweet talk. And she always served wine at her meetings." Jim chuckled. "Not everyone drank alcohol, but the wine always helped set the mood."

"She started the home meal delivery program?" asked Piper.

"All of it," said Jim. "She had everyone define the need as they knew it and had them brainstorm ideas. Within a year we had a well-organized food pantry supported by the churches, and then they started talking about meals. Soon they found a government program for feeding older people and that grew into the idea for a senior center, and the next thing we all knew there was a new program at the Council on Aging and a new agency, the Hunger Alliance."

"It was that easy?" Lynn was stunned.

"No, it wasn't easy," snapped Jim. "It took weeks and weeks of research and getting the cooperation needed, then more time looking into funding and finally leadership. Your mother didn't want the job. So finding the right person and right board for the new agency took more time, but in the end, after a lot of work, it looked easy." Jim sipped more of his soup, then took a thoughtful bite of his sandwich as Lynn placed some cookies on the table. "There should be stories in the newspaper archives. They had a big splash on the twenty-fifth anniversary of the agency and there was a lovely tribute to Helene. I'll look around for a copy. I thought I had it somewhere."

Lynn was quiet as she considered her mother's history. "She left behind a lot of good work."

Jim clasped Lynn's hand. "And everyday you work at the Philanthropies helps all her work keep going."

"That's so sweet," sighed Piper, "I could almost cry." She looked around the kitchen. "Did Dusty eat all of the leftover Christmas candy?" Piper had a short attention span for sentimental.

~ ~ ~

It had been a very productive Saturday afternoon. Once she had visited with Jim and learned about her mother's influence in the Hunger Alliance, Lynn had felt energized. If her mother could accomplish so much, then Lynn could at least vacuum the living room and maybe dust a few things. Although she couldn't understand how it all related, she just felt that her mother would appreciate a clean floor.

Of course, one thing led to another and soon she found herself washing some windows and using that vacuum extension to dust the drapery. If that wasn't enough, she even ran a cloth over the tops of picture frames hanging on the wall. And before she could stop herself she moved into the room they used as an office and started dusting bookshelves and emptying the paper shredder.

Carrying the trash bag filled with shredded paper into the kitchen she stopped, surprised to find her mother-in-law sitting at the table reading the newspaper. "Flora!"

"I didn't want to disturb you, dear," said Dusty's mother. "When someone gets the bug, I say just let them work till they come to their senses."

Lynn flopped into a kitchen chair. "I think I'm there."

"Good, because we're all coming here for dinner."

"What?" Lynn leaped to her feet and, clutching the bag of shredded paper, looked for a place to hide. "There's no food. Who's coming?"

"I don't know," explained Flora, "Herschel dropped me off and told me he was getting his wife and the food."

"Oh, good," said Piper as she walked into the kitchen. "Will said dinner is here, but I didn't know if you were home, so I came over to do things."

"What things?"

Piper shrugged. "Food things. Maybe help Flora make biscuits.

"I'm not cooking," stated Flora. "Hershel invited me out. Why haven't you offered me a drink?" She looked at Lynn who had returned from hiding the shredded paper in the laundry room.

"Tea? Milk?"

"Beer."

Piper grabbed two bottles from the refrigerator, handed Flora one and took one for herself. Then she pulled out her phone and texted cryptic instructions. Lynn scowled at her and got her own beer. Just to be a good hostess, she found some pretzels to offer. Jeff came charging into the kitchen with three six packs under his arms.

"Is this what you wanted, Mom?"

"Is that all there is at home?" He nodded. She used her phone again, texted another secret message and settled back to wait.

"Tell me about this award you and Dusty won," suggested Flora.

That was enough. Piper took center stage and talked about the rookie training program until the food arrived. And would have kept on talking but the food smelled too good.

It turned out to be an impromptu meal with two of Dusty's brothers and their wives and food, along with Will and an assortment of beers and anything he found along the aisles in the grocery store. Dusty tumbled in, surprised at the crowd.

"I thought we were all going to Will's." He gave an apologetic glance at his wife. He had more beer and was followed by Mars carrying a bakery box. Nathan followed, much to Lynn's surprise. He wasn't usually a part of the Saturday night junk food crowd. But he took one look at the crowd and placed his own secret call. Within twenty minutes his nephew Buck and his wife, Penny, arrived with two Uncle Chicken family platters.

"Is there a reason we're all here?" Lynn asked the air.

"Wine," said Will. "We gotta make some plans."

Nathan smiled. "I've always wanted to be a vintner."

"How did you get involved in this?" Lynn asked her good friend.

"There are some aged oak casks in the basement of Palmer Mansion," – Nathan's home – "and Will says that would be my contribution to the process." Nathan was delighted with his new role as associate vintner and oak cask owner.

CHAPTER TWENTY-ONE

It was Sunday evening and Mason was restless. After spending three nights at Yolanda's he had returned to his father's house to finish cleaning. The house on the mountain was slowly emptying. He had been packing things all day. He needed a break. Maybe Yolanda needed dinner. He cleaned up and drove into town.

"You hungry?" he asked as she answered the door. She stepped aside and he walked in.

He followed her into the kitchen where she had a half eaten sandwich on a plate. "I've had dinner."

"No, you haven't," he argued, "that wouldn't feed those dead mice." As he spoke Umberto walked into the kitchen from the basement.

"I thought I heard the guys," he said.

"What guys?" Mason couldn't imagine Yolanda entertaining a bunch of guys on a Sunday night, or any night. The doorbell rang. Mason had never been in a house with such an active doorbell. It rang at all hours and brought in all sorts of people and surprises. Umberto could be heard talking with someone at the front door. Soon two strangers were in the kitchen.

Yolanda made the introductions. "This is Bertram Luft." The black man gave a hundred kilowatt grin and held out his hand. Mason grinned back as he shook hands. "And this is Father Ed."

"A priest?" Mason asked before he could stop himself.

"Not just a priest, but a Jesuit," replied Father Ed as he shook hands with Mason. Of course, he didn't look like a priest, and he was wearing a ratty sweatshirt that said 'Loyola.' He looked as though he was about the same age as Yolanda and Umberto.

There was a shuffling at the kitchen door and Danny walked in. He was followed by a youngster. The men all greeted the young detective. He said, "This is Johnny, one of my guitar students." The youngster, clearly Latino, shook hands around the kitchen.

"Lots of music tonight," said Umberto, clearly happy.

"Music?" asked Mason.

Danny said, "Piano," and pointed to Bertram, "bass," Umberto raised a hand, "two guitars," and he indicated Johnny and himself. Mason looked at the priest. Danny said, "Vocalist."

"What do you play?" asked Bertram. He had assumed that Mason was also a member of the band.

"Drums," he said, "but it's been a while." All the men thought having a drummer was a great idea and hustled Mason to the music room on the lower level. Yolanda was left standing in the kitchen staring at her half-eaten sandwich.

Downstairs, Danny reached into a small under-counter refrigerator and handed out beers to the men and soft drinks for himself and Johnny. Everyone began prepping their instruments and talking. "You play oldies?" asked Umberto, looking at Mason.

"How old?"

"Real old," said Bertram, "maybe before you were born. The real classics."

"I'm pretty old," replied Mason.

Nineteen thirties?"

"Not that old."

"We're helping the two kids," said Bertram as he looked at Danny and Johnny, "learn the oldies because our combo gets a lot of calls for that stuff at the country club."

"Your combo?" Mason was learning another facet of small town life. "The priest?"

They all laughed. "I'm in town visiting my mother," said the priest. "Umberto and I had a group when we were in high school. I always sing with him when I can."

"And his mother still doesn't like me," bragged Umberto. "She thought I would keep him away from God."

"She's changed her mind," said Ed, "She thinks you make great cannoli." The baker bowed to the praise.

Umberto pulled over two music stands and spread out some sheet music. He gave some instructions to the young men and using his bass to set the beat got everyone started on the first song. They played it slowly, rehearsed a few times, brought it to tempo and Ed started to sing. Mason kept up on the set of drums that had been stuffed in the corner of the room. The older musicians were slowly helping Johnny and Danny develop a repertoire of musical standards.

"You boys are doing great," Umberto praised the guys after an hour of rehearsals.

To Mason's surprise Ed had sung lyrics to every song. And he said, "You learn all these songs in the seminary?"

Ed laughed. "Yes. We have a group of guys that play and sing for fun and we visit nursing homes. Those folks enjoy us, even when they don't know where they are." Now Ed wasn't smiling. "We do what we can to nudge their memories. You should see them – sometimes they even sing and dance." He sighed. "But when the music stops, so do they."

"You're bringing us down," chided Umberto. Then he turned to Danny and Johnny, "Maybe some weekend we go to that place where Bergy did rehab." The guys nodded in agreement, ready to pay a visit to the assisted living center.

Yolanda walked into the room wrapped in the best smell to reach Mason's nose in a long time. "Is that your mother's pizza?" Ed asked.

"She's my mother-in-law, remember? But when she heard you were in town, she started baking for you," said Yolanda. "My cousin just brought it over."

Bertram sniffed the air. "She's going to heaven, right Father?"

The guys took a break and enjoyed the pizza and a few more beers. Then Umberto got everyone back on task. This time Yolanda stayed and sang duets with the priest. By ten Danny and Johnny were gone, they had work and school in the morning. Bertram left at eleven. Umberto, Father Ed and Mason spent another two hours working their way to the Beatles and the Stones.

Yolanda finally told them to leave. At the door she noticed that it had snowed again. To Mason she said, "You stay here. Your mountain will be slippery." Too tired to argue he ambled down the hallway to the guest room.

CHAPTER TWENTY-TWO

Monday morning Dusty found his staff huddled around the white board, unaware that he had arrived. They seemed very excited. "Now what?" he asked because he could tell by the sound of their voices that they weren't talking about a murder investigation.

Teniquia grinned at him. "Mars got Jackson's father a job at Taft Manufacturing." Dusty had been correct. His unit was excited about improving the prospects for the three students who had been working as runners for the murder victim. He listened as Teniquia continued. "Danny and Piper are working on something for that single mom, maybe a job at Will's place. Piper's arranging some testing for her at the community college today and she said she might squeeze a scholarship out of Lynn. She wanted to help because the two siblings at her school are really smart."

"That leaves Polly's friend." Dusty waited.

Danny blew out his breath. "He's not that easy. But we have a plan. We're going to arrest him and get him into the juvie system, get him paroled and into foster care. There's a slot open at the group home for teens."

"That's a lot of balls in the air that have to bounce in the right direction." Dusty couldn't wait to hear that plan.

"I talked to the group home supervisor," said Teniquia, "Mars cleared the hearing with Judge Dunn and Danny has Grady at Juvenile Probation all lined up. We're arresting John, that's his name, not Elwrath, after lunch. He'll be in the group home by dinner."

Dusty grinned at his three social

worker/detectives. He knew this kind of instant response and networking was only possible in a small town. Because as Mars always says, "We take care of our kids."

"We do have four dead bodies to deal with," he reminded them.

~ ~ ~

Dusty and Danny made a trip to Asheville. They met Dusty's old friend Detective Dundee. They had been friends for years, going back to their high school days when they had played for regional championships on opposing basketball teams – the tall center and the short point guard. Two skinny teens, both with the joy of the game and a respect for their opponents. That past relationship helped them create a long term, mutual professional respect that helped both of their departments work together. Only today Dundee wasn't that skinny teen point guard – more like a barrel of a man wearing a side arm and a grin.

"How's your wife?" he asked as he clapped Dusty on the back and smacked Danny on the back of the head. "You're lucky she met you first. I'd'a swept her off her feet the first time we met."

"Yeah, like you did last summer at Will's party." Dundee had played against Will back in the day, too.

"I just spilled that drink on her so she would remember me," he explained. "But she'll have to get over me. I gotta girl."

"I hope she's over eighteen," mumbled Danny.

Dundee heard him and smacked him again. "She's a woman. Forty-five. Used to be in the Marines."

"A match made in heaven," said Danny as he moved away from Dundee's hand. He spun around and raised a fist.

"I won't slug you," said Dundee, "Your uncle would

have me iced. Did he send any cannoli?" Danny handed him a small box. Dundee grinned and allowed the two men to enter his office. Sort of like a troll collecting a fee for crossing a bridge or something. "What case can I solve for you?" He kicked the door shut.

"You and Mars went to visit that guy about Gibson, the dead body we found in Verona," replied Dusty. "Since then we've had two more deaths. Two Mastersons."

Dundee savored the cannoli, taking small nibbles to make it last. "Yeah, I saw the bulletins. Now you got two less Mastersons." Another nibble. "You got four bodies in two weeks by my count."

"And we think they're all related," replied Dusty.

"You got something?" Dundee settled back in his chair to enjoy the rest of his cannoli and listen.

Dusty reported on the investigation, Darwin's videos, the evidence of concrete dust, enhancing the video to ID the killers in the warehouse and what they had learned from the kids.

"Woo-eee!" exhaled Dundee. "You ready to arrest those guys?"

"We have to find them first," said Danny. "Your guys say they worked at the same place as Gibson."

"What can we do for you?"

"Can you run a stakeout at the tire shop for a few days?" asked Dusty. "We can cover the overtime."

"You got a deal," agreed Dundee.

~ ~ ~

Polly walked into the room. She wasn't happy about this. Everyone had so many ideas about what she should be doing. She would show them and give them a little attitude. She couldn't get out of this town fast enough. She looked around the room.

There were three other kids slumped on the chairs. She knew them from school. They had dead parents?

She wasn't the only orphan? The woman who seemed to be in charge said, "You must be Polly. We've been waiting for you. I hope you didn't have trouble finding this room."

Polly looked at her and shook her head. "I just walked slow."

"My aunt dragged me here," offered one of the two boys in the room. "I don't know why I have to be here." Attitude, Polly thought, she would have to top him if she wanted to get tossed out.

"I know what you mean," said the only other girl. "He's dead, what am I supposed to do?" Then she began to sob. The three other youngsters looked at her. Polly felt tears gather in her eyes. The boys were both looking at their shoes.

"I'm Fran," said the group leader, "and we're all here because we've each had a great loss. And we're going to support one another because our friends don't understand what it feels like."

"What about you?" challenged the other boy.

Fran smiled sadly. "When I was your age, I lost my twin sister to a severe heart problem. For years I felt as though half of me was missing. I was so angry with everyone, especially her. She left me. How could she do that? But I started attending a group like this and things started to be better for me and better for my parents. I didn't understand that my attitude was affecting the recovery of my whole family. I thought I was the only one who lost someone." She looked at each youngster. "But my parents were in pain, my grandparents, my sister's friends, our other siblings. And the worst part, every time they saw me, because we were identical, they saw her." She sat quietly and let the youngsters absorb that information.

Fran had been there before, had been in their shoes. She laughed to herself. They were all trying to be tough and hostile to hide their pain and anger. She knew that, too. She had sure tried. She cleared her throat and the kids all looked up. "Let's get started."

They all frowned at her. So she jumped right in. "I know you're Polly. So, as the only other girl, you must be Kaitlin." The girl nodded, then scowled. Fran turned to the boys, "Let's see, Carson?" A boy looked up and then down. "So you must be Tyler." She nodded to the oldest youngster in the group. "The senior." Tyler looked at the floor.

"I know you don't want to be here," she began. "I was that way years ago. And I challenge you to prove that your pain and suffering is worse than mine was. You see, I miss my sister every day, even fifteen years later. But I've survived this far because I had a secret plan." She was silent.

Finally, "What kind of a plan?" asked Carson.

"She said it's secret, doofus, so why would she tell us?" snarled Tyler.

"Because I want to help you?" Fran answered. "Or, because I want to help me?"

"Help you?" asked Kaitlin.

"That's my secret," replied Fran. "I found that it was hard to maintain a lot of attitude," all the kids looked uncomfortable, "when I was thinking of someone else and not myself. I had promised my twin, because even if she was dead, she was still part of me. I promised her that we would get through this pain together and I would figure it out."

"So, what, she talks to you?" Tyler asked, daring Fran to talk about ghosts or something.

She smiled softly as she nodded. "We spoke a lot before she died and I knew what kind of person she was. So I decided to measure my action by her standards."

"I don't understand," said Polly, squirming in her

chair.

Yes, you do, thought Fran. Aloud she said, "I knew my sister was kind and funny, and even when she was close to death she talked about the future and challenged me to live for both of us. It took me a few years but I finally understood. I could pout, grieve, be angry and drive my family crazy, or I could live."

She waited as they thought about this. Then she said, "Each one of you knows the person you lost. They gave you ideals, memories of their character, things to take you into the future – ways to move forward that will allow you to live with them inside of you."

The kids were somber, sullen and silent. Fran sighed to herself, meeting one. Aloud she said, "I think that's enough for you to think about until our next meeting. See you next Monday after school." She left the room and the kids quietly collected their belongings and trailed out, not acknowledging one another.

~ ~ ~

Yolanda was diligent about reviewing every request for Foster's money. Many applications were routine funding requests. However, some programs required lots of money and Yolanda wondered how those programs would be sustained after the first year when her money was gone. These were things Lynn had told her to consider: sustainability – once Foster's money runs out how would the program continue; another consideration was community need. She knew that was hard to determine. Sometimes you wouldn't see a big community need because the need was being addressed. The need would only be apparent if the program shut down. A real conundrum, thought Yolanda. Lynn had also suggested that she look for programs that were cooperative, two or more agencies working together to provide a service that many different clients needed. She looked at her pile. Only another million to read. Sigh.

The next presentation was a joint proposal from the Hunger Alliance, the women's shelter and the Council on Aging. What did Lynn say about cooperative ideas? Yolanda read the proposal then re-read it. It was really exciting! The team was laying the groundwork for a program that they all agreed would be managed by the Hunger Alliance to help everyone's clients work on money management issues. Money management had been a big issue last fall when that fellow who worked for that financial group was murdered – and several agencies had wished that the victim had been able to help their clients. Those agencies vowed to explore the possibilities the victim had suggested before his death. She remembered Lynn using that as an example of cooperation. This proposal demonstrated that the agencies were really following through with their vision.

She rested the papers on her lap and rested her head on the back of her chair. She recalled all the problems that surfaced when they found that dead man in Glenda Llewellyn's barn. Although Dusty and Lynn solved the crime, Yolanda had learned about the needs of clients in so many agencies who had money issues – paying bills, buying food. Here was a proposal that laid out a blueprint for building that sort of community support for agency clients. They even had made contact with similar groups in other states, and were asking for the funds to pay for consulting support so that they could be up and running within the year. Yolanda slapped her knee with the request. Here was something that made sense. She dropped it on the pile for consideration.

Then she yawned – it was bedtime. All this paper would still be here in the morning.

CHAPTER TWENTY-THREE

In Asheville the gambling boss reread the newspaper report on the double murder in Portage. Jasmine Fuller, as usual, had done her best to report all details and present a complete picture of the tragedy to her readers. This caused the boss to say to himself, "There were three of them!" Inspired by that thought he drove to his cabin in Bristol.

Entering the cabin he shouted as he waved a newspaper. He was on a mission. "You missed this guy." The news photographer had captured a poignant photo of Darwin Masterson watching the bodies as they were removed from the warehouse. "I want him gone, too."

Antwan opened his mouth to speak. Gilly shook his head. There was silence until the boss spoke again. "It's been a week and no police. No one knows it was us. You can go back to that shit hole of a town. Get in and out before anyone notices."

The two men nodded. They had been hiding out in the boss's cabin near Bristol for a week, feeling sorry that it was winter because in the summer they could have caught some races. Ten inches of snow and an unreliable satellite hook up diminished the forest charm. The boss, fortunately, brought along some supplies, a few movies, more beer and a lot of snacks. The beer and chips had been running low.

"How you want this done?" asked Gilly.

"Just put a bullet through his head," came the reply. "Then get the hell back to the cabin. Tomorrow they got that funeral. Portage will be pretty quiet."

~ ~ ~

Another pleasant afternoon helping Yolanda review grant applications and Mason found himself intrigued by the proposal for a Black History Forum with a focus on local community members. They weren't asking for much money, but the schedule of presentations, once a week for the month, was thoughtful and would certainly be informative and provocative. He couldn't help but think it needed something more – that little punch to make it stand out as a regional attention getter. Something to kick off the first forum with a bang! He put down the proposal.

"Who wrote this?" he asked, looking to the other end of the sofa, always charmed to see Yolanda in her grant review get up – sweats and reading glasses.

Yolanda looked up from her own papers. Today she had her hair tied back at the nape of her neck. It looked like she had used an old shoelace. "Two young women who thought we needed this history lesson. The genealogical society is excited. They have loaned some photos and taped interviews."

"Could I meet them?" He noticed she was barefooted today, her slippers nesting on the carpet. And she had dazzling red toenails. She always surprised him.

"The genealogical society?" She looked over the top of her reading glasses. She told him she had twenty pair scattered around her house, her daughters' houses and her car. She bought them at one of those dollar only stores. Some of the designs were outrageous – stripes and plaids and strange color combinations. Mason enjoyed that secret, too.

"No, the young women. I wanted to offer some suggestions." He straightened and handed her the papers.

"Really? What do you know about being black?"

"I'm from South Africa."

She scowled at him. "I'm serious. What can you offer?"

"Please, may I meet them?"

Yolanda picked up her handy cell phone and placed a call. "Can you or Jasmine drop by the house? I have some questions about your grant proposal." She ended the call and said to Mason, "Five minutes."

"Five minutes?"

"She drives a car with a siren." Then she smirked at him.

Sure enough, within five minutes Detective Teniquia LaMont was standing at Yolanda's doorstep, pushing through the front door, calling out, "What? Jasmine will be here in a minute." She barely closed the door and Jasmine rang the bell. Tee opened the door and let her in.

"In the living room," Yolanda called out. The young women followed the sound of her voice and walked through a dining room, its floor littered with papers and its table covered with more paper and two laptops, and into an equally messy living room. Mason stood as they entered.

Teniquia had lost weight during her hospitalization and recovery. Her patrol uniform sort of sagged, but she was back to her smiling, vibrant self. Yolanda thought it was those kids she and her husband adopted. Jasmine was very professional in her pantsuit set off with a colorful scarf. She always managed to look girly, but with the steel that she had acquired in the military.

"Mason—" began Yolanda.

"The boyfriend?" asked Tee.

"Old news," replied Yolanda. "Anyway, Mason is helping me review grants and wanted to hear more about yours." Both young women stared at him. He stared back at two lovely young black women, both of whom were professionals in the community. He had read all that information in the proposal.

He cleared his throat. "I thought your proposal sounded good."

Tee gasped and challenged Yolanda, "He's deciding on the grants because it's his father's money?"

Yolanda slipped off her reading glasses and frowned at the detective. "No, he's helping me wade through this gibberish."

"Our wasn't –"

Yolanda waved her hand in surrender. "I know. I'm just tired of reading–"

Mason interrupted. "And I asked about your grant because I think it has possibilities."

"But?" challenged Jasmine, the reporter.

"It needs a hook."

The pair stared darts at him. "We designed a great program," stated Jasmine. "We have it well-organized, well-advertised–"

"But," Mason interjected, "you need a hook. So I was thinking you could use a lead off speaker."

"But Mr. Obama costs a lot of money," sneered Teniquia.

"So why not," and here he named a well-known black mayor of a large American city, "Skeet Turnbull? He would generate a lot of interest." They stared speechless. "You know who he is, don't you?"

With that Jasmine lost it. "Of course, we know who he is," she almost screamed, "but he'd cost money, too."

Mason picked up his cell, punched a number. "This is F. Mason Donovan, of Donovan World Wide Engineering, may I speak with the mayor?" He waited and glanced at the young women. Yolanda sat quietly, enjoying the drama. She sensed something was about to happen.

"Hey, Skeet," Mason shouted into the phone, "you at your computer? ... Go to this website." He gave the reference site for the forum. "Looks like a great program, right? ... No, those aren't my daughters, they're the organizers ... How old's your son? ... Wait, I'll ask." He looked at the young women. "You both single?"

Teniquia gasped. "What are you, a pimp?"

"I'm single," said Jasmine, "and I have standards. She's married."

Mason turned back to his phone, "One married and one single with standards ... That's what she said ... So you want to be our featured speaker to kick off this series?"

He waited. The women held their breath.

"Yeah ... covered ... covered ... covered. Oh, and bring your sax. ... See you in a few weeks, pal." He ended the call. "You got a featured speaker. I'll help you anyway I can." He smiled at them.

The young detective cleared her throat. "Can we afford him?"

"I can afford him," said Mason. "He's coming to visit me and will have time to speak at your event."

Jasmine sprang across the room and into his arms. "Thank you."

Teniquia stood still and wiped a tear that had strayed down her cheek. Yolanda laughed.

"Why is he bringing his sax?" asked Yolanda.

Mason grinned. "We're going to have a little musicale. He and I haven't played together in over twenty years. Bertram, Umberto, Danny, that kid, Johnny – we'll have a real old fashioned jam session in your music room."

"Can I come?" asked Jasmine.

"Me, too," said Tee.

They looked at Yolanda who said, "If we move the

drums into the living room and move some furniture we can have a few folks in to listen."

"That's my girl," said Mason. "Now let's get down to business." He ushered the two young women into the kitchen for their first marketing meeting.

Yolanda sighed and returned to the million grant proposals.

~ ~ ~

"This is the fourth time we've had to walk her home," complained Jeff as they dodged dirty snow that was melting fast in the sunny parts of the greenway. They were on Janet's list to escort Polly home from the bakery after school. The boys would ride bikes to Janet's and then walk the greenway into town. Ricky had a longer bike ride home, but he would have pedaled to Portage to walk Polly home. He just worried that he would slip up and everyone would see through his coolness.

"But Umberto always gives us something to eat," Ricky reminded his friend, coolness in place.

"Yeah, but she doesn't want to be our friend." Jeff spoke a truth that cut into Ricky's heart.

"Only because she doesn't know how cool we are." Ricky tripped over some gravel.

"Maybe we should ask her to play some of our games." Jeff didn't seem to be bothered by Polly's charms.

"She plays games?" Privately Ricky thought that had possibilities. He and Polly on a couch, lights low, murder and mayhem on the TV screen.

"Yeah, once when she was living with Lynn and Dusty we played while the adults hung out in the kitchen. She's not bad." He looked at Ricky. "She probably still won't think we're cool. But at least she won't think we're boring."

Ricky was depressed that being 'not boring' was his

best option when dealing with Polly. And it was difficult to keep his feelings under wraps – how embarrassed he would be if Jeff figured out he was interested in Polly.

They kicked through more snow along the greenway. "Maybe we can ask her over to Lynn's on Saturday, or something," Jeff proposed.

Ricky thought Jeff had a great idea. "Yeah, she might want to get away from Janet," he said, intellectually gripping his coolness.

"Janet's not bad," said Jeff.

"She's not bad, she's just out in space."

"Yeah, I know what you mean," offered Jeff, "She came to our careers class to talk about computer jobs, but she got distracted by some notes on the white board about signing up for the senior play and forgot what she was talking about."

The boys knocked on the bakery alley door and slipped into the sugary warmth of the kitchen. Polly was sitting on a tall stool helping Umberto box cookies. "These are for your mother," he told Jeff. "Those are for you." He glanced at two cartons of milk and a small plate of broken cookies. The boys made quick work of the snack while Polly finished her task and got her coat. She never said a word, just stood at the door and waited.

The three youngsters left the bakery, all looking anywhere but at each other. It was not late but it was winter so the streetlights guided them toward the greenway and toward home. No one spoke. Until, "Do you want to come to Lynn's and play some games, Saturday?" Jeff asked.

"Who me?" she asked.

"Jeff said he played with you before and you're good," Ricky blurted out.

"So you wouldn't ask me if I couldn't keep up?"

Polly had been frightened by the episode with the dead man, but she figured she could still find ways to show attitude.

"I would..." Ricky couldn't make himself say anything more that might suggest he just liked to be around her.

"How would I get there?" she asked. And there was the boys' dilemma, a life with no driver's license.

"If you want to come over," offered Jeff, "we'll figure something out."

"Okay."

Ricky almost felt dizzy. How did Jeff do that? He was so cool. Saturday night with almost a date. He hoped neither Jeff nor Polly noticed, but he thought it was almost like a date.

CHAPTER TWENTY-FOUR

Today was the double funeral in Portage. Char and Lester were laid to rest in the family cemetery. Everyone turned out. The Masterson clan members were drawn to a violent death. It had been awhile since a family member had such a notorious end. It was reassuring to the older members that the new generation could still cause trouble. Of course, no one acknowledged that this kind of trouble meant the end of a portion of that younger generation. No matter. It was still reassuring that violence and crime ran in the family – just too bad it ran over some of the family.

Darwin stood aside and watched. There were only two other cousins his age and they had left Portage years ago. Neither of them made it back for the funeral – one was in prison in Oregon, another family hero. And one was in the Army – he was the disappointment. He was successful and not interested in family lore or carrying on traditions.

Darwin stubbed his shoe into the dirt of the old cemetery. It was a sorry place. Someone kept the grass trimmed and the weeds pulled during the summer, but it always looked forlorn, especially in the winter. And now his two partners were taking up residence. What next?

Well, he knew what. The family had already decided. They had demanded that the church be shut down and the church funds, a small bank account needed to establish its legitimacy, be cashed out to pay for funeral expenses. He had done that. Then Char's father had scoured her trailer for anything of value.

Lester's parents had done the same thing. That stupid boy was thirty-seven and had still lived with his parents. Both families had assumed there was big money and riches from the church just waiting to be claimed.

They had been disappointed. No money. Darwin kept his face pious. He had the money but it was nobody's business. Years of growing up with those two had finally paid off. They had ignored him, bullied him and laughed at his computer skills. He had learned to stay in the background, observe and keep quiet. That's why he knew Chartreuse kept her money in Gran's barn in an old tin box buried in the corner of an old stall. That fool Lester kept his money and valuables in the warehouse behind some loose siding in the loft. Darwin was lucky that neither one of them trusted banks. The money was now his, and he did trust banks – a small bank in Kansas that he dealt with over the Internet. He had a comfortable sum of money that would allow him time to plan for his future.

A secret smile warmed him. He would have time to devote to his various Internet scams and not have to worry that the payoffs would be small at first, and grow as he got better.

The family returned to Gran's for food and further discussion of this latest chapter in family lore. Darwin listened to all the talk and was surprised that the family assumed he had only been a fringe member of the church operation. They thought Char and Lester were the brains. They were also concerned that the two brains of the operation had no money to show for the work.

"What do you think?" Char's father asked Darwin, "Where's her money? Wasn't that place making money?"

Darwin thought for a moment, scowling to

emphasize his pain and sorrow, then answered, "I think Char said there had been a few big winners lately and they had to build up the cash again."

"She meant that Nevada Utley," an uncle confirmed. "I was there the night he won everything." He turned to Darwin. "Wasn't there someone else that night, too?"

"Yes," Darwin nodded. "I wasn't there. But she talked about it."

"Of course, you weren't there," complained Lester's father, "we all know you weren't in this deal. They just let you live in the apartment upstairs." He studied the skinny, beaked nose, family geek. "They was just being kind to you so's you would keep their computers working." Everyone laughed and nodded. Darwin kept the computers working for the whole family. As a result he knew a lot about all of them but never found it necessary to say so.

The conversation was also interesting to him because it suggested that Char and Lester never let on what his exact role was in the organization. No one knew about his cameras and his share of the profits. He was happy, beak-nosed, bullied and now, rich.

With that conclusion, he gave a sad and hapless nod to the family and headed back to his place.

~ ~ ~

"In all this time we've spent talking," Yolanda said as she began clearing the kitchen table after their afternoon snack – Umberto's biscotti and coffee, "I haven't learned much about your women." She gave him an impish grin. Teasing Mason was great sport.

Mason liked to push back. That's what made it fun. "So, sex talk?"

"After you tell me something about them personally," she offered, "that is if you can remember anything personal, like the town they live in, or the color of their hair."

"Are you suggesting I only meet up with them for some machine gun sex act and then go on my way?" He watched her blush. "I do know their names and even their addresses. Some of them I know color preferences and dress size."

Yolanda stood and looked at him. "Maybe we should make ourselves comfortable in the living room. David will be asleep for another hour at least." Mason followed her into the living room where she settled into something she called a chair and a half. It really looked comfortable when she pulled her feet up under her and rested against the upholstered arm. He thought, if he ever settled somewhere, he would get a chair and a half – it was a great American invention.

He paced the room, then stopped at the windows to stare at the winter landscape. Turning he said, "The women have changed over the years." He sat on the sofa facing her. "When I was young they were young, as I've gotten older, some of them have gotten younger."

"Just like a man," she said, and it sounded insulting to him.

Defensively he replied, "I don't get rid of them because of their age. We both move on. Sometimes literally. A lady I saw for years in northern Africa accepted a promotion to New Delhi, working for the state department. Another lady, a widow, remarried and left Istanbul for her new life in Dublin."

Yolanda gaped, and finally said, "Talking to you is like reading a National Geographic magazine." Then she couldn't resist, "How young is the youngest?"

He smiled at her. "In age, they're all pretty much over forty. Some I've known for years and some only once. For example, there's one whom I met-"

"And seduced?"

"Met and negotiated a pleasant few days." He sat

forward and placed his elbows on his knees. "I was on vacation, taking a few days in Casablanca after finishing a job. We were in a Muslim country where things are conservative, so we took a quick flight to Funchal in the Madeira Islands. It was a great few days and then Sweetheart called because of Pop. I got her back to Casablanca and made my way here. I may or may not contact her again."

"You didn't see him before he died?"

"I came into town for a few days when he was in hospice care and we had a great visit." Mason sat back and stretched his arms out along the back of the sofa. "He told me he had his church rites all settled and said I didn't have to return for his funeral because he knew I didn't feel comfortable in churches." They were both silent. Finally Mason sighed, "I wish I had."

"I was at his funeral," said Yolanda. "Father Nick did a great job of celebrating Foster's life." She could feel Mason's sadness and regret. To change the topic she urged, "Tell me about your longest relationship."

Mason smiled at her. "You won't believe me." Yolanda gave him a look that said, Try to surprise me. And he did. "My longest relationship is with a South African woman named Riva Biyela. And we never have sex. She runs an orphanage for mixed race children. I think they come from all over the continent. She tries to only get girls because she feels they are at the greatest risk for exploitation." Yolanda gasped. "But recently with all the upheaval, she takes everyone without regard to age or gender." He stared up at the ceiling, lost in memories. "She's quite a girl, or woman. She's about my age. And she's been badgering me for money and materials and construction repairs for decades."

Yolanda watched him speak and noticed the glow in his eyes. Hmmm.

"She's tiny. Sometimes I can't figure how she does all she does without collapsing. And her hair," Mason grinned, "It a continual struggle between her African, Asian and Irish ancestry to see which will win. And her eyes, they sparkle and change color everyday," he sighed, "but they always smile." He proceeded to tell Yolanda more stories about his history with Riva. Yolanda laughed at the woman's bold requests and cried when Mason told about the challenges in caring for her orphans.

They were quiet as they both thought about Riva and her life's work. Finally Yolanda said, "She's a worthy woman. Too bad she isn't attracted to you or you to her. She's who you need in your life, and all her children."

Mason opened his mouth to reply, but David cried out from his nap and the mood disappeared.

~ ~ ~

Piper walked into Lynn's kitchen and flopped in a chair. "It's beginning," she moaned, sounding as though a giant alien spaceship was zapping River Bend neighborhoods and it was only a matter of time before the zap with her name on it found her.

"You got the e-mail," Lynn guessed. Several of Tee's friends had received an e-mail this morning announcing that she was ready to meet everyone back at the gym for her training and workout sessions. She had warned everyone that the initial sessions would be mild because she had to build up her endurance and strength after her hospitalization.

"Next Tuesday night?" Piper dropped her head on the table, burying her nose in the newspaper that was usually spread out. As Lynn told friends, she and Dusty were probably the last print media readers.

Lynn handed her a glass of wine. "Maybe you can say you have parent conferences that night."

Piper raised her head and had print ink smeared on her nose and chin. "But what would be my excuse for the following Tuesday?"

"Death?"

"You're no help," the tiny principal growled at her best friend. "How can she be ready to go back to the gym? She was shot – with a gun!"

"It'll be an easy workout," said Lynn. "She still only goes to work about half a day. How sweaty can we all get? She'll be too tired."

"She can just sit on those exercise balls and count out a thousand crunches. We'll be the ones sweating, not her." Piper gulped her wine. "It's been almost two months. I haven't got a muscle left in my body. They all turned to chocolate over the holidays."

Lynn sat at the table with her own wine. "I know what you mean."

Jasmine Fuller knocked on the door and barged in flopping into a chair. "Two days before the forum and she wants to exercise!" Lynn poured her some wine. "Serve her right if I died and she has to do it all alone. The forums I mean."

Piper raised her glass and clicked a toast with Jasmine. "I'm telling her I have parent conferences every Tuesday."

"That's lying," challenged the skilled journalist.

Piper scowled. "Maybe just every other Tuesday."

"I'll be there," said Lynn and poured more wine.

"Me, too," agreed the reporter.

The principal with the chocolate muscles swore and they knew she would be there, too.

~ ~ ~

In the late afternoon Darwin returned to his apartment. No one in the family had suggested he move or start paying rent. He decided to continue as things were. If they wanted rent he could always move. He'd hate to because he had all his equipment organized. His security system was extensive. His cameras kept watch over downtown Portage.

He parked his car behind the Asian grocery. He didn't like using the warehouse since the murders had taken place there. He had locked it up and was waiting for the family to determine its fate. Locking his car and loosening his necktie, he entered the building through the alley, locked it back up and dashed up the stairs to his rooms. He carefully removed the tie, still noosed so that it would be ready for the next family function – wedding or funeral. He took off his parka, slipped on a sweatshirt and settled before his array of security screens.

And panicked!

The truck that had been tracked from the warehouse on the night of the murders was now moving slowly through Portage. It parked in front of the Asian grocery and one of the murderers ran inside and came out quickly with two bottles of some soft drink. The truck continued down Main Street as Darwin watched his screens and followed its progress through town and down the side street toward the back of the building.

Fear crawled up his back. The truck parked on the street behind the warehouse. No one got out. Darwin reached for his phone. When his call was answered he screamed, "Mr. Dusty, they're here looking for me."

"Darwin, calm down," said Dusty, "Who's there?"

"Them murderers. I just got in from the funeral and their truck's in town. I can see them in my screens." He was glad Dusty already knew how extensive his security was. The detective easily understood the situation. "They're parked in the lot behind me. What do I do?"

"Stay out of sight," advised Dusty. "I'll get someone there. I'm going to put you—"

"Not on hold," screamed Darwin.

"I'm going to put you on the line with Ms. LaMont. She'll stay with you until someone can get to Portage." With that Dusty passed the phone.

"Mr. Masterson?" asked the woman's voice. "I want you to tell me if they move while Dusty gets you some help." Darwin heard some whispering at the detectives' office. The woman's voice came back, "There is no one close so we're calling in a fire alarm. When the volunteers come, they will break in the front door and rescue you. We want you to be ready to leave with them. Dusty will be there in about ten minutes."

"Yes, ma'am," came the whispered, frightened replied.

Darwin heard the siren, then heard the glass shattering. He ran to the head of the stairs as he heard, "Darwin, you asshole, what have you done now?" Two volunteer firemen ran up the stairs grabbed him and dragged him out to their truck. He thought his backbone hit every step on the way down and his shoulder crashed into the door on the way out of the building.

Two more volunteers arrived and made a show of carrying gear into the building. Another three volunteers showed up and delighted in hosing down the church facade. Darwin sat huddled in the fire truck.

As he sat there he watched three sheriff's patrol cars fly into town from two directions and veer off behind the buildings toward the parking area in back. A dark SUV followed close behind. He blinked and thought he heard some gunfire. Things were happening and he couldn't see a thing. The firefighters even stopped and stood close to the truck for protection. The radio in the truck chattered. One of the volunteers reached into the cab and answered. More chatter. One final spray of water, now turning to ice on the sidewalk and the volunteers began to pack up.

The dark SUV pulled up beside the truck. Dusty lowered his window. "Get in my car," he told Darwin.

"My stuff," Darwin argued, not wanting to leave his equipment unattended in a building with no doors and broken windows.

They'll," Dusty nodded to the volunteers, "clean up and board it up. We'll just go sit down at the fire station." Darwin stumbled out of the truck, finding his knees a little weak. He crawled into Dusty's car and they moved the few blocks to the station. "There's some coffee and chili," said the detective as they walked in through the empty engine bay. "They were getting ready for a training session webinar."

"Was there some shooting?"

"They tried to distract us," replied Dusty referring to the murderers. "One of them had been trying to open the back door. The driver attempted to delay us so his partner could get back in the truck." He patted Darwin's shoulder. "We got them in custody. You were a big help. We hadn't been able to find them."

Dusty dished up some firehouse chili – in his mind nothing could beat it. In the meantime, the volunteers started to straggle in, laughing at the fun they had had, getting the hose lined out to clean and repack. The captain of the volunteers sat with Darwin and Dusty.

"We got a couple of my boys covering your windows and doors with plywood. We'll give you a report so your insurance will replace the glass." He helped himself to the chili. "We were glad for the distraction. Our webinar was not coming in. That damn hookup just wouldn't work."

Dusty looked at Darwin and raised an eyebrow. Darwin put down his spoon. "Maybe I can help."

And that's how Darwin found his new life as tech support for the Portage volunteer fire department and, subsequently, all the other volunteer departments in James County. He found himself a respected computer consultant among his peers. He vowed to himself that once his Internet scams started, he would only cheat people in other states.

CHAPTER TWENTY-FIVE

"**S**orry I missed dinner last night," said Dusty as he kissed Lynn on her toothpasty lips. "We got the two guys that killed the Mastersons. They went back to Portage to kill one more cousin." He yawned in her face.

"That's all right," Lynn said after rinsing her mouth. "I had a girls' pity party here." He raised an eyebrow. "Tee is ready to get us all back exercising. She says we start next Tuesday. Piper and Jasmine drank two bottles of wine in despair."

Dusty finished with the toothpaste. Swished, spit. "I'll send a note that I like you with love handles, so Tee can excuse you."

Lynn swatted him with a towel. "I'm not fat." She walked out of the bedroom.

In the kitchen she had the coffee going when Dusty ambled in. "I'm not hungry. I ate at the Portage fire station last night. I think I'm too old for their chili." He rubbed his stomach.

"Would you rather have tea?"

He glared at her. "I'm not that old!"

Lynn gave him an English muffin and a cup of coffee. As he spread butter on his muffin she asked, "What did your staff do about Polly's friend?"

"It all worked out." Chew. Sip. "Polly's friend is in the group home and being very cooperative. The other two kids' parents got jobs. The woman Piper knows is taking Internet classes as well. My staff came through." He grinned.

"What about your murders?"

"That seems to be working out, too." He was sure his stomach was feeling better just thinking about all the success. "We got the guys who killed the Mastersons. They told us the two Mastersons killed their friend, the guy we found in Verona, and they thought those people killed Nevada, too."

"Wow," Lynn trilled, "Not yet February and you've solved four murders and saved three kids!"

"Yeah," grouched Dusty, "And they think I need less money in my budget. The county manager said I was making the county so safe, why spend any more money."

~ ~ ~

Mars quietly listened to the conversation at the other desk. Tee was talking to a realtor. He knew she and Lonzo were looking for a larger place – adopting three kids with the stroke of a pen sort of filled up Glory's little cottage.

"How much will we have to put down?" she asked. Mars kept his eyes on his computer screen. "What else will the bank want us to do?" She shuffled some papers. "Yes, we'll try to get all that information together. It's just that it's the perfect place ... Yes, I understand." She ended the call and hung her head.

Mars waited a minute, then asked, "You all right?"

She looked at her friend. "We're trying to buy that house I told you about. There are so many hoops to get through for a loan. The realtor thinks the bank will want a bigger down payment," she shrugged, "even though we have two incomes. The realtor said we'd know something by the end of the week and then we go from there."

They worked quietly, Mars wondering how he could help his friends and Tee wondering what she had gotten herself into by adopting those three angels.

There was no going back. She and Lonzo loved them all.

~ ~ ~

Samson Teaberry, a young, black man, strutted into the detective's office. He had been a sheriff's deputy for almost a full year now and he had finally, FINALLY taken part in an exciting arrest. He had to drop by and visit his rookie instructor. "Detective," he nodded as he tried to appear cool and nonchalant. He took a seat beside her desk.

Teniquia laughed at her former student. "I know. You were in on that arrest."

"With shooting," he reminded her. "I was perfect." He had to bounce out of the chair and pace the room as he gave her a detailed report on the take down. "I blocked the alley and used my car like a shield. I even shot out a tire on their fancy truck."

She had already heard from another of her former students. This was a good day for the squad. Dusty had been unable to get Mars and Danny to assist when Darwin Masterson called for help. He had to rely on the deputies on patrol and they had performed as they had been trained. Of the three deputies responding, two had been on staff less than five years. The third deputy was a very experienced fellow. In Teniquia's opinion, it was just the right mix to help her trainees learn the correct way to respond in a dangerous situation. "Has your shift captain held the situation review?"

"No, ma'am," said Samson. "He says we'll do it tomorrow at roll call because he wanted to talk with Dusty first." He sat again. "You don't think we did stuff wrong and Dusty's mad?"

"I think Dusty wants to meet at roll call, too. He wants your shift to know what you fellows did right." Samson grinned. Teniquia smiled back at him, so happy that he was maturing into a well-trained professional in law enforcement. He had been doing his monthly rotation at Piper's school and was very successful in that phase of his training also. She was sorry that his grandmother, Nettie Teaberry, had died before knowing he succeeded.

"She knows," he said as though he read her mind. "I can feel her smiling at me."

They both were silent as they thought about the day Nettie Teaberry was found beaten and close to death at her small trailer. She had died several days later, still in a coma. Those days had been a trial for Samson, and Tee had worried that he would not successfully complete his training. But something had sparked in him and now he was on his way to a solid law enforcement future.

~ ~ ~

Mars walked into the bank, bypassing the tellers, the lines, the security guards and entering the restricted area. The tellers and guards all nodded. He walked into the office of Renfro Bartlett, regional VP of the First River Bend Bank, years ago known as Palmer Bank.

"Mr. Healey." The man jumped to his feet.

Mars wasn't certain how to flex his influential muscle. He had only consented to serve on the bank's board a few weeks ago because his uncle, Hutch Dunn, had badgered, cajoled, threatened and finally begged until Mars had agreed. His family had helped organize the original bank over a hundred years ago. They were still stockholders. Various mergers and buyouts had only increased the value of their holdings. Being one of the wealthiest men in town had not kept him from pursuing a career in law enforcement. It was the wealth he tried to ignore.

He took a seat and waited for Renfro to settle at his desk. "Thank you for accepting my offer for a brief orientation after your first board meeting. Do you want me to start with any particular operation or organization?"

"I want to learn about our lending operations." Mars had taken time to dress for the occasion wearing one of his designer suits and all the accessories that screamed wealth. He'd have to go home and change back into his regular clothes before he returned to the unit office.

"Loans?" Renfro gulped. "Do you need some funds? We have some very flexible rates and conditions for directors who need some financial support." He wanted to loosen his collar.

"I'm interested in loans we make to the public, things like home mortgages." Mars got comfortable in the visitor's chair. It was one of the tools he used in his interrogations.

Renfro sat up straighter. Was this new director interested in making more loans or in making money more difficult to obtain? He always walked a fine line when dealing with members of the bank board. "We are probably the only local lender in the county. Folks can go to other counties or find something online, but we are the home town bank."

"Is it difficult to get a loan?"

"We do have standards and there are banking regulations." The banker began to relax. This might just be a bland lesson in mortgage lending. "Over the years we have tried to help our citizens and customers find capital when needed. Of course, we protect our money. We look at income, neighborhood, background."

"What does neighborhood mean?" asked Mars as he adjusted his shirt cuff at his wrist.

"Let's just say there are some places that loaning money would just be throwing good money after bad."

"Those places?"

Renfro thought about his response. He didn't know Mr. Healey well enough to understand his political preferences. "We aren't eager to loan too much money in South End. We look at the people applying." Here he chuckled. "If one of our regular clients is borrowing money to buy rental property in South End, we usually oblige. But it is more difficult to lend money to an applicant investing in a personal home in South End."

"Why?"

"Mr. Healey, you're in law enforcement. You know we're talking about minorities here. People who might not be trustworthy or have no long term solid employment history." The banker was getting uncomfortable; he couldn't read this board member. The others were so transparent in their politics.

"You're telling me," began Mars, "that I could get a loan for rental property in South End, something on which I could potentially charge high rents-"

"And make money, a good return on your investment." Renfro wanted to make certain the man saw the plus side of being a slumlord.

"But if I wanted a home," Mars continued, "a good solid home for my family, maybe something near the elementary school, where there are some solid older homes. If I wanted something like that, I couldn't get a loan?"

"You could get a loan." Renfro did pull at his collar. There was an undercurrent he didn't understand. "Not everyone could get a loan."

"What would stop someone from getting a loan for a house as I've described?"

"Background, lack of income, social things."

"Social things?"

"Really, Mr. Healey, I know you haven't been active in our industry and in on all the historic discussions about loans and special populations–"

"Special populations?"

Renfro was disgusted with Mars' disingenuous attitude. "We look at race, of course. South End blacks and Latinos don't always pay as they should. We make the process difficult. Often they find another lender or finally just rent."

Mars sat in the chair, masking his fury as he brushed some lint off his expensive lapel. "I have two black friends who want to buy a house in South End near the elementary school. They have two solid incomes. My friend, Teniquia LaMont, just returned to work after taking a bullet on your behalf, protecting this community. Her husband, Lonzo Stonemill, an EMT, wouldn't care that you were white, or old, or pompous, if he were called here in a life-threatening situation. He would do his best to see that you arrived at the hospital in a condition that would encourage your survival." Mars stood. "When I return to my office I expect to hear that they have a loan approved with only a 10% down payment and at a very favorable interest rate like a board member might be offered, or better." He walked out of the office, nodded to the teller and the guards and got into his fancy sports car. He had to get home and change his clothes before he returned to the office.

CHAPTER TWENTY-SIX

Lynn stirred her cocoa as she sat in Yolanda's kitchen. One of the gift baskets Yolanda had received included some great cocoa packets. Lynn was focused on sampling the Dutch chocolate – marshmallow-hazelnut offering. It smelled heavenly. And Yolanda chose to serve it mixed in whole milk, not skim or water. Lynn tried to pay attention to the point her hostess was trying to make. What was it?

She sipped. "Where can I buy this?" she asked, knowing that was not the topic she had come to discuss.

"Look at the Marketeer," suggested Yolanda. "It has a lot of this kind of thing. But if you want this brand, it's a trip out of town to a Trader Joe's, either Asheville or Greenville."

Lynn had to consider whether she wanted this cocoa enough to drive down to South Carolina. She hated the traffic in Asheville. Back to business, she urged herself. "You don't have to award the money on this timeline you created," she advised her hostess.

"I want it done," moaned Yolanda. "It seems to be running my life. Besides, Mason has been helping me. I used his father's giving history as a guide. He kept a journal of his donations and made comments about how he thought the money was spent and if it met his expectations."

"A journal?"

"Mason said that was his way of doing business," replied Yolanda. "He said that Foster kept a work log, like a daily diary, in his business because field work in third world countries needed to be managed daily. He said you never trusted anything to get done if you didn't keep notes and remind everyone the next day what they promised to do."

"That sounds like dealing with Dusty sometimes," said Lynn as she licked her cocoa spoon. "So what did his diary say?"

Yolanda had made herself the milk chocolate-French cream-mint cocoa. Lynn was having second thoughts about her choice, the French cream mint aroma was so heavenly. Yolanda, always a good hostess, said, "Want a sip?" Lynn wiped her spoon on a napkin and collected a taste. "Want to trade?" asked the hostess.

"Can't I finish mine and then have another cup?" asked Lynn, never shy about heavenly treats.

"As long as you listen to my choices," said Yolanda. She took a sip of her cocoa and opened her notebook. "To start, Foster had given money to a lot of local groups and left notes about how he thought they met their mission and used his money. Most groups were reviewed favorably. You won't be surprised at the few that didn't measure up in his log, because they don't measure up in anyone's." Another sip. "He did have his favorites – those that serve children and those he thought were innovative. He was my guide, and drum roll," she riffed on the kitchen table, "here are my awards."

Lynn accepted the notebook and began to study the presentation. She finished her cocoa. Yolanda made her another using the milk chocolate variety and waited as Lynn worked through the report. "This is marvelous," grinned Lynn, the chocolate stain extending the curve of her smile. "You have spent five hundred thousand dollars, and made almost everyone in town happy."

The report gave a sizable donation to the Youth Center in South End to upgrade their computer and technology labs. The provocative grant was an incentive to the community college to hold training for parents of the youth members as a preliminary to qualifying for credited course work at the college. There would be additional funds for a second year if credited courses were added at the Youth Center for both parents and young adults in the community. The other large grant went to the financial management program that was proposed as a cooperative effort among several local agencies. Yolanda suggested that this be a three-year proposal with the money coming for each successive year as the program met its planned goals.

On the last page as the running total of all grants got closer to the actual funds available, Lynn saw that the final fifteen hundred dollars was assigned to Dusty and Piper for training. She laughed. "Did your son force you to make a grant to his boss?"

Yolanda said, "No, Piper did. She came into the bakery for her usual Thursday afternoon cookie buy and mentioned that little Moses had been so shy in school until he met Samson who had come to school for a week of his training. I don't think she connected me to the grant." Yolanda thought a moment. "In fact, I don't think she or Dusty knew anything, they just sent in the proposal using Piper's parent/teacher organization as the fiscal agent. I guess that was the only nonprofit they could think to use in the short time they had to respond."

"Pretty clever of them," concluded Lynn. "How do you want to handle this?"

"I'll drop this off to Robert first because he has to approve everything, then I'll need your guidance."

Lynn nodded and looked into her empty cup. If she

kept eating like this, she would have to start running again before the snow melted. Ah, but she had a date on Tuesday at the gym. Maybe she could have another half cup. "If Robert says okay, I'll prepare a letter for you. One will be to all who got no funding to say thanks but no money. And the other will be an individual letter to each agency with any comment or further instructions you're adding to the award. Once you sign everything, my office will write the checks and take care of the mailing. Would you like a press release?"

"Why? I don't have any more money. I'd be happy to disappear from the funding scene."

"How about a release that states that the following agencies received grant funds from the Foster Donovan funds at the Philanthropies?" Lynn asked. "It will highlight his generosity and his commitment to our community. I could include a little bio."

"That would be nice. He was so quiet but so generous. I told Mason I wish I had known him better because I would have given him a thousand kisses."

~ ~ ~

Mason's phone rang as he paced the living room with David. The baby had been crying all afternoon. Yolanda thought it was a tooth, or his ears, or gas. She was concentrating on cleaning up the grant paperwork littering her home. "Yeah?" he whispered into his phone because David had just calmed down. He listened, then shouted, "What do you mean arrested?"

David screamed. Mason shouted again, "Yeah, you hear a baby. Answer me." Yolanda rushed to take the screaming baby, but couldn't leave the room. Something was happening and she wanted to know what. Mason's face was bright red. His eyes were popping out of his head. Was he having a heart attack? He continued to shout, using several languages. Finally he took a breath and began to speak in a more coherent manner. "Okay, I'll wait to hear from you. ... Do anything you have to ... I can't leave here for a few days. Skeet is coming to visit. ... Yeah. ... Call me as soon as you can."

He ended the call and continued to pace the room. Finally, he turned to Yolanda. "Riva was arrested and accused of fomenting civil unrest. Sweetheart is on the job. He'll call me back."

"In South Africa?"

"Yes."

"Is she in danger?" All of a sudden international news became a reality to Yolanda. "Can Sweetheart help her?"

David had stopped crying watching Mason pace around the living room. Mason began speaking, "She always takes risks. Never weighs the consequences. Always thinks everyone will see her point of view." He turned to face Yolanda, tickled David's toes as he rested against his grandmother's chest. "She won't listen. I've argued for years. She laughs in my face. Do you know what she tells me?" Yolanda shook her head. "She says I need a little fire in my life. She says I need to charge into life like my parents." He paced again. "I don't know what she means." He turned back as though he expected David to answer. The baby giggled.

Yolanda took a deep breath. "She means you live on the surface. Maybe it's because you've moved so often, nothing has stuck, or ruffled you, or inspired you, or scared you."

"I'm scared now," he admitted. "Jail for a woman in any country is an ugly experience." As he spoke he paled and gripped the back of a chair.

"Are you all right?"

"I don't want to talk about it. I think I'll go back to my place and do some cleaning. I'll have to leave as soon as I entertain Skeet and help the girls with their first forum presentation."

Yolanda nodded. David seemed to be following the discussion. Mason's voice had taken on a somber tone. He kissed them both and left the house.

~ ~ ~

Lynn worked all afternoon, organizing the paperwork for Yolanda's grant awards. She had called Robert to make certain there would be no changes before she invested time in the process.

"It looks good to me," he growled into the phone. Lynn thought the snow better melt soon. Robert needed to golf. "I didn't think she'd pull it off so soon."

"She worked hard," acknowledged Lynn. "We met several times and she seems to have made awards that are coherent and to agencies in a manner that, in my opinion, will strengthen our nonprofit community."

"That's quite a statement," said Robert. "Why do you say that?"

Lynn replied, "She funded several cooperative programs. She set some performance standards that no one else ever thought of. Just look at her two big grants. The four or five agency initiatives to start that finance advisory project. If they succeed, the whole community will benefit. And that idea of hers to encourage the community college to move some classes to the Youth Center in South End. That's inspired."

She heard Robert huff into the phone as he seemed to think about her assessment. "You're right," he said, "she's taking some risks though. Some of these folks may fail, or not reach her expectations."

"That's the great part," laughed Lynn. "Challenging people usually makes them more successful than they thought possible. They'll be more creative and maybe deliver something even better than Yolanda expected. Win-win!"

"You're too optimistic for such a miserable day."

Lynn looked out her office window. It was sort of raining and all the dirty snow piles in the parking lot were looking disgusting. "It's another day closer to golf," she reminded Robert.

"That almost puts me in a better mood. Go ahead and give that damn money away."

~ ~

Mason got back to his father's house. Funny, he thought, I just can't think of this place as mine. Then he thought about some of the things Yolanda had said over the past few weeks. She called him a child of the world. She called him superficial. She had made millions of insulting comments on his dating habits. Damn, she challenged his whole life.

As he walked into the house, his phone rang. "Yeah." His caller ID told him it was Sweetheart.

"I got her out of jail."

"Is she OK?"

"Just a black eye."

Mason swore in three languages. "Where is she?"

"With me. She'll stay at my place until you get back."

"Let me talk to her." There was a shuffling and some whispering.

"Hello," came the bright, soft, enchanting voice that he enjoyed.

"What were you thinking?" he raged into the phone. "You're lucky I'm not there, I'd ... well, I wouldn't have given you a black eye. Are you all right?"

"Mason, I'm fine. Sweetheart has taken care of everything. We have security protecting the building until we find a new space. My children are being cared for by some people he found."

"What about you?"

"I can't go back to the building or see my staff." She

giggled. "So we're skyping with them. Sweetheart is being very helpful."

"I mean, are you hurt? Did they ... did they ..."

"Mason, I am fine. I took a few hits as they say, but no one did more than that. I was only in jail for three hours. Sweetheart got me out very quickly." The lilt in her voice began to calm him.

"Let me talk with him again." As Sweetheart took the phone Mason went into a language that they shared and Riva didn't speak. "Tell me the whole story."

Sweetheart went into some detail. "I bribed the jail committee. I have hired our security contractors to protect the orphanage from anyone coming on the grounds. I have hired a nursing team, made a donation to a convent to send staff. And I negotiated with the buyer to pay him by the week to rent his space until we find a new location. I estimate all this may cost—"

"I don't care," Mason yelled into the phone, "Just get it done. You have a good plan. If you can't find something suitable, start building. I want it to be a campus with several buildings. I want some staff housing and a small medical clinic."

"Maybe we should ask Riva what she wants," Sweetheart cautioned.

"No," replied Mason in a harsh warning. "She won't ask for enough."

He heard a hiss in the phone. Sweetheart finally said, "We are now in the orphanage business, I see."

"Damned straight."

Another silence, then, "Are you courting this woman?"

"What ever gave you that idea?"

"I'm gay, remember. I sometimes see what you straight men miss. You know, nuance -outrageous out of character behavior. Knighthood antics that suggest a deeper motive."

"She just needs help."

"Yeah. So do the whales and melting ice caps." Sweetheart chuckled. "You're acting different. More like the guy your dad wanted you to become. And you're acting like a guy who cares very much about this woman. Think about it."

"Let me talk to her." Mason hated being manipulated by his assistant.

Riva came back on the line. "Why did Sweetheart speak so I couldn't understand him? Are you ending your support?"

Mason growled into the phone. "No! We had to talk about some business and I didn't want to disturb you." He listened for a response and she said nothing. "Why do you think I wouldn't support you? I got you out of jail."

"Sweetheart got me out of jail."

"On my orders." Mason was miffed. "How could you think I wouldn't be concerned?"

"You always like to keep your distance from me and my orphans."

"Maybe I'm finished with keeping my distance." He heard a small gasp. Throwing away the last threads of caution and sanity, he said, "Maybe it's time to get closer to your orphans ... and to you."

She was very quiet and finally whispered, "I think I would like that."

Mason snorted. "Of course you would, you've been after my money for years, decades." He softened his voice, "And maybe I should have paid more attention to you."

Another small gasp. "Mason, are you courting me?" He heard a guffaw in the background.

"Tell Sweetheart he's fired. And tell him to call me tomorrow with an update."

"I love you, Mason," she whispered into the phone.

"Me, too." And the call ended.

CHAPTER TWENTY-SEVEN

"It's a wonder you bother to knock anymore," Yolanda said as she opened the door to let Mason enter the house. "You seem to be here a lot."

He smiled at her, kissed her on the cheek and walked in looking for something. He turned back and asked, "Where is he?"

She laughed. "The little angel is taking a nap. He was here very early this morning and wore himself out. He'll be getting up soon for lunch, I'm sure." She led Mason into the kitchen where she was preparing some chicken salad. "There's enough for you to join us." They heard the baby cry out.

"I'll get him," offered Mason as he dashed down the hallway.

Yolanda follow behind saying, "He'll need to be changed before we do anything else."

After a challenging time, trying to control Mason who kept distracting David, she finally got everyone back into the kitchen and settled for lunch. Mason had a great looking sandwich and hot coffee. David had some pieces of chicken, Cheerios and his sippy cup. Yolanda regretted not having an open bottle of wine available for herself. She studied her guest. "You've had an epiphany."

Mason choked on his food. "Are you a witch?" She just smiled and waited. "I've been thinking about my women in all those ports, and find that there is someone who means something to me, something more than an X-rated dinner." He sipped his coffee and helped David sample some chicken. The baby squealed as Mason played with his toes. "I've learned a lot on my visit here. It got me thinking. None of my regular women friends has ever given me as much pleasure as you and your family have. In fact, remember when you said that you wanted a relationship that was more than a dinner and maybe never meeting again?" She nodded. "There's a woman in South Africa. I see her often because I have offices there. We don't, well, we don't."

Yolanda nodded again. "The lady who got arrested – Reba, Riva?"

"You are a witch," he said with amusement. "Riva runs a nonprofit that takes care of orphans, as I told you. Every time I'm in my offices she appears. Like she has someone call her when I'm in town. She just seems to materialize and talks about her work and talks about the kids and suggests that my company build something or repair something or give her money for something."

They quietly watched the baby destroy his lunch. Yolanda cleaned him up and carried him to the living room where she and Mason could sit while David explored. "Do you give her what she needs?"

"I almost always do, " he replied, "and sometimes I take her to lunch because I enjoy the sound of her voice." He got a look on his face that she recognized as embarrassment. "In the past I've thought about seeing her more intimately, but she's mixed race and that's sometimes a challenge still, especially when a person is a portion of every race. And yet, when I think about the things I've enjoyed in River Bend, I think of her as someone I want to tell about my experiences."

"Don't you talk to your other women?"

"Very superficially," he shrugged, "weather, our travels, the dinner we just shared, our next dinner."

"Worldly banter," Yolanda named the script.

"Yeah, nothing meaningful." He helped David find a toy under a chair. "But when I talk with Riva, we talk for hours about everything. We argue, sometimes even agree and share ideas. She helps me see the world in different ways, through different eyes. Just like you and my pal here do." Yolanda grinned.

"Does that mean you're going back to redesign your relationship? Is race an issue with you?"

"It's not an issue. But I think the politics of it just kept us from exploring a relationship."

"You or her?" Yolanda smiled to herself. He was ready for a new way of life. He was finally catching on. His father would be proud.

"That's a good question. Both, I think. We're similar in age so we grew up with the old mindset. Things are different now." He stood and paced. "She's been arrested for trying to protect her orphanage from some developer. Evidently her landlord sold the property out from under her." Yolanda gasped. "Don't worry." Mason smiled to calm her. "I talked with Sweetheart and we have some temporary plans for her kids and he's out shopping for a piece of property. And of course, he bailed her out of jail."

Yolanda rushed over to hug him. "Now you're in the orphanage business."

David crawled over and began pulling on Mason's shoelaces. He picked up the baby. "I think I am. Thanks to my pal here, I can even be hands-on with the little folks she takes care of."

"Is that important to you?"

"It is. I've been thinking a lot. When I told you we weren't finished, I think I misunderstood what I wanted from you."

"What you needed from me," she identified more eloquently. "You came here and found family and babies and life. You never realized how much you wanted all of it." He opened his mouth to speak, but she held up her hand. "You found a small town life, and I think you now know how you can have that caring type of life in South Africa with a woman who may be different than your average American girl, but you're different, too. I've told you before, you were raised a child of the world. I've heard you speak Chinese with Mr. Lee. I've seen you work with Tee and Jasmine and you are colorblind – a middle aged white man working to help put on a black history presentation and suggesting recipes to a Chinese cook."

"Does that mean we're finished here?" he asked with a smile.

"I think we are," she replied, "you've found what you're looking for, even if you didn't know it was missing in your life. Maybe that's what your father was praying for all these years when he sat in church." She cupped his face in her hands and gave him a gentle kiss. The baby babbled.

~ ~ ~

Late Saturday afternoon found Ricky Mitchell pacing in his bedroom. This was the night of his almost date with Polly. They were all going over to Ms. Power's for pizza and games while the adults talked and stuff. He couldn't believe it. The kids would be alone in the living room. He laughed at himself. Alone to do what? He knew he didn't have the nerve to do anything, even if he knew what to do. Besides there was Jeff who was only planning on playing games. Ricky paced some more.

His mother was dropping him off at Jeff's where he would spend the night. She called, "It's time to leave, honey, or you'll be late for dinner." Ricky wasn't hungry, but he dashed to the car.

Once at Jeff's he gathered his things from the car – several graphic novels, a few video cartridges, a couple of movie CDs – and hoped he had remembered to throw in some pajamas and clothes for tomorrow.

The boys ran to Jeff's bedroom, looked over all of Ricky's stuff and returned to the kitchen for a snack before it was time for dinner at Lynn's. Janet was bringing Polly and planned to spend the evening with the adults talking about whatever.

The plan worked just as Ricky expected. Janet and Polly arrived. Dinner was served. Janet ate a lot. The adults talked. The kids helped clean a little then moved to the game console in the living room. And Jeff was correct – Polly was good competition. They played for a while. Then Jeff broke the spell by talking. Ricky would have been just as happy to sit on the sofa with Polly between them and not be challenged to be sociable.

But he couldn't control Jeff, who asked, "Why'd the police pull you out of class? It was all over school last week."

Polly was silent for a few minutes. After wrestling with herself she decided to be honest. These guys were okay to hang out with. "Mars heard that some people saw that dead guy in town. They looked at security tapes and saw some kids walking through the parking lot behind the bakery and near the bank. I was one of the kids. The police wanted to know if we all saw him talking to anyone or doing anything."

"Wow," Jeff replied, "did you?"

"Not me." Polly killed a few more images on the screen. "Some of the kids talked to the guy. They got more questions." She looked toward the kitchen. In a lower voice she said, "Janet heard about it, 'cause Mr. McElvoy had to tell the parents, and she lost it. She didn't eat all afternoon until Lynn explained stuff."

"Wow," both boys gasped.

"Janet wasn't happy about me hanging with those

kids."

"Neither were we," offered Jeff. "They're losers."

"No," Polly defended the kids, "they all have family problems. I heard Lynn tell Janet that Dusty and his team helped some of the kids, or helped their parents or something." She hung her head. "I have to find new friends according to Janet and I have to go to a group counseling thing at Hospice." With that admission she killed a few more screen images.

Ricky wanted to tell her that he would be her friend. But Jeff was quicker. "We can be your friends."

She looked at both boys. "You already are." She almost smiled. "I think Janet wants me to get back with my old friends from before. I'm thinking about it."

With that confession Jeff took control of the conversation by dissecting students at school and making recommendations from his perspective as to who would please Janet. Ricky sat quietly wondering if she would speak to him at school and wondered if he should ask. But Jeff suggested a movie and the moment was gone. But not the urge to strangle Jeff.

CHAPTER TWENTY-EIGHT

Mason was ready for Super Bowl Sunday. He had been one of the seven people who had selected the two finalist teams on Play-off Sunday. Today he would see if he was one of the big winners. They were all going to a mansion to see the game. "Who is our host?" he asked Yolanda as they drove into the Dancing Creek neighborhood to a beautifully restored mansion.

"Nathan Taft," she reminded him. "He was at Lynn's for the play-offs. He's one of the finalists like you. And he's so excited that he volunteered to host the party. I think this will be a bigger crowd. Danny will be there."

"And David?"

"He's with his other grandparents." She directed him to the parking area already crowded with cars and SUVs. Nathan, always the perfect host, had rented extra TV's to spread around the party rooms – and enough food in every TV room to feed the excited mob.

Lynn caught sight of them. "Hi," she gave Yolanda a hug. "I haven't seen this many people here since Buck's wedding." She moved on.

Will said, "Hey, Mason, come help." Will was hanging the names of the seven finalists on a portable easel in the big living room. "You might go home with some cash." The two men hung the papers, secured the easel in an out of the way corner and went to find the beer. The rest of the day was as it should be – food, games, joy and disappointment.

"I really enjoyed myself," Mason said as he made his way to Yolanda's front door. He held on to her tightly because he was very drunk. "Those are great people. They didn't care that I was from out of town."

"Why should they?" Yolanda was holding him up. "I think you should spend the night."

Mason grinned at her. "I was wondering if I would ever wear you down." He sort of leaned on the house.

"You're too drunk to drive up that mountain to your place." She pushed him into the house and locked the door. Before she could turn out the lights, he had disappeared into the guest room. She ran to check on him. He was sprawled across the bed, still dressed. She slipped off his shoes and threw a comforter over him. Mason had another American adventure checked off his list. She wondered of he would remember Super Bowl Sunday.

CHAPTER TWENTY-NINE

Mars walked into the office on the Monday after Nathan's Super Bowl Party carrying a small bundle of food. Danny followed right behind with his own bundle of food. "Any of those wings?" asked Dusty. He had been surprised to walk into an empty office this morning and now he knew why.

"How did you know it was Nathan's food?" asked Danny.

Dusty waved his phone. "Nathan texted me, asking if we needed any more."

"Buck brought this when we ran," explained Mars. He, Buck and Danny ran through River Bend every morning before work. Buck, Nathan's nephew, bragged that he was the fittest executive in town. "He said there was so much food they were packing up a lot for the Hunger Alliance soup kitchen, but he knew we would appreciate a few things."

"Damn straight," agreed Dusty as he read Cook's inventory on the outside of each package. He opened the one labeled 'Breads, Cookies and Cakes.'

"What smells so good?" asked Teniquia as she floated into the office. Mars hadn't seen her since his visit to the bank. She reached around Dusty and rescued a chunk of peanut butter cheesecake. "I'll make some fresh coffee." She bustled over to their small break area and had the coffee dripping in seconds. Returning to her desk and her prized piece of cheesecake, she smiled at her friends. "We got the house!"

The men all made comments and each gave her a

hug. "When did this happen?" Mars was curious.

Tee shook her head. "It was weird. One minute the bank was throwing up these roadblocks and the next our realtor was setting a closing date." Dusty and Danny glanced at Mars. He stared back and dared them to speak. Tee continued, "The realtor called Friday before I left for work. That's why I didn't come in. She wanted us to move fast in case they changed their mind. Our closing is in three weeks." She grinned and hugged her friends again.

"Where did we get all this food?" she asked after she sampled her cheesecake. And the guys told her about Nathan's Super Bowl party. After more food sampling and then cleaning up the mess and putting the rest of the food away for lunch, she said, "I think I'll delay my gym class for a few more weeks. I'm going to be so busy with this house." She attacked her computer, composing an email.

Dusty thought that every woman in her class would be grateful, and then he wondered if he could wait until lunch to sample those wings.

~ ~ ~

Mason couldn't open his eyes. His mouth was full of cotton. Then he remembered. That damn Will Zubov. He said winners had to drink a shot for every touchdown scored. And Mason had been one of the winners of Super Bowl Sunday. He didn't even know anything about the teams! He sat up then flopped back. Wait a minute, he thought, those guys didn't make anyone else do shots. There had been three winners. Mason, beautiful Marianna and a young kid named Jeff. Mason nodded to himself. He was the only winner that Will could intimidate with impunity. His lips went dry just thinking about "intimidate with impunity." No one would badger the beautiful Marianna into doing shots. Mason had recognized her from all her old TV appearances. Even though she said that had been thirty years ago, she didn't understand how behind third world TV was. She was a big star in some obscure parts of Asia.

And that Jeff kid, his mother, that tiny woman, would have killed Will. Wait, Mason was confused. Weren't they married? He sat up again, slowly. He was still in his clothes from yesterday. He looked around the room. Then he heard a baby squeal. He was at Yolanda's!

Mason pulled himself together, stopped in the bathroom to comb his hair and squint at his reflection. He hoped he hadn't been rude or insulting or something to Yolanda last night. He shuffled toward the kitchen ready to face the music. And he winced, because David was beating a rhythm on his highchair with a wooden spoon.

David squealed a greeting as he walked into the room. "Hey, buddy." Mason could always find a smile for his best friend. He flopped into a chair. Yolanda placed a glass of water and two aspirin in front of him. And she tried not to laugh. That relaxed him. Her attitude suggested that he had been drunk and pitiful but not rude and insulting.

"It's almost noon," she remarked. "Are you able to eat anything?"

He took the medicine and stared at her. "I can't possibly eat another thing."

"Nathan always has a lot of food." It was an understatement. Nathan Taft had Googled Super Bowl Party snacks and provided every recipe he found – three kinds of chili, deep fried appetizers of every kind, an endless variety of chips, dips and salsas, hot wings, honey wings and sesame wings. And the alcohol! Mason wondered how many guests had just collapsed at the mansion and were probably being thrown out this morning.

"And you were so generous with your winnings." She massaged the back of his neck. She was certain his head was pounding.

"I was?" He hadn't been this hung over since college.

"Don't you remember?" She grinned at his discomfort. "You gave your share to Jeff and told him to take a girl on a date. I couldn't hear what else you told him, but his face turned so red I thought it would explode." She put David on the floor and the little scamp bustled to Mason's side and pulled himself up, grinning in triumph.

Mason lifted him onto his lap and spoke to him in Italian. David squealed and Yolanda said, "I understood that. And, no, I won't put you out of your misery. But I will heat you some chicken soup."

"That sounds good," replied Mason, surprised that it did sound good and comforting. "I can't believe all the food last night. American food is sure different than when I was in college. Then I think it was just pizza, burgers and fries."

"You're probably right," she said as she began heating the soup. "Nathan can also put on a very sophisticated spread – pate, shrimp, wines. He has a flare."

"I didn't embarrass you or myself, did I?"

Yolanda laughed. "You were a perfect guest. Don't worry, Piper got so mad at Will–"

The doorbell rang.

She ushered Will into the kitchen. Mason hung his head. Will laughed. "I'm sorry. My wife is so mad at me. She thought I probably killed you." Will pulled up a chair and sat at the kitchen table. Yolanda put a bowl of soup in front of him. "But you have to blame Dusty, too," continued Will. "He said we had to get even with someone because all season everyone won the pool but us."

"What are you talking about?" Mason thought he needed two more aspirin.

Yolanda explained. "There was a football pool going on this fall and everyone won at least once except Will and Dusty." She shrugged. "I think even Dusty's mother won once. So here you come to town and don't know much about football and you win the Super Bowl!"

"I think it was too much for Dusty," admitted Will.

"But you were the one giving me all those shots," Mason pointed out.

"Yeah, but I had to do something to boost Dusty's morale."

"That doesn't make any sense," said Mason.

Will looked sheepish. "I guess I needed a morale boost, too. And now I have to please my wife who thinks you suffered unfairly."

"Bless her," said Mason as he sipped his soup.

~ ~ ~

The day after the first Hospice group meeting, Polly had been sitting at an empty lunch table in the school cafeteria, staring at her lunch. Tyler, the senior from the hospice group, walked up with his tray of food. "You saving this table?" Polly shook her head and he sat down. Neither youngster spoke. The next day he had returned to her table and they were joined by the other two kids from the group. They all ate in silence. By Friday they had become an established lunch table group. Tyler, the oldest said, "I have to go to that therapy because my dad died of cancer." He looked around the table.

Kaitlin said, "My brother died in the army fighting in some strange place I never heard of."

"My mother had a heart attack. No one knew she

was sick." Carson hung his head to hide the tears. Then the three youngsters stared at Polly. They waited.

She finally said, "My mother was murdered by my father. Then somebody murdered him."

They all gasped. "If this was a contest," said Tyler, "you would win." No one knew whether to laugh or cry.

"You can all read about it. It was in the papers and everything," explained Polly. "It happened just before Thanksgiving."

"That big explosion?" asked Carson. "That was in my grandmother's neighborhood." Polly nodded. Everyone thought about her situation.

Polly decided to ramp up her winning streak. "Now I don't have either parent," she looked at the boys, "or siblings," she looked at Kaitlin, "or grandparents or aunts and uncles, or anyone else you all have."

"You're an orphan?" asked Tyler.

"Yes."

"You live in that burned out house near my grandmother all by yourself?" Tyler swatted Carson on the back of the head.

"No," said Polly, "I have guardians and some people want to adopt me and friends of my mother's keep checking on me."

"Where do you live?"

"I live with the Bergmans, you know, the old sheriff. Their daughter and her husband want to adopt me."

"So you're not alone," stated Kaitlin, as she started to think about some of the things Fran had said, and things her brother had said before he left home. "Your mother left people behind to take care of you."

"Well, I guess," admitted Polly, "but I'm still alone."

"You're as alone as the rest of us," said Tyler. "We lost someone but we have other people who care about us." He had been thinking about things Fran had said, too.

Fran was delighted with the second meeting of her teen group. It seemed that they were bonding at school, according to the assistant principal. She didn't ask questions but she listened. They were becoming more familiar with one another, sometimes even teasing and joking – little insider comments that she didn't get, but they understood.

CHAPTER THIRTY

Mars and Danny hadn't gotten much out of the two guys who murdered Char and Lester. The guys showed their experience with law enforcement and demanded an attorney before answering any questions. Once the attorneys saw the security videos of the executions, they recommended cooperation.

As law enforcement officers had surrounded the men in Portage, Gilly had managed to text a prearranged code to Angelo. Two days after the shootout when Dusty, accompanied by Dundee and his support staff, got to the residential address for the Pontelli family, nobody was home. The place was stripped and there was no forwarding address. Dusty had been pissed.

Exploiting all the resources available when tracking a criminal only proved to Dusty that he was dealing with a well-organized operation, probably working in several states. And he couldn't find Angelo Pontelli anywhere. Damn.

Four days later he got a call from Dundee. "That tire place is back in operation."

"I'll meet you for lunch," replied Dusty and he took off for Asheville.

They arrived at the tire yard and saw the same three workers pulling and stacking tires. "Where's the boss?" asked Dundee. One of the men nodded toward the office building. Inside the officers met a young man talking on a phone.

He ended the call and asked, "May I help you?"

"We want to see Pontelli," replied Dundee as he and Dusty both showed their badges and ID.

"He quit. I'm Bart Ralston."

"Where can we find him?"

"I don't know. I answered an ad on the Internet and I got hired yesterday." Bart gave them a tentative smile. "I'm sorry. I really need this job and I don't want any trouble with you or with that guy Pontelli if he's in trouble with you."

Dusty and Dundee asked a few more questions, but Ralston seemed to have no information. They walked through the yard and asked those men some questions. Again they did not receive informative answers. Back in the car Dusty said, "This is an interesting place. I wonder where we can find the corporate offices?"

"I bet it's going to be a mare's nest of entanglements," guessed Dundee. "I'll keep an eye on this place. They gotta be up to something."

Dusty agreed. "They really moved Pontelli fast. If you learn anything about this place copy my office and keep me informed if anything happens in the future."

All the way down the highway back to River Bend Dusty rehashed the case in his head. The boss of the operation had disappeared. And in Dusty's opinion, Pontelli was more some middle manager than a boss. He was probably already resettled somewhere with a new identity, along with his family. He had arrested two killers, and also solved the murders of Nevada and Homer Gibson. They had been victims of the dead Mastersons. Pontelli's two guys were on video with the murder of the Mastersons. So it was a case all wrapped up. But a bigger fish had gotten away.

Maybe Dundee would come up with something more ... sometime in the future. He took consolation in the fact that he and his staff had solved four murders – all related to one another. And, as Lynn had reminded him, helped three kids.

~ ~ ~

Mars had listened to Danny talk about Yolanda's

granting adventure. The mice were just part of the story. There was the tale of Yolanda caught in the bakery by Rory and Salley almost demanding money from her funds. He laughed at that story and at the idea of Umberto chasing all of them out of the bakery unless they were buying something.

It was no secret in town now that the bank had sent out a press release announcing his appointment to the bank board. People could read between the lines. Mars would be taking over some responsibilities from his Uncle Hutch. Responding to fundraising requests was one responsibility Uncle Hutch was happy to relinquish. Or as he had stated, "Let you be the bad guy from now on."

Mars frowned. Was that going to be his life from now on? People stopping him to troll for donations? And what if he missed a good new idea and kept supporting something whose time had passed? Maybe he should talk with Uncle Hutch or Lynn about how to give away money. He wanted it to be at arm's length. He had invited Lynn to lunch at the diner today to begin exploring and defining his new role as community donor.

He walked into the diner and saw her speaking with that woman Starr whom they had arrested several months ago. Her mother was now on trial for murder and, if Mars was hearing good gossip, she was getting to know her father, the Reverend Graves, preacher on weekends and breakfast cook here at the diner during the week.

"Lynn," Mars nodded in greeting.

"Mars," she smiled, "you remember Starr?"

"Yes, ma'am," he replied, then to the waitress he said, "I hope you're doing well. I was sorry to hear of your grandmother's passing."

Starr acknowledged his comment. "Thank you,

detective. I guess you can't say anything positive about my mother." Mars frowned because she was correct. She smiled at him. "But you can ask after my father."

Mars smiled back. "I hope he's doing well."

"I was just telling Miss Lynn here that his church is a marvel. And so loving. They make me sorry that I waited so long to join them." She turned to Lynn, "As I was saying Daddy is purchasing some property to have what he calls growing space for his congregation." Mars held in a secret smile as he recalled the bank board meeting where he almost demanded that the Reverend Graves be given the loan and preferential treatment as a bank customer. What chaos! What fun!

"It's growing that fast?" asked Lynn.

"Not that fast," explained Starr. "His idea is that we can use the property to have gardens and grow vegetables until we're big enough to need a new church." Mars and Lynn smiled at her. "What can I get you? I still got a job here." They knew the menu so well, they ordered their favorites and Starr bustled to the next table.

"Why are you buying me lunch today?" Lynn asked Mars after Starr moved on.

Mars straightened the napkin holder and ketchup bottle and brushed some imaginary crumbs from the Formica tabletop. "I'm taking over some of Uncle Hutch's responsibilities. I think he's going to give me control of giving away our money."

"Maybe you should be talking with Yolanda. She learned some lessons about giving money away." Lynn studied the young man. He had so much to offer yet he seemed shackled by his sadness.

Mars blew out his breath. "I've heard about her adventures from Danny. So here are my thoughts. I want to understand a bit more about that criteria you helped her work out. I want to stay at arm's length. I don't want people stopping me on the street angling for a donation. How does Nathan keep people at bay?"

Lynn thought his concerns were valid. "My advice is to decline service on any nonprofit board. They'll expect big donations once you join the board. Nathan keeps everyone at arms length by requiring that all requests for donations be submitted through the Philanthropies office."

"Really?" Mars gasped, hearing something useful. "I thought he walked around town with his checkbook in his pocket."

"Nathan is a good businessman and expects a businesslike process from any agency wanting his money. Let me explain." Starr returned to the table with their food. Once served, Lynn began again, "Nathan has taken advantage of the Philanthropies grant forms and also of our knowledge of local agencies and their organization and program success. He has time to give thoughtful consideration to each request."

"I don't," Mars shrugged. "He's given Buck responsibility for Taft Manufacturing. I have a day job."

"You might consider creating a family foundation or just a donor advised fund at the Philanthropies," suggested Lynn, "and select some folks to be an advisory board to help review grants, maybe quarterly or every six months."

"What kind of advisors?"

"Why not start with you and your uncle and his daughter, the judge?" suggested Lynn. "The three of you know a lot about what goes on in town. That way your uncle will still be involved but with reduced responsibilities. Your fund can invite requests at set times. The three of you could meet for dinner and discuss the requests. You could send out invites for specific types of projects each quarter such as funding programs that serve children in the first quarter, programs that serve homeless in the second." Lynn smiled at him. "It's your money. How much you give away and when is up to you."

They ate for a while as Mars thought about her ideas. "You've given me a place to start. I'll talk to Uncle Hutch. This sounds like a way to work on making this donation stuff easy for the three of us. I think the judge will agree if it means she doesn't have all the responsibility."

Lynn laughed. "I know judging and fishing demand her time. Let me know how I can help."

They talked more as they finished lunch. "Thanks for your help," said Mars as he pulled out her chair and she stood.

"Any time." They waved to Starr and left the diner.

~ ~ ~

It was interesting working at the bakery. Polly was learning a lot about folks and their sugar addictions. She laughed to herself, Dusty was there every Wednesday afternoon for his share of the broken pieces of biscotti. Talk about an addiction. No one touched the pile of pieces until he had his fix. And Lynn, she was always ordering sweets for some meeting or social function and always managed to sample something from the box as she left the store. And that tiny principal, she came in every Thursday evening for three-dozen cookies because each week she picked one of the classes in her school as the "winner" and she gave them cookies as a treat. Polly could never figure out what made them a winner, but Piper always had some screwy reason.

And everyone gave her a hug when they came in, even Dusty. Umberto must not have told anyone about finding her in the alley with those kids. Tim had told her that everyone was concerned about her and would take care of her. She couldn't figure that out either. They didn't have to be kind, and she had a feeling they weren't pretending. They liked her. She knew they had liked her mom.

Even those boys, Ricky and Jeff, came by the bakery. Sometimes they said it was because Janet sent them to walk her home. As they walked they complained about never getting old enough to get a driver's license, or something. They made her laugh.

But her favorite times were when Teniquia and Lonzo brought the kids in for cookies. They always came after school on days when Lonzo wasn't working. The kids sat at the bar by the window and ate a cookie and drank milk. They always smiled at her and little Moses hugged her sometimes. What a difference from their days in the hospital when they didn't even talk. Maybe that was what Mars meant when he said "we take care of our kids." He had told her that at Thanksgiving when she wondered what would happen to her. When those little kids were in the bakery, everyone smiled at them and congratulated Tee and Lonzo on their beautiful family. They weren't orphans any more.

That got Polly thinking about her status. Tim was on the carrier and he sent her texts and photos all the time. He reminded her to keep an eye on Janet. At first she thought he was being silly, but a few weeks with Janet and she understood. Who could get out of a car and leave the engine running? Janet! Who could leave a teakettle on the stove until the bottom burned? Boy, did that make Thel angry! So these days she kept an extra eye on Janet and remembered her own mother saying that moms had eyes in the back of their heads. A few weeks with Janet and Polly was wishing she had those extra eyes.

Hmm, thought Polly, maybe it's time to think about what the Hospice lady said about attitude and happiness.

CHAPTER THIRTY-ONE

Dusty drove into the old farmyard. He had been invited this time. Granny Masterson had called and asked him to visit. It was February and the trees were suggesting they might consider blooming soon. He noticed a few crocus grinning at him from under the porch.

The old woman came to the door and walked out onto the porch as he climbed from his car. She waited until he stood at the porch step and nodded, indicating that she wanted him to enter the house. She turned and walked in, holding the door for him. He noticed there were two cups at the table and the smell of coffee. The mid-morning sun was throwing welcoming light around the kitchen. It was a very pleasant scene. Dusty was taken aback – not the image he had of a Masterson home – warmth and fragrant coffee.

"Thank you for coming, law man."

He was back at OK Corral, but with sunshine and crocus. "My pleasure, ma'am."

She indicated that he take a sat. Once he did she poured coffee, offered him cream and sugar, poured herself a cup and sat down at the table. There was a small dish of Oreos that she slid across the table toward him. He took one. "My kin killed that Utley boy." She made her statement and was silent.

"Yes, ma'am," replied Dusty. More silence.

"Thank you for looking out for my grandson." She held onto her cup, staring into its depths.

"He was in danger." Dusty thought for a moment. "He didn't know the Utley boy was attacked." The detective wasn't certain what Darwin knew, but he sensed that the old woman needed to think he was an innocent bystander. "He's been helping the fire department with their computers."

"He's a good boy," she replied and sipped her coffee. Dusty ate his cookie and sipped his coffee. The sunshine danced around the room. "He's my only grandchild, now."

"He'll look out for you," said Dusty.

"They shouldn't a killed Adele's boy." The old woman was silent again. "They suffered for their sins. Life always balances."

"Yes, ma'am," replied Dusty. "Life balances. Since you take care of your kin, that boy will take care of you."

"Even with all my sins?"

She was a sad woman, a lonely woman, Dusty realized. "Ma'am, everyone sins and everyone finds forgiveness. Isn't that what they said at the funeral? You always looked out for your family. They will take care of you."

She stood. "Thank you for coming by. Thank you for looking out for my boy."

He stood. "Yes, ma'am."

~ ~ ~

Once word got out that Skeet Turnbull, the well-known black mayor, would be the featured speaker at the kick-off of the Black History series, tickets were in demand, the community college offered a larger venue, at no charge, and reservations came from throughout western North Carolina.

Mason had helped the young women organize the evening's presentation to share local history as part of the introduction to Skeet's speech. They had invested their funds in well-placed advertising. In addition, they had listened to Mason's advice and also invested in quality methods to preserve the tapes and old photos.

Nathan Taft had offered a room at the historic Taft Manor, now a respected regional museum, as the home for the collection.

The plan came together. The forum was a success. Tee and Jasmine were on an emotional high. Or as Lonzo remarked, "One more smile and I'll be holding your ankles like you're some helium balloons."

And now it was time for fun. Skeet had brought his sax, but not his son. Jasmine was relieved. She was sort of dating Samson Teaberry and didn't know if the mayor had expected her to take an interest in his son.

A select audience assembled at Yolanda's place. Bertram arrived with his wife, Ling, the lovely Chinese woman he had married twenty years ago, and their two children, nineteen-year-old twins, Archie and Jin. Johnny, the young guitarist, arrived with his mother and father and a quiet uncle. Lynn and Dusty arrived as Piper, Will, Jim and Marianna snuck in behind, trying not to be noticed. Yolanda had made certain to invite her in-laws. Danny brought his wife and Mars and Mr. Taft. Tee and Lonzo came with Jasmine and Glory. Lonzo's mother baby-sat the kids. The only missing link – the Jesuits had called Father Ed back to work.

Yolanda had given a lot of thought to arranging instruments. The piano was already in the living room. She brought the drums up from the basement. She pushed the sofa and chairs against the wall, got rid of all tables, lamps and other stuff, leaving only two floor lamps, creating a great atmosphere. That gave her an idea. She borrowed a few card tables and chairs and set up the living room as a small jazz club, with, she hoped, enough seating for everyone.

Once the atmosphere was in place she sent out requests for food and drink. Everyone came with enough food for an army. Her mother-in-law brought a great antipasto and freshly baked bread and pizza. Johnny's mother brought two flan. Umberto delivered an array of bakery goods while Nathan brought along appetizers prepared by his cook. Dusty and Will came loaded with beer and soft drinks.

Skeet looked around the room and shouted, "Can everyone say diversity?" as he looked into the faces of River Bend's multi-cultural community. And the music began.

CHAPTER THIRTY-TWO

Mason had been staying with Yolanda since the Super Bowl. His house was being readied to go on the market in the spring. Since she had the space, Skeet was a houseguest, too, for his River Bend stay. They were sitting in her kitchen fighting over the last piece of flan and the few rolls and cookies that remained from last night.

"You got something going with this lady?" Skeet asked, hoping to divert Mason's attention from the flan. "She has a lot going for her. Great looks, great family. Great voice."

Mason let him take the flan. "She and I have an understanding." Skeet almost spit out his coffee. Mason glowered at him. "She was a friend of Pop's. She helped me settle his estate and she," he sighed, "she helped me think about my life."

"Think about your life?" It was too early for Skeet to do philosophy. "You're a hedonist. What's to think?"

"Friendships, family, loving." Mason went to the refrigerator to get the butter.

"Now you're scaring me, man."

Mason sat back at the table, pensive, organizing his thoughts. "If I can make you understand," he told his old friend, "maybe I'll understand it better." Skeet poured them both more coffee and settled down to listen as Mason continued, "When I came here I was the guy you knew. But this lady welcomed me into her family, shared her life, shared her heart and helped me see another way to lead my life. It didn't happen overnight. And I tried every way I could to get into her bed." He buttered a roll.

"I think she's just lucky her son wears a gun."

Mason laughed. "Yeah, you should have seen him when he caught us kissing behind the high school gym."

Skeet choked on a bite of flan, laughing at that image. "Really, the high school gym? What are you, fifteen?"

"You had to be there," replied Mason. "Then I met her grandson and everyone else in this storybook town—"

"Storybook?" challenged Skeet. "I heard about the dead mice and the murders."

"Storybook, as in the small town America idea of family and friends and service to the community." Mason thought as he chewed. "Let me tell you a story to illustrate small town, big heart kind of stuff." He lowered his voice. "This goes no further. It's confidential."

"Small town confidential," grinned Skeet. "I like it already."

"Not that kind of confidential," explained Mason. "Yolanda, who has relatives everywhere, has a cousin who is the secretary to the bank board of directors. That guy Mars, the detective."

"You mean that male model quality detective?"

"Yeah, him. He's real rich and sits on the bank board to represent his family interests. They had a meeting last week and the bank approved a loan to that other detective, Teniquia and her husband, at conditions usually only available to bank board members."

"The male model?"

Mason nodded. "Yeah, he was responsible. Then he brow beat the old white guy board to give a loan and small business banking privileges to a small black church. You can't say anything, but the cousin told Yolanda because Mars is a friend of her son's."

"Damn," grinned Skeet. "He was so quiet last night. I woudda never guessed he had that kind of heart."

Mason nodded. "That's the kind of stuff I learned here. Then when Sweetheart called to tell me Riva Biyela was tossed in jail and I talked about her with Yolanda, Yolanda knew before I did that I had to go help out. She also knew before I did that maybe Riva is someone I should have a relationship with."

"The orphanage lady?"

Mason nodded again. "South Africa's changing. Maybe they're ready for me and a mixed race lady to be together without too many eyebrows going to the heavens."

"Good for you," said Skeet, in a serious tone Mason had never heard. "Foster used to worry about you."

"How do you know?"

"We talked from time to time, once he retired here," confessed Skeet. "He wanted you to find the joy he and your mother found in sharing their lives with others, through charity and caring about friends. All those things you seem to have found here."

"Yolanda says Pop prayed for me to find something."

"He did. And you have." Skeet spoke in a solemn voice.

They stopped talking as Yolanda walked into the kitchen from the garage. David was in her arms. He squealed at the sight of Mason. The man jumped to his feet. "Hey, pal," he greeted the baby as he took the little bundle from Yolanda's arms.

As Mason spoke to the baby in Italian, Skeet watched the exchange and understood what Mason had been trying to explain. Mason found his heart in River Bend.

Yolanda broke into his thoughts. "Danny got the car gassed. If you guys want to make that plane you're going to have to leave for Charlotte by ten." They all looked at the little teapot clock on the wall. Only two more hours.

And what a hectic two hours – everyone stopped by to thank Skeet and Mason.

In the end, Mason and Yolanda stood on the driveway. "This isn't over," he whispered as he hugged her. "You're coming to South Africa to meet Riva and bring all the news from this crazy place."

They hugged. She cried. And they were gone.

~ ~ ~

Polly had joined those boys to play video games. It was kind of fun. Janet seemed to enjoy taking her to Lynn's house and eating all the food that always seemed to appear.

And she had some new friends, those Hospice kids. They were eating lunch together regularly. Maybe she could join the practice for the lacrosse team? She smiled to herself. What was happening to her attitude? It had made things interesting for a while, but was it still necessary? She was sitting on her bed sketching. As usual, as she thought about life, she drew her mother.

"What do you think, Mom?" she asked the sketch, "Am I figuring things out?"

The sketch gave her a conspiratorial grin. "Yeah, you like me to solve my own problems." The next sketch was an outright grin. "I know, you always said you wanted me to think for myself. It still hurts without you, though."

Susan's loving smile looked out from the paper. "I'm working on being better. I hang out with some new kids." Susan's new face sort of scowled. "I know. I'm more selective. You would like these kids. We all met at a grief counseling group." Another new face gave her a sidelong look. "You caught me. Even though I tell you things are fine, I still need help. And I play video games with some guys." Susan's face looked surprised, her eyebrows raised. "Not weird guys. Remember that Ricky kid who helped me at the library? And Jeff, his friend. They walk me home from my job."

Susan's next face looked surprised. "I didn't tell you about my job? I work at the bakery after school." Susan's face licked its lips. Polly laughed. "I know. I want to gobble up everything. Those boys walk me home or Mars gets me if Janet promises him dinner." Polly looked at the loving faces of her mother as they spread across the sketchpad. "Yeah, I'm getting along, but I still miss you." A tear appeared in Susan's loving face. Polly placed the sketches on a pillow and rested on her side reviewing each expression. As Lynn had told her, remembering was always sad and comforting. Polly had wondered how it could be both. She didn't understand it any better, she just knew that remembering was both – she was sad but comforted by these talks with her mother.

CHAPTER THIRTY-THREE

The second forum was occurring later this week and Lynn was so excited. Once Skeet Turnbull came, other regional black leaders and performers hinted at their interest in being a part of the presentation. At the next forum, after the presentation about the history of local rural blacks in James County and the role of DeLand Beaumont, a man Jasmine billed as the black horse whisperer, the crowd would be entertained by a mixed racial group of musicians from Brevard College who had a program of regional music of the period.

And the rest of the series was aligning in the same way. The series had drawn the attention of a black officer in the North Carolina National Guard and a black physician active in state health clinic certifications. Lynn was proud of the young women who had organized the series and proud of the people who had helped, including Mason Donovan.

Thinking of Mason – and Yolanda appeared at her office door.

Lynn blinked. Then she smiled. Robert O'Hara told her he had sent Yolanda her check for twenty-five thousand dollars with taxes paid – also part of Foster Donovan's plan.

"What are you going to do with your money?" Lynn asked as she walked around her desk to give the woman a hug.

"I'm going to South Africa," replied Yolanda. "I've been invited to a wedding and to the grand opening of the Foster and Marian Donovan Children's home." She wiped a tear of joy and excitement from her eye.

"Mason says he'll have the kids all trained and I will get five hundred kisses a day for as long as I stay."

Yolanda had told Lynn the story of Riva's arrest and Mason's response. They had both agreed that Yolanda was correct, Mason had to travel around the world to find what was right in front of him.

"I can't wait to meet Sweetheart," exclaimed Yolanda as she pulled a small notepad from her purse.

"Who's Sweetheart?" asked Lynn.

"Mason's assistant." Yolanda looked around the empty office and whispered. "He's gay and speaks several languages and knew before Mason did that Riva was the woman for him. Mason threatened to fire him for his impudence." She smiled and scanned her notes. "I need to borrow some luggage. Jasmine says I'll need adapters for my hair dryer and iPad charger. What do you have that I can borrow?"

"Anything you need." Lynn was as excited as her friend about this new adventure.

~ ~ ~

A chilling wind rattled the large windowpanes in Mars' loft. He lived on the top floor of the building housing Uncle Hutch's law firm. A few years ago when the firm remodeled the building, and updated its technology, the third floor became extra space. Uncle Hutch had thought about adding a security system and decided to remodel the top floor as living space and offered Mars the opportunity to inhabit one of the first downtown condos. Of course, downtown River Bend was probably as quiet as suburban River Bend, but it was the thought of being at the cutting edge of urban sophistication, and being close to work, that convinced Mars that the loft was a great idea.

So on a windy evening he sat on his masculine sofa, in front of his large screen TV, close to an array of workout equipment that rivaled any gym, and thought about his life in the new year.

Uncle Hutch had instigated a new facet of his life. Mars was finally going to step out of his safe trust fund baby existence and move into his new role as rich community manipulator. Wait, that's not what Uncle Hutch said, and Mars certainly wasn't some idle trust fund baby. But moving into a role on the bank board was going to add something new to his life. He doubted that it would be scary, no one would shoot at him, and he didn't think it would take a lot of time. Uncle Hutch just wanted him there to protect the down trodden. Well, no, he didn't quite say that, but he did say that the bank should be more community minded, and sometimes the board forgot the community.

It would give him something new to learn and champion. He flopped back on the sofa and smiled as he thought about Tee and Lonzo signing papers for their new house. It wouldn't be just a house any more. It was on its way to being a home – children, joy, laughter. His quiet role in helping the new family get that new home made him appreciate Uncle Hutch even more. He wondered how many times his uncle and Nathan and Jim Hoefler, and those other community leaders who had come before him, had manipulated community actions to help deserving families.

And local congregations. Part of the bank board agenda had been to discuss a loan to Reverend Graves' small church. Some of those old men on the board had no interest in developing a relationship with the small black church. Mars had an interest. And when he argued in favor, he saw it in their faces. He was more of a challenge than they had anticipated. Uncle Hutch would be pleased.

Mars didn't think that bank board service would make him forget Nancy and their hurtful parting. If he wanted a wife and family, he would have to start acting like he was interested in ... a life without Nancy.

In the meantime, he had found a new role in the New Year – bank board member, community donor and backroom manipulator. Wait! Did Uncle Hutch intend that? He grinned.

~ ~ ~

It was almost mid-February and Jason was already signaling his plans for March Madness and the method he would use for playing his 'official' basketball pool. Lynn had listened to Will and Dusty go on for what seemed like hours talking about picks and byes and regions and conference champions and a lot of other jargon that went in one ear and out the other. In fact, she had finally told Will to go home. Piper had gone home two hours earlier, leaving Will at the kitchen table, speculating non-stop with Dusty.

At last, she was washed and tucked in bed, trying to get the chill out of the covers. Dusty was still downstairs waiting for the dog to finish his nightly check of the yard. He better hurry, she thought, the covers weren't warming quickly enough. They needed his body heat. She thought that maybe she could use his body heat, too. Her mind sort of wandered and the next thing she knew he was pulling back the covers letting in cold air.

"You still awake?" he asked as he pulled her close.

"I am now," she grumbled, trying to act disinterested in his warm presence. "You just let all the warm air out of the blankets."

"I'll warm you," he said and she smiled to herself because that was the answer she wanted. "I can feel you smiling."

"No, you can't. I'm too cold to smile." She hated to be so easy to read, especially in the dark.

He kissed her neck. Smelled her hair. Got comfortable for a more intimate exchange. "You're heart rate is up and you're breathing has changed."

"I have a smile heartbeat?" That was kind of a nice idea.

"You have an I-want-some-sex heartbeat." He coughed because she elbowed his ribs. It was a soft cough because she couldn't move easily when he held her so tight. "I guess I'll leave you alone."

"No, I mean, we could talk before you ravage me." She embraced him. "You could be romantic and–"

Dusty had moved quickly and had her pinned under him. "I've got incentive tonight to get you in my power." He felt her stiffen. "Now you're suspicious."

"I have a suspicious heartbeat?"

He rolled off her. "You have a suspicious sound in your voice."

"So, what do you want?"

"Sex."

"You want something else. You're talking too much. You can tell by my heart rate what I want. I can tell by your, well, your you that there is a subtext to this exchange."

"I just kissed you and you see subtext?" He seemed to withdraw and consider falling asleep. Lynn waited because she was now certain there was a subtext.

He turned on his side and pulled her close again. Ah, ha, she told herself.

He brought his lips to her ear. "It's not really subtext. We just might need your help."

"We?"

He kissed her. "Thank you for that grant for our training program."

"It wasn't me. It was Yolanda's decision."

"But I can't be as grateful to her as I can be to you." More kisses and caresses.

She snuggled closer, kissed him in return. "So what help?" she whispered.

"Oh, yeah," he mumbled coming back to the discussion. "You have to be the treasurer of Piper's parent/teacher group." He felt her stiffen again. He held tighter. "She doesn't have a parent who understands the kind of reporting and money handling this grant requires."

"It's only fifteen hundred dollars."

"The parents' treasury has only three hundred dollars." Dusty chuckled. "Will pays for most of the things at the school. He finally told Piper he wants receipts for his taxes, so with the money from Yolanda, and Will wanting receipts, Piper needs a treasurer and we elected you."

"We? Me?"

"You can do this in your sleep," he cajoled. "We need you to help and to mentor one of those parents to learn how to keep the records in the future." More kissing and exploring other parts of her body. "Now you can give in to my way of asking. Your knees will be weak and you'll have this great, long lasting afterglow, or Piper can come at you with both guns blazing and you might not be able to stand up to her methods but you won't be glowing either."

"Those are my choices?" asked Lynn, "your persuasion or Piper's?"

"That's about it." He settled her comfortably in his arms.

"You know I would say 'yes' to both of you."

"But you'll have more fun my way." He pulled off her nightgown.

"Did Piper put you up to this?"

"No, she just said I got the first round and if I failed she'd come in guns blazing."

"She did not."

"Well, it was subtext," he replied. "She knows I'm asking. My reputation is on the line. You say 'no' to me and what will she think? I couldn't score, my style is no guarantee of a slam-dunk. I missed an easy lay-up."

"Is everything sports and sex with you?"

"When I'm with you, it's just sex."

"But I said yes, so we can just go to sleep." She gave him a fake yawn.

"Not tonight, sweetheart."

Thank you for reading.
Please review this book. Reviews help others find
Absolutely Amazing eBooks and inspire us to keep
providing these marvelous tales.

If you would like to be put on our email list to receive
updates on new releases, contests, and promotions,
please go to <u>AbsolutelyAmazingEbooks.com</u> and sign
up.

About the Author

Renee Kumor has lived in North Carolina for over fourty years. The setting for the River Bend Chronicles series reflects her early life in Ohio and her later years in western North Carolina. She was a stay-at-home mom for several years developing a personal ethic of community service. Through the years as her children aged, she became active in the political and non-profit life of the community. She began writing a political opinion column for the local newspaper, but retired from writing when she announced her candidacy for local political office. After eight years as a county commissioner, she returned to non-profit service and began writing a monthly column for the newspaper on non-profit management and service issues. Renee has been married to her husband for fifty years. They have four children and four grandchildren.

Next in the River Bend Chronicles Series:

There's No Explaining Love

It's springtime and Lynn is enjoying all the flowers throughout River Bend. To his chagrin Dusty is assigned extra work, appointed by the sheriff to a nonprofit board, Home Again, a program to help parolees re-enter society. He is not thrilled. And he is immediately suspicious when a local bank is robbed just days after the parolees settle into life in River Bend. During the investigation he stumbles onto a new romance between Amelia Shipley, owner of Amelia's Maids and Zackary Rawlings, a wealthy businessman. Dusty is joined by an FBI team responsible for investigating the robbery. While the investigation proceeds, Lynn and her friends encourage Amelia to accept Zackary's proposal of marriage. Before the wedding plans can be finalized Lynn and Amelia are kidnapped by the robbers who try to escape River Bend during the annual Memorial Day festivities. Big time FBI professionals meet small town crime solvers.

Look for the next installment in Renee Kumar's River Bend Chronicles – *There's No Explaining Love* – available soon at: www.AbsolutelyAmazingEbooks.com and other online booksellers.

ABSOLUTELY AMAZING eBOOKS

AbsolutelyAmazingEbooks.com

or AA-eBooks.com